THE SIXPENNY CROSS COLLECTION

THREE ENGLISH VILLAGE COSY MYSTERIES

BOOKS 1 - 3

VICTORIA TWEAD
NEW YORK TIMES BESTSELLING AUTHOR

Ant Press

CONTENTS

A IS FOR ABIGAIL 5
B IS FOR BELLA 99
C IS FOR THE CAPTAIN 221
A Request... 315
Preview of Chickens, Mules and Two Old Fools 317

The Old Fools series 325
New! The Stillwater Murders by Victoria Twead 327
New! The Bone Garden by Victoria Twead 330
Dear Fran, Love Dulcie 333
About the Author 334
Contacts and Links 335
Victoria's Bookstore 336
More Ant Press Memoirs 337

A IS FOR ABIGAIL

SIXPENNY CROSS 1

Abigail Martin has everything: beauty, money, a loving husband, and a fabulous house in the village of Sixpenny Cross. But Abigail is denied the one thing she craves... A baby.

I'm old now. My hair is the colour of the ashes in the fire and my skin is no longer smooth and tight like yours. But although my voice quavers when I speak, I still feel young in my head.

Like you, I was born in the village of Sixpenny Cross. Now, eighty years later, I'm still here. I've watched new families arrive, and old ones die out. I've seen babies born and watched them grow into adults. So many stories!

Sometimes I don't sleep so well because memories crowd into my head.

But you, little one, with your soft golden curls, you are asleep now, but I'll tell you a story while I watch over you. It's hard to choose which tale to tell first.

A is for Abigail. Yes, I'll tell you about Abigail Martin.

When I saw the travelling people drive through the village this spring, heading for Sixpenny Woods, I was reminded of nice, young Abigail Martin.

Poor Abigail had a deep yearning, a hollow part in her soul. I am sure it was because of that terrible need, that great gnawing emptiness she felt inside, that she made a bargain.

And twenty-four hours later, when she heard that tiny snuffling sound, she could have ignored it.

But she didn't.

And life for Abigail was never the same again.

2

"It isn't fair, Daisy," Abigail complained. She began counting off points on her manicured fingers. "Look at me! I have naturally blonde hair. (Well, almost.) I'm happily married and I live in a great big, beautiful house. Sixpenny Cross won the Prettiest Village in England contest three years running. I'm not short of money and I don't need to work. I have friends. I even have you, Sam."

She reached forward to fondle the retriever's golden ears. Sam's brown eyes stared into Abigail's green ones.

"Oh come on, Abigail, cheer up!" said Daisy, setting down her coffee cup. "It's really not like you to moan so much. You should be grateful for all your blessings."

"I have a sister with three children," Abigail continued, ignoring her friend. "And a brother with two. I even volunteer at the school so I'm *surrounded* by children."

"Listen, you can always adopt."

"I told you, Aiden won't even entertain the idea. He says he could never love a child that wasn't his."

She broke off to stare through the window. In the distance an old lady, a shawl thrown over hunched shoulders, trudged along a lane, dragging a small child by the hand. Travellers.

"How long are the gypsies going to stay in Sixpenny Woods?" asked Daisy, following her gaze. "You know our lawnmower went missing last week? Simon is positive it was the gypsies."

"I expect they'll move on soon. They always do."

"Look at the time!" exclaimed Daisy. "I promised Simon I'd cook steak for supper tonight. I'd better hurry or there'll be nothing left at the butcher's."

She gathered her stuff, kissed her friend on the cheek and headed for the door.

"Now stop feeling sorry for yourself, Abigail. It'll happen when you least expect it."

"Will it?" Abigail asked Sam as Daisy closed the back door behind herself. "Will it really? Will it *ever* happen? Aiden and I have been married nearly five years. We hardly see each other because of his job. And how many children do we have? None!"

***

Aiden stared out at the iconic skyline. The hotel room was expensive, a penthouse commanding a spectacular view of London's most famous landmarks. He could even see the silver-grey Thames threading through the city. Behind him, a woman was dressing.

"Help me with this zipper, would you?" she said, her accent unmistakably American.

She stepped forward and stood with her back to him, blocking his panoramic view. Even though she no longer attracted him, he couldn't help admiring her shapely curves. She was perfectly aware of the effect she had on men and unhurriedly lifted her long hair to allow him access to the fastenings. Aiden zipped, then battled with a tiny pearl button.

"There you go," he said. "Nice dress."

"It wasn't cheap. So little choice. The stores here are nothing like back home. So *rural*. Gee, I'll be glad when I get out of this grey country."

"It won't be long now."

"Okay, I'm going out for a couple of hours. I'll see you later."

She stepped away, and Aiden's view of London sprang back. But it wasn't London or Martha he was thinking about. It was Abigail and Sixpenny Cross.

———

Abigail sat in the kitchen, deep in thought. In the background, a newscaster on the radio relayed news of the Falklands war, but she was deaf to it all.

"*Whoof.*"

Sam expectantly eyed the leash that dangled from the hook on the back of the kitchen door.

The phone rang and Abigail picked up the kitchen extension, switching off the radio and Margaret Thatcher at the same time. Sam lost hope and flopped onto the floor.

"Abigail?"

"Oh, hi Hilary, how are you?"

"Abigail, I'm sorry to 'ave to do this to you at such short notice..."

"What's up, Hilary? You sound stressed."

Hilary was the Martins' cleaning lady.

"It's my older sister in Wales. She's 'ad a fall, poor thing, a serious one. I'm going to 'ave to go up there and 'elp out. I 'ate letting you down, but..."

"Oh Hilary! How awful! Of course you must go! Don't worry about me, I'll be absolutely fine. You know it's just Sam and me in the house and it hardly gets dirty."

"Are you sure?"

"Of course I'm sure! This house is much too big for Aiden and me, most of it is never used. It just won't be a problem." She paused, and then added quickly, "Of course your job will be waiting for you when you get back."

"Thank you, if you are absolutely sure..." There was relief in Hilary's voice.

"Don't worry about a thing, just go to your sister. I do hope she gets well soon, and I'll see you when you come back."

Abigail sighed as she rang off.

"Okay, time for your walk, boy."

Sam jumped up and danced round the kitchen, his eyes never leaving the leash on the back door.

The phone rang again.

Sam flopped down on the floor once more, his head on his paws.

Abigail picked up the receiver, convinced it would be Hilary again, but it wasn't her cleaning lady this time.

"Abs?"

"Hi Aiden, how's things?"

Aiden phoned daily, and she loved the opportunity to chat. If only he had more time.

"Good, good."

"Job going well?"

"Yes, we're really close to getting that contract, just a few loose ends to tie up with the client."

"I'll be glad when they finally sign. This has been going on for so long. Are you still coming home on Friday?"

"Of course I am, Abs. I can't wait!"

"I miss you so much, Aiden."

"I know... But I'll be home soon. Any village news?"

"No, not really. Hilary phoned to say she's gone to Wales so won't be cleaning for us for a while. Her sister had a fall. And Daisy came round for coffee. That's it really."

"Well, we'll be able to catch up properly on Friday evening. Oh, must go, my client is here. Bye Abs, love you."

The phone went dead and Abigail sighed. Sam opened one eye hopefully.

"It's your turn now," she said, clipping the leash to his collar.

Locking the door behind her, Abigail and Sam set off down the path for their walk, their legs brushing the daffodils that leaned towards them.

Turn left or right? Which way along the lane? Sam faced right, straining the leash, hoping Sixpenny Woods and its wealth of scents would be today's destination.

"Sorry, Sam, but all the time the travellers are camped in the woods, we're not going there. We'd better turn left and walk to the village."

Abigail tugged Sam the other way and together they headed along the lane in the direction of the village. Sam snuffled happily in the lush grass, reading messages left by rabbits and other animals. Abigail watched a newborn lamb in the field trying out its legs as it danced around its grazing mother before butting its hard little head against her side, begging for a drink.

In the distance, she could see a tractor gouging neat parallel lines in the soil. She guessed it was Archie Draper, and waved. But Archie was too busy concentrating on ploughing straight lines to notice her.

It should have been idyllic, and it was. Except... Except for the hollowness inside Abigail. A deep, dark hole of cold nothingness that only a baby could fill.

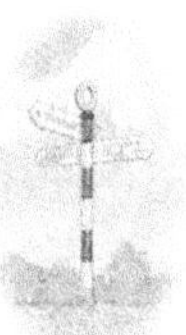

3

The expensive Harley Street specialist said there was nothing wrong. He had pronounced Abigail fit and well. There was nothing wrong with Aiden either. But still no baby appeared.

Abigail tried to put the whole painful subject out of her mind.

"Hello, Stan," she said as a familiar figure pedalled past her.

"Afternoon, Mrs Martin. Lovely day!"

Crime in Sixpenny Cross was almost non-existent and for years Stan Cooper had been the village police officer. Unless it was urgent, he travelled everywhere on his bicycle. In an emergency, he used the police car which had become a fixture in front of the police station.

Aiden always said that Stan had the easiest job in Sixpenny Cross and the only job he could think of that was easier than Stan's was being a weather forecaster in the Sahara Desert. It was probably a good thing that Sixpenny Cross wasn't gripped by a crime wave. Although Stan was a well-liked and diligent policeman, his clumsiness was legendary.

"Did you find Daisy and Simon's lawnmower?" she called after him.

"Yes, they forgot they lent it out to Frank Jones."

"Not stolen then?"

"No!" Stan shouted over his shoulder, wobbled dangerously, righted himself and pedalled away.

Abigail and Aiden's house was half a mile from the village green. They'd found it in the glossy pages of *Country Estates*, a magazine they subscribed to when they lived in London. Abigail had fallen in love with the house even before they viewed it. It had a hefty price tag, but for such a beautiful house, with its extensive grounds and separate guest cottage, what did one expect?

And they could afford it. They could also afford to pay for a cleaning lady and gardener. Abigail's plan was that she'd soon fill the house with children who would play in the grounds and attend the village school. But the house remained scarcely lived in. With Aiden away so much, Abigail used only the kitchen, sunroom, bedroom and bathroom.

Higgledy-piggledy cottages, some thatched, some with red roof-tiles, lined the approach to the village. Yellow daffodils swayed in the spring sunshine and bees were already busy visiting the flowers, one by one. Here the road was better, and there was a pavement to walk on.

The Dew Drop Inn was quiet. Angus McDonald, the landlord, was busy sweeping the floor and didn't see Abigail pass.

Abigail passed the little school, listening to the hum of learning. She glanced at her Tiffany watch. Soon the bell would ring and the children would spill out into the yard. One day, maybe, her own children would be among them.

At the centre of Sixpenny Cross was the large village green. In summer, cricket matches took place against rival village teams. There was a pond fringed by reeds, and a willow tree that trailed branches into the water and shaded a bench where old folks liked to sit.

Today the green was empty apart from a pair of mallard ducks guarding an untidy nest. Cars were slowly arriving and mothers were beginning to migrate towards the school, preparing to collect their youngsters. Abigail greeted a few that she knew by sight.

At the village shop, which was also the Post Office, Jayne Fairweather, the postmistress, waved to her as she passed.

"Hello, Abigail!" she called. "Is your husband coming home soon?"

"Yes, this weekend!"

It was good to be known and to exchange friendly words with fellow villagers, but Abigail had never felt wholly accepted. She was very aware that many of the villagers' families went back generations. The headstones in the churchyard were proof of that. Abigail and Aiden would always be 'newcomers'. However friendly people seemed to be, they'd still give her sidelong glances when they thought she wasn't looking.

When she'd mentioned it to Aiden, he'd shrugged.

"They're just jealous," he said.

"Jealous of what?"

"Our money, probably."

The irony of it was that Abigail would have exchanged all her money, her Audi car, her jewellery, and the house for a baby.

"Once round the green, and then home," Abigail told Sam, who was already panting. "And I'm keeping you on the lead, I don't want you chasing Mr and Mrs Duck."

Two figures sat on the bench, an adult and a child. They seemed familiar. Abigail had no intention of walking anywhere near them until a movement caught her eye. For the first time, she looked directly at the pair. A blackbird sang in the willow tree.

Was the woman beckoning to her? Surely not!

The old lady wore something shapeless that almost reached the floor. Her feet, encased in ancient suede brogues, sat side by side on the ground, peeping out from under the hemline of her skirt. A shawl was thrown over her head and shoulders, so only her weather-worn face and hands were visible. It was the gypsy and child Abigail had seen earlier, walking down the lane.

The child sat still. Only his hands moved, making restless shapes in his lap.

The old woman beckoned again, and Abigail glanced over her shoulder, checking that the signal wasn't intended for someone else.

"Sit for a moment," commanded the old woman.

"Me?"

"Yes. We mean you no harm. Sergei, move along and make space for the pretty lady."

"Honestly, it's quite okay…"

"You don't want to sit with us?"

Abigail didn't, but she was far too well-mannered to say so. Sergei shuffled along and regarded her steadily with small dark eyes set in a pale face. His fingers never stopped their manic dance.

Abigail sat, and Sam flopped down at her feet.

"Bufniță has been waiting for you," breathed the old woman.

4

"*P*ardon?"

Abigail caught the scent of wood smoke on the old woman's clothes. Her breath smelled of onions. She leaned in closer and Abigail tried hard not to recoil.

"You come from the big white house down the lane. The one with the long gravel drive and grounds," said the crone.

It was a statement, not a question.

"Er...yes. That's right. My name is Abigail. And you are..."

"My real name doesn't matter. I am a wise woman who has watched the years pass. They call me 'the owl' in my language, Romanian. Bufniță."

"Well, I'm very pleased to meet you, er...Bufniță," said Abigail, and turned slightly, meaning to offer her hand for shaking.

For the first time, she looked directly into the old woman's eyes. It was as though the returning, unblinking gaze was sucking her in and Abigail felt the sensation of swaying, spinning, falling. She stopped breathing.

The blackbird in the willow tree burst into song again and Abigail shivered, snapping herself out of it. She was being ridiculous!

"You said you were waiting for me?"

"*Da.*"

Abigail waited.

"*Da.* Life is made from many crossroads. We walk our paths, so smooth and flat, then suddenly, *poof!*"

The old woman's small clenched fist struck her other palm, making Abigail jump.

"Bufniță will put crossroads in your path, Abigail. Bufniță has something for you worth more than all the gold in the world. But only if you choose to take that path."

"What path? I'm sorry, I don't understand."

"You will. If you want to."

"What do you mean?"

"Bufniță has told you. She has been waiting for you. At last you are sitting beside her. Bufniță can offer you something priceless. Be warned, it won't be easy and later you may feel as though your heart is being ripped from your chest. But that will pass, and you will be happy. Bufniță can say no more until you cross her palm with gold."

"Gold? I don't have any gold! I just came out to walk the dog!"

The old woman's eyes were transfixed by the watch that flashed in the sunlight on Abigail's agitated wrist. The small boy's fingers stopped their crazy dance in his lap.

"My watch? But that's a Tiffany watch! It's worth..."

"The choice is yours."

"I can't just give you my watch! In exchange for what? None of this makes any sense and it's time I was going."

"Wait."

The old woman's claw shot out and clutched her arm. Her eyes bored into Abigail's.

"You can go, yes, and forget this day. You can go and live your empty life, and tell the time by the gold watch on your wrist. Or you can give Bufniță the watch and she will change your life. What is the time now?"

Abigail glanced at her wrist.

"Nearly a quarter past three."

"Abigail, listen to me." The old woman gripped tighter, her nails digging into Abigail's skin through her sleeve. "Give Bufniță the watch and she will give you her promise. You know the woods where we camp?"

Abigail nodded.

"Come to the woods when the sun reaches that same spot in the sky tomorrow. Come to the place where we travellers camp, by the Wishing Rock, and all will be revealed. If Bufniță does not keep her promise, you may call the police and report that Bufniță stole your watch from you. Look, the lady in the Post Office sees everything from her shop. She will have noticed that you are sitting with Bufniță and Sergei. She will back you up."

Abigail looked across the green to the Post Office in the distance. Jayne Fairweather was sorting a display outside the shop. Abigail waved, and Jayne waved back.

Abigail wasn't really the impetuous type. She liked to think about all her decisions, weigh them up, and consider them from all angles. But for some inexplicable reason, she was ready to take a risk that day.

With one smooth movement, she unclasped the watch and pressed it into Bufniță's dirty hand. Bufniță's claw closed round it. Sergei's fingers resumed their crazy dance on his lap, but his expression never changed.

"You have done well, Abigail Martin," whispered the old woman. "You have chosen the right fork of the crossroads."

Abigail was in shock.

As she walked back over the green, past the mothers collecting their children now that the school bell had rung, she shook her head. Had she really just struck up a conversation with a gypsy woman? Had she *really* handed her the Tiffany watch Aiden had given her last Christmas?

Crazy!

The remainder of the day crawled by and that night she slept fitfully, visions of Bufniță's craggy weather-worn face entering her dreams. The next day was no better, and Abigail kept catching herself checking the time.

Aiden phoned, as he did most days, although Abigail couldn't help noticing that his calls had become shorter and shorter.

Perhaps that's because he's coming home very soon, she thought, her stomach flipping with excitement at the thought.

"So, any news in the village?" he asked.

"No, not really. Just one strange thing happened when I went for a walk yesterday, but I'll save it until you come home, then I can tell you about it properly."

"Strange thing?"

"Yes, I met an old gypsy woman."

"Sorry, Abs. I have to go. I'm looking forward to hearing the whole story when I come home this weekend. Must go, love you, bye…"

Abigail leaned back in her chair, her hands around the coffee mug decorated with two intertwined *A*s that Aiden had given her last Valentine's Day. It was only two-thirty, and her appointment with Bufniță was not for another half hour.

What was Abigail expecting? A box of treasure? She certainly wasn't short of money. Did she want some abstract wish granted, like happiness? Abigail wasn't normally the type to believe in the supernatural.

No, she told herself, when she met Bufniță in the woods, she'd ask for her watch back, give her some money, and that would be the end of the whole silly business.

The phone rang again. It was Daisy.

"Abigail, sorry to be a pest, but can you give me that carrot cake recipe again, please? I can't find it and I've searched everywhere."

"Oh, like the lawnmower?"

"Oh, that was embarrassing!" laughed Daisy. "It wasn't the gypsies at all! Which reminds me, I saw them leaving this morning."

"You what?"

"The gypsies left Sixpenny Woods this morning. I saw their convoy go past my house. Simon is delighted, and I bet all the villagers…"

"Daisy, I'll find you the recipe. Something's come up. I must fly."

Abigail slammed the phone down, her hands shaking.

Gone? The gypsies had gone? She was furious with herself. How could she be so gullible?

5

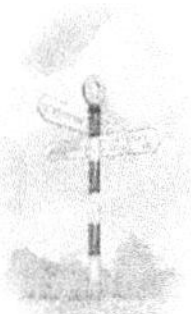

"**S**am! Come on! Walkies!"

Sam couldn't believe his luck. He jumped up, thrashing his tail, and together they left the house. At the gate, Abigail turned right, heading for Sixpenny Woods, and Sam's tail beat even faster.

Resisting the urge to break into a run, she marched along the track that led into the woods. Soon, the track petered out but Abigail knew exactly where she was heading. She let Sam off the lead and he trotted ahead, occasionally stopping to sniff something irresistible.

Branches swept at her face, and the canopy overhead largely blocked out the spring sunshine. Her footsteps fell silently on the rotting leaf litter. Then the trees thinned out and she was at the clearing where the gypsies camped. The ancient granite Wishing Rock stood silent.

Apart from the remains of a bonfire in the centre, with weak wisps of smoke still curling from the charcoal, there was no sign of life. She noticed a tree with the initials CD gouged out, but it didn't look freshly carved.

No vans. No vehicles. No people. No dogs. No Bufniţă.

No question. The gypsies had moved on.

Abigail kicked a tree trunk in frustration.

"Bufniţă! Where are you?"

No answer.

"Bufniţă! You broke your promise!"

Her voice rang through the woods but there was no reply.

How could I be so stupid? Did I really hand over my expensive watch to a complete stranger? To a gypsy woman, no less? And for what?

"Come on, Sam," she said, her heart heavy. "Let's go. We'll take a walk to the police station and have a word with Stan. Report my watch stolen."

She looked around for Sam. He was a particularly obedient dog, not given to ignoring commands. He had been trained as a guide dog for the blind, but he hadn't quite made the grade.

"Sam?"

It was a rare occurrence, but this time he refused to come to her call.

"Sam! Come on!"

Silence. Nothing stirred. Abigail squeezed her eyes shut in exasperation and concentrated, listening.

Then she heard something. A noise coming from her right. Not the noise of a dog snuffling through undergrowth, but a tiny whimper, almost a mewling.

Oh no! The gypsies have abandoned a puppy!

She swung round in the direction of the tiny sniffle and spotted Sam. He was sitting quietly beside a small bush at the edge of the clearing, his tail sweeping the ground as he looked at her.

She approached the bush carefully, and peered round it.

"Sam, what have you got there?"

What she saw turned her bones to liquid and her heart nearly beat out of her chest.

"Ohhh…"

In a straw moses basket lay a baby.

Not trusting her own eyes, she squeezed them tight, then opened them again.

The baby was still there.

Abigail drew in a long breath, then crouched beside the basket. She touched the baby's rosy cheek with the back of one tentative finger. The baby fluttered its golden eyelashes but didn't wake.

The basket looked new, as did the lacy white coverlet tucked around the baby. The baby's face was clean and beautiful, flushed by sleep.

"This is it," she whispered. "This is the treasure worth more than all the gold in the world. This is the gift Bufniţă promised."

Legs shaking, she sat crosslegged beside the basket, never tearing her eyes from the baby's face.

"Who are you?" she whispered. "You don't look like a gypsy baby. Did they steal you? Is your mother looking for you?"

The baby waved a tiny fist in sleep but didn't open its eyes.

Except what she'd learned from having nieces and nephews, Abigail didn't know a lot about babies. She knew this one wasn't very old. Maybe a few weeks? As her heart thudded, she knew she had to pick up the basket, with its precious, tiny occupant, and do the right thing. She had to take it to the police station.

A little distance away something caught her eye. A bag. She leaned over and grabbed it, pulling it towards herself. She fumbled with the fastenings, curious to see what it held.

Like the basket, it looked new. It was one of those cleverly designed bags that opened out into a changing mat. And it had pockets stuffed full of all manner of baby items: bottles, formula, talcum powder, nappy cream, nappies, a pacifier and a teething ring. Everything was brand new, unused.

It's almost like a baby starter pack! she thought. *I think I was meant to find the baby and keep it!*

But Abigail wasn't a bad girl, and she wasn't stupid. She knew she couldn't keep it.

With aching heart, she slung the bag over her shoulder, then carefully lifted the moses basket with its sleeping occupant. Somewhere not too far away, she heard a car door slam and an engine start up and speed away, but her thoughts were only on the little mite asleep in the basket.

Sam followed obediently behind as she walked out of the woods and down the lane towards home. As she reached her gate, she knew she must continue past, and walk into the village and to the police station.

Stan might not be on duty. Then what? Perhaps it would be better if I just kept the baby until the morning. It'll need feeding and changing soon. I can do that.

Her heart hammered. Straight on to the village, or home?

Instead of walking past her gate and heading for the village, she turned and followed Sam who had already swung up the path to the kitchen door.

The decision was made.

A deep feeling of contentment washed over Abigail and the gypsy's voice rang in her ears.

You have done well, Abigail Martin. You have chosen the right fork of the crossroads.

She would keep the baby.

For the moment, anyway.

Just one night wouldn't hurt.

As she turned the key in the lock, the baby stirred. The little fists flailed, and the eyes eased open for the first time.

"It's okay, baby," whispered Abigail, "we're home."

6

*A*bigail locked the door behind her and placed the moses basket on the kitchen table. The baby was more agitated now, kicking at the coverlet and beginning to screw up its face and turn its head as though searching for milk.

"Are you hungry? Just hold on, little one, I'll soon sort something out for you."

Was the baby a girl or boy? She realised she didn't know.

The first priority was food, so she pulled the tin of formula out of the bag and quickly scanned the instructions. She didn't have a steriliser, but she boiled the kettle and poured boiling water into the bottle, hoping that would do the trick instead.

How much formula to make? According to the tin, it depended on the weight of the baby.

Very carefully, she lifted the baby out of the basket. It felt warm through the little stretch suit it was wearing. A wave of tenderness swept over her as she cradled it in her arms. So young, so perfect, so innocent. She walked slowly to the bathroom and stood on the scales. She knew exactly how much she weighed, and could now calculate the baby's weight. Okay, so she needed to make about 500ml of formula. She was doing well.

She placed the baby back in the basket. Using the scoop and following the instructions to the letter, she made up the feed and set it aside to cool.

Next came the nappy change, and the revelation.

Boy? Or girl?

She opened the changing mat and gently lifted the baby into the centre of it. The baby kicked and she sensed it was getting agitated. As quickly and gently as she could, she removed the little sleep-suit and nappy.

"You're a little girl!" she breathed.

First she wiped the baby clean, then fitted a new nappy around her, pressing the adhesive strips to keep it in place.

"Well, that wasn't too hard," she said and lifted the baby into her arms.

The nappy promptly fell off.

The second attempt was more successful. Next, Abigail offered her the bottle and the baby sucked enthusiastically. She held her to her shoulder and patted her back as she had done for her nieces and nephews. She was rewarded with a fat burp. An hour later, the baby was clean, fed and drifting off to sleep again. As Abigail tidied the kitchen, a contented feeling enveloped her and she realised that the cold, gnawing sensation, deep inside her, had vanished.

With the baby asleep, she made herself something to eat and relaxed, always keeping one eye on the basket. In addition to the large table and chairs, there were two easy chairs in the huge kitchen, Aiden and Abigail's favourite places to sit on cold winter days. Abigail made herself comfortable and reached for the phone. Two messages awaited her.

The first was from Daisy.

"Abigail, don't worry about the carrot cake recipe, I found it. I've made a batch so put the kettle on tomorrow morning, and I'll bring some round. Oh, and is Aiden back early? I thought I saw his car pass our house today."

The second message was a puzzle. The caller was female, with an American accent, and the message was baffling.

"Hah! So that's how you sound! I was curious."

Who on *earth* was that? Could this day get any stranger? She played it back twice more. It made no sense at all. It must be a wrong number.

She shook her head, trying to clear it. There was no time to worry about mysterious phone calls, she had to make a plan.

Bufniță meant me to find the baby, she said to herself.

There was no doubt about that. But it didn't mean she could keep it. She couldn't keep a baby a secret, and Aiden would never allow her to keep it. No, she'd have to report it to the police.

Or did she? *What if she just packed the two of them up and left? Ran away?*

But what about the baby's mother? There may be distraught parents somewhere, desperate to find their tiny daughter.

Exhausted, Abigail fell asleep, only to be woken a few hours later by a hungry baby demanding a feed.

The bathroom door was open, framing Martha as she applied her make-up and brushed her hair.

Aiden looked at her. Had he ever really been attracted to this woman? What had he been thinking? Risking his marriage for a romp with this cold-eyed, unfeeling ice queen?

There was no question about it, she was beautiful to look at. But behind that soft skin and those wondrous curves beat a heart of granite.

"Why are you staring at me?" she asked, looking straight at Aiden. "Are you going to miss me? That's a laugh! Believe me, I won't miss you or your horrid little country. Go back to your waiting angel in Ten Cent Dump or whatever your precious village is called. Me? I'm counting the hours until I get back to New York where I do belong."

By morning, Abigail had perfected the maternal art of carrying an infant on one's hip whilst carrying out chores. She had tidied the kitchen and sorted all manner of stuff without needing to put the infant down, but she still hadn't decided what to do next.

The problem was, she didn't want to do *anything*. She wanted time to freeze and the world to leave her and her baby alone.

She jumped as somebody knocked on the kitchen door.

"Abigail? It's me! Put the kettle on."

Abigail took a deep breath and unlocked the door to let Daisy in.

"Oh my! Who is this adorable little munchkin?"

"Um, I don't actually know. It's quite a story…"

"Well! I can't wait to hear this one! What do you mean, you don't know? Is Aiden back?"

"No, I'm on my own, except for this little sweetie, of course. Aiden will be back this weekend."

"Hold on, let me make coffee and cut us some carrot cake, then you can explain."

Daisy listened carefully as Abigail told her story, only interrupting when something didn't seem clear.

"Hang on, you gave the gypsy your watch?"

"Yes, I don't know what came over me really, I just felt I had to take the risk."

She continued the story.

"And there was nobody else in the woods?"

"Nobody. I didn't see anybody. All the gypsies and their stuff had gone."

"But the baby made a sound?"

"Yes. Thank goodness I heard her, and Sam had already found her. He just sat there beside the basket, waiting for me to go over."

"And were there no clues in the bag? Or in the basket?

"None."

"Abigail, you know you can't keep her, don't you?"

Abigail cast her eyes down. She didn't answer.

"Abigail, are you listening?" Daisy's voice was gentle. "I know how much you want a baby, but this isn't the way. Imagine the despair of the parents of this little munchkin. You *have* to report this."

Abigail lifted her head and stared back at her friend with hurting eyes.

Loud banging on the front door made them both jump.

"I'll go," said Daisy.

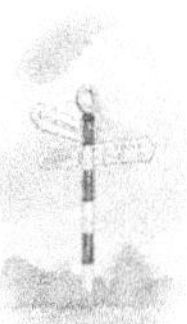

7

*A*bigail buried her face in the baby's neck, inhaling, breathing in the scented warmth. She heard Daisy opening the front door and talking to somebody, then she popped her head round the kitchen door.

"It's a delivery. Don't worry, I'll handle it. No need to disturb the little munchkin."

She vanished again and Abigail could hear thumping and moving noises coming from the hall. By the sounds of it, it was quite a big delivery. Perhaps Aiden had ordered something and forgotten to tell her about it?

At last the noises stopped, the front door closed, and Daisy came back into the kitchen.

"Whew," she said, dropping an envelope onto the table beside the untouched carrot cake and heading for the sink to wash her hands. "That was a big delivery! I got them to pile it all up in the hall."

"Thank you," said Abigail, tearing the envelope open. "I wasn't expecting anything. I wonder what it is?"

She unfolded the contents and stared. The name of the company that had delivered was Baby Magic, and Abigail ran her eye down the list of items delivered.

"What…"

Daisy looked over her shoulder and read aloud.

"Baby bath, blankets, steriliser, bottles, nappies, nappy cream, a dozen tins of formula, travelling cot, clothes, more clothes, high chair, car seat, stroller… Abigail, did you order all this?"

"No! Of course I didn't!"

"Well, then who did?"

"I don't know!"

"Does the delivery note show who ordered?"

"No, it just says 'paid in full with cash' and my address."

"Do you think it's a mistake? Delivered to the wrong address?"

"Nobody has a newborn baby around here."

The two women stared at each other.

"Or was it the gypsy woman?"

"I doubt it. Why would she buy all this for me?"

"What does it say on the envelope?"

Abigail picked it up, and stared at the neat typed words on the front.

Tiffany Martin
  12, Sixpenny Lane,
  Sixpenny Cross.

Daisy saw the blood drain from her friend's face and snatched the envelope to read it for herself.

"Tiffany?"

"My watch…"

"I know. This is surreal."

Abigail clutched the baby closer to her. In that moment, she knew that if she was allowed to keep this baby, her name would be Tiffany. But her heart was full of dread. This baby would soon be taken from her. Very soon.

"Does Aiden know about any of this?"

"No, of course not. You know how he feels about adoption."

"Abigail, before this gets any deeper, I want you to phone the police station. You need to tell them everything, the whole story. You *can't* just keep this baby."

"I know."

"Do you want me to do it for you?"

A tear trickled from the corner of Abigail's eye.

"Yes. You do it."

"Right. I'll find the number."

Abigail stood up and began to pace the floor, cradling Tiffany in her arms. The baby was already asleep, but Abigail walked up and down, up and down, as Daisy dialled.

"Hello? Is that Stan? ... Hello, Stan, this is Daisy Grainger. ... Yes, I'm fine, thank you, and so is Simon. ... No, it's nothing about lawnmowers! I'm actually phoning from Abigail Martin's house in Sixpenny Lane. We have a bit of a situation here. ... No, no, it's not an emergency exactly, but it is a police matter, and I think it might be a good idea if you could come round as soon as possible? ... No, it's a bit delicate, I'd rather we explain when you come. ... Good. We'll see you then. Goodbye, thank you."

Abigail paced up and down, up and down, her head bent low over the sleeping child.

"Well, that's good then," said Daisy brightly. "Stan is going to hop onto his bike and come round right away."

Abigail didn't reply. Instead, she began humming a tuneless song as she walked up and down, up and down.

Martha snapped her pink designer suitcase shut.

"That's it then, all packed. I'm gonna walk right out of your life. New York, here I come and it just can't come soon enough for me!"

"No hard feelings, eh?"

"Aiden, don't be an idiot. You never meant anything to me."

"Martha..."

"Come on! I don't think I ever meant much to you either. We worked together, we played together a few times, hey - we even lived together! We got that contract together, but this is where it all ends. We both gained from the arrangement, but we draw the line now."

"Will you be okay?"

"Of course! I came to England with one thing on my mind. I wanted to make me a load of bucks. And I have. We got paid handsomely for that contract, as you know, but your little, er, contribution, was the icing on the cake!"

"Will you keep in touch?"

"Nah, what for? I'm done here. I'm ready to start frying other fish."

Aiden held out his hand to touch her arm, but Martha backed away.

"So long," she said, her ridiculously high heels clacking on the marble floor as she and her pink suitcase headed for the private lift. She pressed the button and the lift doors slid apart.

"Martha…"

"Enjoy your life in Ten Cent Dump. Enjoy your dull little wife. I'm outta here."

The lift doors whooshed shut behind her, but Aiden remained transfixed for a very long time.

8

"Come on in, Stan. Mind the boxes. Abigail's just had a rather big delivery, but we'll explain about all that. She's in the kitchen."

Stan side-stepped round one box, but managed to trip over a smaller one poking out cheekily.

When they reached the kitchen, Sam wagged his tail and Abigail looked up from her easy chair. She was still cradling Tiffany, but at the sight of the policeman, her grip tightened.

"Morning, Mrs Martin."

Abigail said nothing, but gave the police officer a half smile.

"Please sit down, Stan. I'll make us all a nice cup of tea while Abigail tells you the story."

Stan pulled out a chair and sat down. He looked from Daisy to Abigail and then to the tiny baby she held in her arms.

"It all began the day before yesterday on the village green," said Abigail dully. "And now I have Tiffany, and I don't think I can let her go."

Stan waited.

"She's very upset," said Daisy, plonking the teapot on the table. "Abigail, shall I tell the story? You can stop me if I forget anything."

Abigail nodded, her blonde head bowed over the infant.

Daisy sat down, poured tea, and started. As soon as she got to the part where Abigail handed over the watch, Stan held up his hand.

"Hold on, Mrs Grainger, I think I'll take notes as you talk, if you don't mind."

He slipped out a notebook and patted his uniform pockets, searching for a pen. He found one and began writing.

"Did the gypsy woman give you her name?"

"Bufniță," whispered Abigail. "She said it meant 'owl' in Romanian."

Stan scribbled in his notebook. The ink was refusing to flow properly but he'd be able to read the dents in the paper later.

Daisy continued, with Abigail supplying further details when asked.

"And this is the basket you found the baby in?" asked Stan, pointing with his pen.

The pen lid fell off, bounced on the floor, and rolled under the table. He bent down to pick it up, bumping his head on the table edge as he straightened up.

"Yes, that's the basket," said Abigail, ignoring the incident.

Daisy went on to describe how Abigail had brought the baby home and cared for her overnight.

"And the next thing that happened was a banging on the door. I answered it for Abigail, and it was the delivery. Well, you've seen the packages and boxes in the hall. Piles of baby stuff, all brand new. Here is the delivery note."

Stan looked at the envelope with interest.

"Tiffany? Wasn't your watch a Tiffany watch?"

Both Abigail and Daisy nodded.

"Well, this is quite a story," said Stan, closing his notebook with a decisive snap. "I think we have quite a bit to work on. I'm going to go back to the station and make a start. The gypsies won't be hard to track down, so they'll be interrogated. We also have this delivery note to check up on. Do you mind if I take it with me?"

Abigail shook her head.

"Then there's the watch. Perhaps it was offered to pawn shops recently. Also, we need to search Sixpenny Woods thoroughly, there may be clues left behind. And of course we'll check that no babies have been reported missing or kidnapped."

"And Tiffany?"

"I was coming to that. Social Services are terribly overstretched, and I was wondering whether you would be kind enough to consider looking after the baby for the moment? I can see she's very comfortable here, and this case may take a little while to sort out."

Abigail's whole demeanour changed. She sat straight in her chair, and a huge smile lit her face.

"Oh, I'd *love* to!" Abigail bent down and kissed the baby's head. "Hear that, Tiffany? You're staying for the moment."

"Brilliant!" said Daisy. "That's great news."

"Right," said Stan, getting up and making the table rock. "I'd better get the ball rolling. Mrs Martin, you will get a visit from the local Health Visitor, just to check the baby is okay. And a visit from Social Services to sign a few papers about the fostering. Of course it'll need a signature from your husband, too. Is he due back home soon?"

Had Abigail's head not been bowed over Tiffany, the policeman would have seen a flash of fear cross her face.

"Yes, Aiden is coming back tomorrow evening," said Daisy.

"Right, thank you, I'll be in touch. I'll see myself out," said Stan, going out into the hall.

The ladies heard him stumbling over the boxes in the hallway, then close the front door.

"Well, that went well!" said Daisy. "I think Stan has loads of good leads to chase up. Bet nothing so exciting has happened in Sixpenny Cross for decades! And you get to keep the munchkin for the moment."

"But what am I going to tell Aiden?" wailed Abigail. "He'll never sign any papers to foster a baby!"

"You don't know that."

"I do! You know how much I love him, but that's one thing we have *never* agreed about. We've had this conversation so many times. I've always said I'd consider adoption if we can't have children of our own. He always said he never would. He says if I don't fall pregnant, then we aren't meant to have children. He's an only child, you know. I don't think he has the same need to have children as I do."

"Let's wait and see, shall we? You are only fostering after all. Perhaps he'll fall in love with the little munchkin, just like you did. Remember how he didn't want a dog? And then one day you brought a puppy home. Look how he loves Sam now!"

Sam heard his name mentioned and swept the floor with his tail.

Abigail said nothing. She knew that Aiden would never agree to Tiffany staying, temporarily or permanently.

The next day and a half flew past. The Health Visitor called and checked Tiffany over and pronounced her wonderfully fit and well.

"How old do you think she is?" asked Abigail.

"I'd say she's about three weeks old, and doing well. We'll keep an eye on her weight to check that she's gaining weight steadily, as she should be. I must say, you are doing a grand job! Any problems or questions I can help you with?"

"No, thank you. She's as good as gold."

"Good, I'll pop in again soon."

Abigail had begun to plunder the boxes in the hall. While Tiffany slept, she read the baby care books from cover to cover. The stroller was now assembled and, when Tiffany was fractious, Abigail pushed her around the house and garden.

"Listen, that's a blackbird singing his heart out. He's probably got a wife and babies somewhere close. And look, there's a robin redbreast. See how bold he is sitting on the fence?"

Abigail couldn't remember when she had been happier. The birdsong, the kaleidoscope of spring flowers, and the baby in the pram, all made her heart dance with joy.

It couldn't last.

9

*A*bigail stowed the tins of formula in a kitchen cupboard, and the steriliser on the counter. The baby bath was in one of the bathrooms and tiny baby clothes were folded and neatly put away in the chest of drawers in the little room next to their master bedroom. Abigail had always thought it would make a lovely nursery.

Mrs Robinson from Yewbridge County Social Services rang the bell.

"Hello, I'm Tina Robinson," she said, showing Abigail her badge. She glanced down at her clipboard. "And you must be Abigail Martin."

"Yes, that's me," smiled Abigail. "Please come in."

Mrs Robinson had a warm manner and kindly smile, but she was also a very shrewd individual. Her eyes darted everywhere, missing nothing, and she approved of what she saw. The house was clearly clean and comfortable.

Abigail led her into the kitchen where Tiffany was asleep in the moses basket.

"Here she is. I'm calling her Tiffany for the moment."

Tiffany sighed in her sleep, and the two ladies smiled.

"What a sweet thing," whispered Mrs Robinson. "It's hard to believe that any parent could abandon their baby, but sadly, sometimes it happens. We're so grateful to you for fostering this little one until we find her mother."

Abigail smiled again.

"It really is my pleasure," she said, meaning it from the depths of her being.

"The Health Visitor tells me that she's very happy for the baby to stay with you. If you could just sign here," said Mrs Robinson, "then I'll come back early next week to get your husband's signature. Is that okay?"

A dark cloud flitted across Abigail's soul.

"Yes," she said.

It isn't 'okay' at all, screamed her heart.

Stan phoned a couple of times to keep her in the loop.

"There are absolutely no reports of any babies being kidnapped," he said. "In fact, nobody has reported a missing child in the whole country for several months."

"That's good to hear."

"We found the gypsies," Stan continued. "They moved into the next county. My colleagues gave them a visit, and found the old lady who calls herself Bufniță."

Abigail's heart lurched. She held her breath.

"The old woman refused to admit to anything except that she met you for the first time on the village green when you were walking your dog."

"That's true," said Abigail. "And Jayne Fairweather at the Post Office will tell you the same. She saw us that afternoon."

"Bufniță said she didn't know anything about your watch, denied even having noticed it. She totally denied leaving a baby in Sixpenny Woods, or knowing anything about an abandoned baby. The gypsies allowed my colleagues to search the camp and there was no sign of the watch, or anything to lead them to believe they might have had a baby in their midst recently."

Abigail felt strangely relieved.

"We haven't got very far with the delivery note, I'm afraid. The goods were paid for in cash so there's no paper trail. The shop is holding a spring sale at the moment, and they've had crowds in. They hired temporary staff for the checkouts, and nobody remembers who served that customer. Their security cameras haven't helped either."

"Did you find any clues in the woods?"

"No, nothing. Just recent signs of the gypsy encampment, as we expected. Never mind, we'll keep investigating, something will turn up."

Abigail quietly prayed that nothing would.

Aiden phoned. Uncharacteristically, she didn't pick it up, but held her breath as she listened to his message.

"Hi Abs, I expect you're out walking Sam. Sorry to have missed you, but I'll be back tomorrow anyway, so don't bother trying to catch me. The contract is all sewn up, and I can't wait to be home! I reckon I'll have packed up by the afternoon, and, allowing for traffic, I should be with you early evening. Can't wait to see you! Love you, bye."

Abigail knew she should be pleased, but she wasn't. Without any doubt, Aiden's homecoming spelled the end of her motherhood. There was no way Aiden would allow Tiffany to stay. No way that he would sign the Social Services fostering papers. And if no trace of Tiffany's parents was found, no way he'd ever agree to adopting her.

There was nothing she could do. Nothing.

Or was there?

Abigail pressed Tiffany to her chest and began to pace up and down, up and down, humming tunelessly.

———

Aiden's eyes flicked to the clock on the dashboard. Half past eight already. A bit later than he'd guessed but rush-hour traffic was always unpredictable, and Fridays were the worst.

His fingers raked through his dark hair, then he drummed impatiently on the steering wheel. Soon he'd pass through Yewbridge.

Even though the wide roads would become twisty country lanes, he estimated he should be in Sixpenny Cross by nine o'clock.

* * *

"You usually complain that there's not enough police work to keep you busy in Sixpenny Cross," said Sally Cooper, smiling and shaking her head.

"I know," said Stan, kissing his wife's cheek. "This case is really unusual. I thought finding the mother of this baby would be a simple matter, but I was wrong. I've got nowhere with it. And I've only just put the phone down and locked the office."

"I wonder who her parents are, poor little mite," said his wife. "Look, why don't you pop over the road for a pint to relax you? I'll have your dinner ready in about half an hour."

"Great idea, thank you. I'll be back in thirty minutes."

Through the window, Sally watched her husband walk across the road and enter the Dew Drop Inn. She put the shepherd's pie into the oven and began to lay the table.

Well, she thought, *that little baby girl was lucky to end up with Abigail Martin. Nice girl, and not short of money either, thanks to her husband's high-powered job. Just a pity it keeps him in the city so much of the time.*

* * *

It was nearly nine o'clock. Being spring, it was still light outside, although twilight was setting in. Abigail kissed Tiffany's warm head and laid her in the moses basket, tucking the coverlet round her securely. The baby lay still, with open eyes, contented after her feed.

Abigail stared out of the window and down the drive, waiting, waiting. Then she stared back at the baby.

I'm sorry, Tiffany, I think our time together has come to an end.

In the distance, up the lane, she saw headlights twinkling and a terror overcame her.

Abigail gasped.

No! No! Aiden will not make me hand Tiffany over to a complete stranger! I won't allow it!

Her heart thudded.

Crossroads time. Come on, Abigail! You have to choose right now. Aiden, or Tiffany? Choose!

10

For a split second she deliberated as the headlights approached.

Then she made her decision.

She grabbed the bottles of pre-prepared formula from the fridge, and a handful of disposable nappies.

Aiden's car swept up the drive, tyres crunching on the gravel.

Stuffing the bottles and nappies into the end of the moses basket, her head whipped round to see what else she could quickly grab. A few items of Tiffany's clothes from the clean laundry pile, the flashlight from the drawer, her jacket from the back of the chair.

Aiden climbed out of his car, opened the boot and lifted out his suitcase. He locked the car and strode up to the front door.

Abigail snatched up the moses basket and her keys. Sam jumped up and wagged his tail furiously.

"Not now, Sam," she hissed. "Lie down!"

As Aiden turned his key in the front door lock, Abigail was slipping out through the back door and into the night.

There weren't many customers in the Dew Drop that night, which pleased Stan Cooper. He'd had a heavy day, and he felt like relaxing. A nice cool glass of beer and then home to a steaming shepherd's pie. Perfect.

"Evening, Stan," said Angus, the landlord, polishing glasses and holding them up to the light. "Your usual?"

"Thanks, Angus."

"Tough day? Caught a cyclist without their lights on? Archie Draper been speeding on his tractor again?"

"Now, stop that!" said Stan, laughing. "As it happens, I'm working on quite a puzzler at the moment."

"Can you talk about it?"

"Yes, I can give you brief details. Who knows, you may be able to shed some light on the matter. I know you hear a lot of what goes on in the village."

Angus passed the foaming beer glass to Stan and waited. He was a good listener, an essential trait for a pub landlord, and one of the reasons that the Dew Drop Inn continued to thrive.

He glanced round the bar. Nobody needed serving at the moment. His regulars, the Captain and his friend were playing dominoes in the corner by the fire, their usual spot. They were wrapped up in their game, and the group by the window were chatting, enjoying their drinks and each other's company. Idly wiping the counter with a cloth, he turned back to the policeman, ready to hear the story.

Stan took a sip from his beer and looked at Angus over his glass, not noticing the beermat still stuck to the base of the glass.

"Somebody found a baby in Sixpenny Woods this week."

"A baby? Oh no! You're joking!"

Being a pub landlord, Angus had heard his fair share of strange stories, but this surprised him.

"No, I'm not joking. Not something that happens every day in Sixpenny Cross, is it?"

"Was it a teenage mother abandoning a newborn, do you think?"

"Unlikely."

"Then it must be the gypsies."

"At the moment we don't know."

"Is the baby okay?"

"Yes, it's a little girl, about three weeks old. Beautifully dressed and looked after which rather blows the theory of an unwanted teen pregnancy."

"Must be the gypsies then."

"Except that we've interviewed them, and they insist they know nothing about any babies."

"Well, you know gypsies. And they have a reputation for stealing babies."

"We'll have to follow every lead. At the moment, nobody has reported any baby missing. So I take it that you've heard nothing here in the pub about a baby? No gossip?"

"Nope, nothing," said Angus, shaking his head, "but I'll certainly be listening out from now on."

***

"Abigail! I'm home!"

The house was silent, apart from Sam who bounded up to Aiden, tail wagging furiously in welcome. Aiden patted him on the head then called his wife again.

"Abs?"

No reply.

Aiden dumped his suitcase beside the boxes in the hall and went into the kitchen. The light was on, and the back door was unlocked, but there was nobody there.

He walked from room to room, calling Abigail, finishing his search in the bedroom. Everywhere were signs of a baby in residence. Aiden's face was white and bloodless. He opened their phone book, searching for a number.

"Daisy, is Abigail with you? I've just got home and there's no sign of her."

"Oh, hi Aiden! Glad you're home. No, Abigail isn't with me. Is her car in the drive?"

"Yes, it's parked as usual."

"Perhaps she's taken Sam out for a quick walk?"

"No, Sam's here with me. Daisy, everywhere I look in the house, I see baby stuff. What on *earth* is going on?"

A long pause.

"She hasn't told you anything?"

"No."

Another long pause.

"Well, Aiden, it's not my place to tell you really. I think you need to discuss it with Abigail."

"But she's not here!"

"If you are really worried, perhaps you should talk to Stan."

"Stan Cooper? The policeman?"

"Yes."

"Thank you, Daisy, I'll consider that."

With a shaking hand, Aiden replaced the receiver, then searched the house again, calling Abigail as he went. He opened the back door and turned on the outside garden lights. Nothing moved. No sounds apart from an owl calling in Sixpenny Woods.

"Abs! Are you out here?"

No response.

Aiden went back inside and wondered what to do. He sat at the kitchen table and put his head in his hands.

In the little guest cottage in the garden, Abigail crouched in the dark, listening. She'd heard Aiden open the back door. She'd moved away from the window when he flooded the garden with light. When he called her, she shuddered and shrank down. She'd prayed that Tiffany wouldn't make a sound, and she hadn't.

The guest cottage was comfortable, with everything provided that a guest might need. It had a kitchen, a living room, bedroom and bathroom. It was brand new, rarely used. It was a perfect hide-out, but not for long. She couldn't stay there, she'd soon be discovered.

What to do? Ideally, she'd get to her car and drive away. The problem was that Aiden would hear her feet crunching across the gravel. She'd have to wait here in the guest cottage until the coast was clear, then get to her car. But she couldn't do that unless Aiden went out or went to bed. And if she did manage to get to the car, then what? Where would she drive to?

Daisy's? No, Daisy was too sensible. She wouldn't approve of what Abigail was doing. She'd make her go back to Aiden, and then there'd be fireworks. Aiden would say they couldn't keep Tiffany, and Tiffany would be taken away. No, she couldn't go to Daisy.

Perhaps her sister in Yewbridge? Abigail considered that one. It was a possibility.

Abigail's thinking was muddled. Distress was eating away at her and she'd lost the ability to make rational decisions. She was mentally exhausted, and her mind was jumbled. Only one idea remained clear in her head: every moment she had with Tiffany was precious. She needed to watch and wait until the lights went off and the coast was clear. She began humming softly.

Inside the main house, Aiden was still in the kitchen, fretting. Should he follow Daisy's advice and phone the police? Or wait? Perhaps Abigail would walk through that door any moment.

But he knew she wouldn't. In spite of the lateness of the hour, he reached for the phone.

11

Flying was not an activity Martha Guttman particularly enjoyed, although Business Class seats did make the experience somewhat less gruelling. Sitting still for long periods of time was not something she found easy.

None of the movies offered interested her and she'd already had a manicure and hand massage. Now she was thirsty. Irritably, she pressed the button to summon the hostess.

In the galley, the two air hostesses on duty exchanged glances when Martha's seat number buzzed and lit up.

"Your turn," said one. "I waited on her ladyship last time."

The other nodded, smoothed her hair and made her way down the aisle to Martha's seat. She drew the curtain aside a fraction and popped her head round, smiling.

"You rang?"

"Tea. Earl Grey. In a proper china cup and saucer."

"Yes, ma'am."

If the curtain hadn't swung back, Martha would have seen the hostess make a face and roll her eyes.

Martha stretched her feet, hoping the flight wasn't going to make her ankles swell. Earlier she had raised her leg and stretched her toes and noticed the man across the aisle gawking at her. That's why she'd drawn the curtain.

Men! Gee, they were so stupid. And so easy to control. She'd been shipped over from the New York office specifically to work on this contract with Aiden. And Aiden was cute, but stupid. A perfect short-term distraction.

Reeling in Aiden like a fish had been child's play. All she had to do was smile at him, and laugh at his stupid jokes. Of course the short skirts had helped, and the way she sat just a little too close when they worked on papers together.

Huh! What's a girl supposed to do to entertain herself when she's so far from home? She was bored, and Aiden was available.

The company, keen to impress the clients, provided them with a penthouse suite in the heart of the city. It served as an office as well as somewhere to conduct important conferences. It also had two separate bedrooms, one of which was abandoned a few times when her strategy to seduce him succeeded. His initial protests about his silly little wife in Ten Cent Dump had been easily brushed aside.

It was all temporary, anyway. Martha didn't want to stay in the UK, she missed the razzle-dazzle and energy of New York City.

It had taken a year of hard work, but they'd won the contract which had earned them both a great deal of money in bonuses. If only she hadn't made that one stupid mistake…

But even that had turned out hunky-dory in the end.

Hadn't it?

Better than okay. Gee, Aiden had handed her *even more* dollars to keep her quiet. She smiled as she thought of her extremely healthy bank balance.

Yep, she'd done the right thing accepting it.

Hadn't she?

Tufty, the Cooper's scruffy brown and white dog, jumped up excitedly and wagged his stumpy tail in welcome.

"Ah, you're back, good timing," said Sally Cooper to her husband.

She opened the oven door and slid the piping hot shepherd's pie out. It was golden brown and slightly crispy on the top. Perfect.

"Dinner's ready. Did you enjoy yourself? Relax a bit?"

"Thanks, yes," said Stan as he washed his hands and splashed water on Sally's clean floor. "I had a good chat with Angus behind the bar, but unfortunately, he hasn't heard anything. My, that pie smells good."

Before he had the chance to sit down, the phone rang. Stan and Sally looked at each other. Phone calls at that time of night were not good news. It usually meant that the call had been diverted from the police station next door, and something needed urgent attention.

"I'll get it," said Stan heavily, and lifted the receiver. "PC Cooper here, how can I help you?"

"Ah, Stan, it's Aiden Martin here, Abigail Martin's husband."

"Good evening, sir."

He waited. Often people needed a moment to collect themselves before speaking to the police.

"Stan, I've just got back from London expecting Abigail to be here, but there's no sign of her. The house is empty, except for baby stuff. I phoned Daisy Grainger and she doesn't know where my wife is, and she wouldn't tell me anything. She told me to get the story from you."

"Right, sir."

Stan looked at the shepherd's pie waiting for him, then at Sally poised with the serving spoon.

"Do you think you could wait half an hour? The thing is, I haven't eaten yet. I'll just have a quick bite then I'll cycle up to you. If Mrs Martin turns up in the next half hour, give me a call."

He nodded at Sally, and the serving spoon descended, digging into the pie. Stan's mouth watered.

"Yes, that's fine," said Aiden trying hard not to sound worried. "Thank you. I'll leave the lights on in the drive and I'll see you soon."

From the dark of the guest cottage in the back garden, Abigail could clearly see Aiden in the lit kitchen of the house. She saw him talking on the phone. Then she saw him put his head in his hands again.

For a moment she was tempted to go to him. She pictured herself entering the kitchen and putting her arms round him, telling him not to worry. But one glance at the sleeping baby in the basket stopped her. Aiden wouldn't understand.

At the first opportunity, she'd get to her car and escape.

She hummed tunelessly under her breath and waited.

In the Cooper household, Stan was mopping his plate clean with a slice of bread.

"Delicious," he said. "The last thing I feel like doing is cycling up to the Martin's house now, but I think I must. Strange that Mrs Martin is missing. I imagine there's a simple reason for it."

"I think it's very strange that Mr Martin didn't know anything about the baby," Sally remarked.

Stan reluctantly climbed on his bike and cycled through the village and up the lane to the Martin's house, turning into their gravelled drive. He dismounted, and walked his bike to the front door, leaning it against the wall. He pressed the bell.

In the guest cottage, Abigail had stopped humming. She stood motionless, listening. Was that somebody crunching on the gravel of their drive? When the doorbell rang in the distance, she jumped. Who could be visiting at this time of the night? From the shadows of the cottage, she watched the illuminated kitchen.

She saw Aiden stand and go to answer the door. Moments later, he returned with Stan and they both sat at the table. Abigail's jaw dropped with horror. *Aiden had called the police?*

This changed everything. How long before they searched the

garden and guest cottage? And they'd hear her on the gravel if she tried to reach her car.

Reason abandoned her completely. Now she saw herself as rescuing Tiffany, and it never occurred to her that she herself might be charged with kidnapping a child.

"Sleep, little baby," she whispered. "We have to move, otherwise they'll get you."

Tucking the coverlet more tightly around the baby, she slipped on her jacket. Lifting the moses basket by the handles, she opened the cottage door and crept outside into the garden. Aiden and Stan were still sitting at the kitchen table, deep in conversation.

The basket was heavy and cumbersome, but Abigail scarcely noticed. Avoiding the rectangle of light thrown out by the kitchen window, she skirted the garden, hugging the boundary, heading for the end.

Luckily she was very familiar with the layout, and didn't need the flashlight. She had no real plan, just a desperate desire to escape from her husband and the police.

The grounds of the house were extensive, and it took her some time to reach the spot that she had in mind. There was a break in the hedge where deer had pushed through, and Abigail planned to use it to her advantage. Now, out of sight of the house, she clicked on the flashlight and ran the beam along the hedge, searching for the gap.

There it was!

Walking backwards to protect the baby from branches that might spring back, she pushed through and into Archie Draper's field on the other side.

Now where?

Sixpenny Woods?

She shuddered. No, too dark and full of unknown dangers. One of Archie's outbuildings would be preferable for the moment. Then, in the morning, she could keep an eye on the lane, and quickly return to collect her car if Aiden went out.

But she had to hurry. Tiffany would soon be awake for her next feed.

Archie's recently ploughed field made the ground soft under her feet. The moon wasn't full, and clouds scudded across it frequently, but there was enough light to see the big open field, and the silhouette of the farmhouse beyond it. Clustered around the farmyard were barns and outbuildings.

Abigail set off. Walking straight was easy because all she needed to do was follow the line of the furrow. Luckily there hadn't been much rain recently or the field would have been a quagmire. But it was a big field, and the basket was getting heavier and heavier. Her arms ached.

The flashlight beam began to dim, so she turned it off to conserve the battery. She could manage without it because her feet had grown accustomed to following the line of the turned earth.

She switched the basket from one hand to the other, trying to relieve her aching arms and wrists. A deer barked in the distance. Something scuttled over her shoe, but she ignored it, concentrating only on putting one foot in front of the other.

She longed to find shelter and a place to set the basket down and rest her weary limbs. Head down, she trudged on, only allowing herself the occasional glance up to see if the Drapers' farm was getting any closer.

She was sweating from exertion, the perspiration running down her face and body. She stopped, unzipped her jacket and laid it carefully over Tiffany, shielding her from the cold night air. The breeze had strengthened, and she felt both hot and cold as the perspiration sprang from her pores to be cooled immediately by the wind.

At last, when she thought her arms and legs could go no further, she reached the gate to the farmyard. Resting for a moment, she put the basket down and leaned on the gate, gathering her strength. Something rustled in the hedge beside her, but she was too tired to take fright.

No lights blazed in the farmhouse. Perhaps the Drapers were out? No. Farmers were early risers and it was more likely they had already retired to bed.

Abigail switched on the flashlight and pushed the gate open, wincing when it creaked. From inside the house, a dog barked. Abigail killed the flashlight, grabbed the basket and shrank back into the shadows.

"Tyson! Pipe down! Whatever is the matter with you?" a muffled voice shouted from inside the farmhouse.

The dog quietened down, and all was still again. The moon cast a cold pale light over bushes and buildings, creating deep shadows. Nothing stirred.

Abigail was shivering now, partly from fright and partly from the cold that had penetrated her bones now that she'd stopped walking. She slipped through the open gate and shone her torch at the first outbuilding. She tried the door, but it was locked. So was the second. She pushed the third door hard. It opened.

Hallelujah!

Inside the building, she looked around and saw bales of straw piled up to the ceiling.

We'll be warm in here for a while, she thought.

And then she had a small stroke of good fortune.

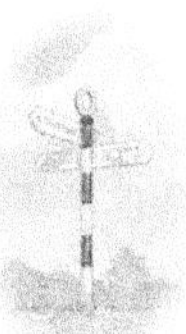

12

To Abigail's delight, the beam of her dying flashlight caught a light switch.

"Tiffany, I'm going to give you your bottle first, because I don't need light for that. By then the Drapers should be fast asleep and I can turn on the light and make us a warm, cosy den for the night."

Tiffany whimpered. It was getting close to her feed time. The fresh night air had given her an appetite and she was making it clear she was hungry. Abigail plucked her from the basket and sat on a straw bale, cuddling her close and enjoying the warmth. She offered her the bottle and the baby sucked greedily.

Abigail's teeth were chattering. She was cold and still a little shaky from the trek, but the shelter from the wind and the baby's natural warmth were taking the chill from her bones.

The building had no windows but Abigail didn't need light for this job, it was already second nature. She never tired of giving Tiffany the bottle. Normally she watched the baby's eyelashes flutter as she fed but tonight it was too dark to see. She loved the closeness, and the little contented grunting noises Tiffany made as she sucked. Abigail hoped that it didn't matter that she hadn't warmed the bottle.

"Slow down, Tiff, you'll choke! There isn't any hurry, you know," she whispered.

No sound came from the farmhouse and even the dog was quiet.

When the baby had drunk her fill, Abigail stuffed the gap under the door with loose straw, partly to block out draughts, and partly to stop any light seeping out under the door. She switched on the light, delighted when the single dirty bulb illuminated.

She still felt cold, and her head ached, but this place would do nicely for the night.

"There we are, Tiff!" she said softly. "We're going to be fine tonight. I'm going to change your nappy, then we'll have a little play, then settle down and go to sleep."

Half an hour later, Tiffany was tucked up in her basket and dozing off. Abigail switched off the light. The straw bales served as a mattress and she curled up round the basket using her jacket as a cover. Her throat was sore and every bone ached. She desperately wanted a drink and something to eat. Eventually, she dropped into a dreamless, exhausted sleep.

As the orange morning sun rose in the chilly dawn sky, Archie Draper pulled on his wellington boots and whistled to his dog. It was his favourite time of day. Just a few chores to do before he went back inside to tuck into the breakfast Molly was making for him.

"Hey, Tyson, did I leave the gate open last night? That's not like me, must be getting old."

Tyson, nose to the ground, was busy. There were strange new scents here that needed investigating. For once he ignored the barn cats and concentrated on gathering information.

Strange humans had passed here during the night.

In the hay store, Abigail opened her eyes a crack, and listened. She felt terrible; cold, shaky and lightheaded. Every muscle ached. Her throat was sore and a desire to cough overwhelmed her. She buried her face in her jacket to muffle the inevitable sound.

"Tyson, did you hear that? Thought I heard a cough."

Abigail froze, but another cough erupted. Tyson was already barking and pawing at the door.

"Tyson, who's in there?"

Tiffany woke and began to whimper. Abigail sat up, grabbed the handles of the basket and took a deep breath.

Archie held Tyson's collar and pushed the door open, allowing the morning light to flood into the dark interior. Disturbed dust particles danced crazily, suspended in the light. Archie Draper gaped at the scene before him. A woman and a baby in his hay store?

"What the…"

Abigail tried to stand, but the effort was too much. She sat down heavily again. At that moment, Tiffany decided that she was ravenous and began to yell. Tyson barked excitedly.

"Ye gods and little fishes! Tyson, quiet! Abigail Martin, is that you? What on earth are you doing in here?"

Abigail stared at him, then shielded her mouth as another cough racked her.

"Here, come with me, I'll take you inside. That's a nasty cough you have there. I reckon the dust from the straw has got into your throat, or you've caught a chill. Have you been here all night? The wife'll get you some hot tea and a spot of breakfast. That'll make you feel better. Then you can tell us the whole story."

Tears trickled down Abigail's pale cheeks.

"No need to get upset!" said Archie, alarmed. "I'll take the basket, you hold the baby and hang onto my arm. You'll feel a lot better when we're inside."

Abigail allowed herself to be steered out of the store room and across the farmyard to the kitchen. Tiffany grumbled, but her yells had subsided. Archie kept up his cheery chatter, and Tyson followed, his tail wagging.

"Our kitchen is nice and warm, and I know my wife will be cracking open some new-laid eggs, and setting the table for breakfast."

Abigail didn't say a word, grateful that he didn't seem to expect a reply from her.

"Emily, put the kettle on, we've got visitors!"

His wife opened the door and her eyes widened.

"Mercy me! Come in, come in!"

"Tyson found them in the hay store," said Archie, as though Abigail was deaf. "She's freezing. I reckon she's caught a chill. Young 'un seems fine though."

As if to demonstrate there was nothing wrong with her, Tiffany exercised her lungs at full volume.

"Oh, my!" laughed Emily, peering at the baby's red, screwed up face. "Reckon I'll concentrate on your breakfast first, shall I? This bottle here ready to be warmed is it?"

Abigail nodded, and the farmer's wife stood the bottle in a bowl of hot water.

"Sit yourself down, my love. Take the weight off your feet. I'll have this bottle ready for this young madam or sir in two shakes of a lamb's tail. Then, when you've got some breakfast and a hot cup of tea or two down you, you can tell us all about it."

About a mile away, the climbing sun was shining down on other early risers. Stan dismounted from his bicycle and pushed it the remaining yards up the gravelled drive to the Martins' front door. He attempted to lean it against the wall, but the handlebars twisted round and it fell. His second attempt was more successful.

"Morning, sir," he said as Aiden swung the door open. "Ready to start the search now that it's light?"

"Morning, Stan, I'm more than ready. And I've just made a bit of a discovery. Somebody has been in the guest cottage. It's unlocked and the door was open a crack."

"Did you search it?"

"Yes, I think she was there, but she's gone now."

"Well, bearing in mind that Mrs Martin didn't take her car, or any possessions really, I don't believe she's gone far. Of course she was weighed down with the baby, too. And I think you would have passed her down the lane last night if she had gone that way. We know she'd only just left before you arrived because you said the water was still hot in the kettle."

"Where is she then?"

"We'll find her, sir. My intention is that we search until midday. After that, well, then we have a bit of a problem. We can't register Mrs Martin as a missing person. She's an adult and can do as she pleases. However, she's taken the baby. Unfortunately, if we go official, then she could be charged with kidnapping."

Aiden sighed. He blamed himself. Abigail had taken flight because of him. He was totally responsible. He'd made no attempt to understand how much she yearned for a baby. No, he'd not only high-handedly announced that he'd never adopt somebody else's child, but he'd also had an affair behind her back. He didn't deserve her.

No wonder she couldn't face him with a baby in her arms. No wonder she'd run away. And because of him she could now be looking at a serious criminal charge.

Aiden had lain awake most of the night, listening out for the slightest sound. His thoughts churned in his head like the contents of a cement mixer. Eventually he'd fallen into a fitful sleep, promising himself that when he found her, he'd beg her forgiveness.

"I'm guessing she didn't cross the gravel at all, or you'd have heard her," remarked the policeman.

"What? You think she may have gone down the garden and across the fields?"

"It's possible…"

"Right! Let's go! No, Sam, you can't come."

Sam's ears were pricked and his delight at an unexpected early morning walk was evident.

"Excuse me, sir, but I think Sam might be able to help us here. He's a retriever, right?"

"Yes."

"Well, perhaps if you let him sniff something of the baby's, he might be able to help with the search?"

"Genius! Yes! Do you know, Stan, I think you may be onto something there!"

Aiden grabbed a towelling bib that was lying on the kitchen table and held it up to Sam's nose. Sam wagged his tail.

"Go find it, Sam, go find it!"

13

*S*am was in his element. This is what he was born for! Feathery tail swishing furiously, he bounded out of the kitchen door and into the garden. Nose down, he trotted along the path until he came to the guest house.

The two men looked at each other. Neither man was surprised, but they were definitely impressed by the dog's sense of smell.

Aiden let Sam into the guest cottage. Sam sniffed around, particularly near the window, then ran outside again, along the hedge, towards the bottom of the garden.

"Hold on, boy," panted Aiden, and clipped a lead onto his collar. "Okay, go find it!"

Sam usually walked perfectly on the lead, but today he was on a mission. Today he was hunting down the little human that smelled of milk. His nose never stopped working and he strained on his lead, pulling so hard that Aiden was forced to jog, the policeman trotting close behind.

Sam skirted the garden, paws soaked by the dewy grass. He followed his nose, and that took him along the hedgerow, exactly where Abigail had walked the night before. When he came to the gap in the hedge, he didn't hesitate. He pushed through, tugging his master behind him.

"Shucks!" said Stan to himself as a branch whipped back and struck his face.

Once in the field, Sam swung his head left and right, until he picked up the scent again, clear and strong.

"Looks like we're going for a trek across the field!" Stan panted.

Aiden felt a little more positive now they had a definite purpose, but he was tortured by the thought of Abigail stumbling across the field in the dead of night, clutching a newborn baby. They *must* find her. And quickly.

Abigail stared hungrily at the plate of food that Emily placed in front of her.

"There you are, my love. Two fresh, lightly boiled eggs, some buttered toast and as many cuppas as you can drink. Everything always looks better after a decent breakfast, you mark my words."

Abigail looked from Emily to the plate in front of her. She still hadn't said a word since she'd been discovered.

"Pass me that little angel," said Emily, "and I'll feed her while you tuck in. Oh my, Archie, were our kids ever this small?"

Silently, Abigail released her hold on Tiffany and watched as the baby sucked furiously on the bottle the farmer's wife offered her. Only then did she nibble on the corner of a slice of toast.

It tasted good. No, it tasted delicious. Abigail polished off both eggs, all the toast and a big mug of tea. For the first time in hours she felt warm, inside and out. Her throat was no longer sore and her headache had departed.

"You look better already," remarked Archie. "You've got some colour back in your cheeks."

"Thank you," said Abigail softly. "I'll never forget your kindness."

She looked round the comfortable, shabby kitchen and thought of her own chic one, knowing she infinitely preferred the Drapers'.

None of the chairs matched, neither did the worn, handmade cushions. In Abigail's kitchen, every chair matched, and the cushion fabric repeated the pattern on the curtains. Crockery occupied every space on the Drapers' dresser, along with a basket of eggs, and some jam jars. At home, crockery was arranged artistically on Abigail's dresser, and rarely used. Here, Tyson lay on a threadbare rug near the cooking range, compared with Sam's elegant rarely-used dog bed at home.

The kitchen table was huge, but dented and scratched, the wood pale from decades of scrubbing. An enormous teapot dressed in a knitted tea-cosy sat in the centre.

"Another cup of tea?" asked Archie, watching her.

"Thank you, yes, I'd love one. And I owe you both an explanation."

"When you're ready, my love, no rush," said Emily.

Nobody noticed Tyson's ears prick up. Nobody saw him jump to his feet, alert, listening.

"I'm ready now," said Abigail, and took a deep breath. "You must be wondering why…"

But she never finished her sentence, because somebody knocked on the kitchen door at the same time as Tyson began barking.

Abigail leapt up, nearly knocking over her chair, and snatched Tiffany from Emily's arms.

"Don't let them take her!" she hissed, terror in her eyes.

"Nobody is going to take your baby from you," said Emily, putting her arm round her frightened guest. "Archie, open that door!"

"Stand back," he said, grabbing the poker.

He opened the door decisively, then gaped.

"Morning, Mr Draper," said Stan. "Sorry to disturb you so early. May I come in for a chat?"

Sam was already in the kitchen, renewing his acquaintance with his old friend Tyson, and greeting Abigail with delight.

"Of course," said Archie and stood back to allow the policeman entry.

"I don't think you'll be needing that!" said Stan, pointing at the poker in Archie's hand.

The intense atmosphere lightened immediately as everyone but Abigail smiled and Archie replaced the poker.

"Is Aiden with you?" she asked, white-faced.

"Yes, he's outside. I wanted to see you first."

"How did you know where I was?"

"Ah, Sam helped us there. Excellent retriever he is! Led us a merry chase through your hedge and across the fields."

Abigail forced herself to blurt out the one question that she really didn't want answered.

"Have you found out anything more about Tiffany's parents?"

"Yes."

Abigail's heart beat like a drum.

"I think the mystery has been largely cleared. We now know the identity of the baby's mother, and the father, and how you came to find her in Sixpenny Woods."

Archie and his wife exchanged glances. None of this made any sense at all.

Abigail's distress was palpable. Her knees were shaking and she sank down onto a chair, tears coursing down her face. Her hold on the baby was vice-like.

"So you are going to take Tiffany away?"

"No," said Stan gently. "No, I'm not."

"It's a trick! You're going to take her! If you *know* who the parents are, then why am I allowed to keep her? Aiden put you up to this!"

Emily rested a supportive hand on Abigail's arm.

"I'm sure that's not the case, my love," she said gently.

"It is! It is the case! Aiden will never let me foster or adopt a baby! That's why I ran away!"

Before anyone could answer, another figure stepped into the doorway. Aiden stood framed, his face strained and as pale as the milk in the chipped jug. The room fell silent.

"Abigail, Stan is telling the truth. The reason why nobody will ever take the baby away is because Tiffany is my daughter."

14

"**R**ight," said Stan, breaking the silence. "I'm going to return to the station and collect my car. Then I'll come straight back and take the three of you home."

"I've chores to do outside," said Archie tactfully. "It's time I got the tractor out, those fields won't plough themselves."

He hurried out of the door, grabbing his coat and boots on the way.

"I'm going to check the ewes and collect the eggs," said Emily, zipping up her jacket and pulling on fingerless knitted gloves. "Help yourself to tea or anything you want."

It was unlikely that either Aiden or Abigail heard her kind words or saw her leave the kitchen, they were still staring at each other, speechless.

Aiden sat down heavily.

"Abs, I'm so sorry..."

Abigail stared back at her husband with ice-cold eyes but her hold on the baby didn't loosen. She felt as if a claw had grabbed hold of her heart. She suddenly recalled the old gypsy's words.

Be warned ... you may feel as though your heart is being ripped from your chest.

Eventually she managed to force out some words. Her tone was flat, expressionless.

"I don't understand."

"Abs, everything is my fault, and I've behaved appallingly. If you never forgive me, I wouldn't blame you."

"I don't understand. Explain."

"You know how I've been working flat out on the contract… I've been away from you and Sixpenny Cross so much. I know that's no excuse, but I kind of lost my way."

"Explain." Abigail's eyes were narrow and flinty.

"I'm so sorry, Abs. I had an affair."

"Go on."

Aiden was gabbling now, eager for her to understand but mortified at having to confess.

"I had to work really closely with a woman called Martha Guttman, and we just kind of began a relationship."

Abigail snorted.

"Martha is American. We had a relationship, well, just a brief fling really. I don't think we ever had any strong feelings for each other. It didn't last long."

"How could you!" Abigail spat. "Didn't she know you were married?"

"Yes, but she didn't care."

"Neither did you, it seems."

"Abs, I'm so sorry, so very sorry. It should never have happened."

"No, you bet it shouldn't."

"And then," Aiden took a big breath, "then Martha announced she was pregnant. It was a big shock, to both of us, especially as we weren't even romantically involved. She was horrified and insisted on having an abortion, but I couldn't bear the thought of that. I persuaded her to have the baby, and then sign it over to me. She didn't take that much persuading as Martha's main interest in the world is money. So I offered her a lot, and she agreed to the deal."

Abigail simply couldn't believe what she was hearing. Had the world gone crazy?

"She gave her daughter away for *money?*"

"Yes, Martha is like that. She doesn't have a maternal bone in her body. She hated being pregnant, but she looked on it as a lucrative nine-month job. And she hated England, couldn't wait to get away when the baby was born and our work was over."

"I still don't understand. What were you planning to do with the baby?"

"At first I thought I'd just tell the truth and bring the baby home to you."

"That would have been the right thing to do."

"Yes, but I couldn't face telling you I'd had an affair. I was so ashamed." Aiden buried his face in his hands. "And so I hatched a plan. One weekend when I was home, I took Sam for a walk in Sixpenny Woods and visited the travellers. I introduced myself to Bufniță and I told her to get you into conversation and persuade you to come to Sixpenny Woods at an appointed time. I told her that you were very kind-hearted and gullible, and that you'd probably give her your watch if she asked for it, in exchange for information."

"It was you! You set Bufniță up! You told her to ask for my watch?"

"Yes. If you hadn't given it, she'd still have told you to go to the woods at an appointed time. I had already given her a lot of money and promised her more if you didn't give her your watch. I just thought you'd be more likely to turn up if she'd taken your watch."

"Did she know about the baby?"

"No, nothing. I just told her to get the gypsies to move on as soon as she'd got you to agree to go to the woods the next day. I needed the coast clear so I could leave the baby there for you to find."

"How *could* you! What if I hadn't come to the woods? What if somebody else found her? What if animals attacked her?"

"I was there watching all the time. You didn't see me. I was worried that Sam would see me though."

Abigail remembered the sound of a car driving away at the time. And hadn't Daisy said that she thought she'd seen Aiden's car?

"And the delivery? I suppose you ordered all that baby stuff?"

"Yes."

"You disgust me."

"Abs. I'm sorry."

"You had an affair. You lied. You cheated. You schemed and manipulated."

"Yes."

"I don't think I can ever forgive you for this."

"Abs..."

"You betrayed me."

"Abs..."

"You tricked me into falling in love with your baby."

"Abs, she could be *our* baby if you'd only forgive me," he begged. "I'll do anything, go to counselling, anything. My brief affair with Martha made me realise how much I love you. What a fool I've been!"

"I can hardly bear to look at you."

"Abs..."

Aiden's eyes beseeched her and his hand snaked out across the table to reach hers.

"Don't touch me! I told you, I can't even bear to look at you."

Abigail looked down at the baby and stroked her soft cheek with one finger. Her mind was in turmoil. She began humming a tuneless song.

Martha paid for the postcard and walked out of the store. Central Park wasn't particularly busy, and she headed for an empty bench, her high heels and the sway in her walk attracting the attention of several men in the vicinity.

She pulled the lid off her pen, thought for a moment, then wrote a sentence. Then she wrote the destination address on the other side. She had no trouble remembering it.

12, Sixpenny Lane,
Sixpenny Cross,
Near Yewbridge,

Dorset.

Gee, what a darned stupid address!

A sparrow hopped a few feet away, searching for fallen crumbs from picnickers' packed lunches. Two fledgelings hopped behind her, beaks agape in hope. A pair of joggers ran by, then two young mothers, deep in conversation, pushing strollers. She watched them until they were out of sight.

She read her message again, nodded with satisfaction, then slipped the postcard into the nearest mailbox.

15

Stan wrapped his hands round the mug of tea his wife had handed him. Last night, when Aiden Martin had admitted to his affair and to being the father of the baby, Stan had been very surprised.

"Good gracious! Well, that's not what I expected!" Sally had said, just as surprised as her husband.

Stan had just returned from delivering Aiden, Abigail, and the baby back to their house in the lane.

"So what happened when you drove them back to their house?" Sally Cooper wanted to know now.

"They were hardly speaking. Mrs Martin looked as though she was in shock. And Mr Martin just stared out of the window. When they got out of the car, they were very polite, but you could have cut the atmosphere with a knife."

"Who was carrying the baby?"

"She was."

"Good. She hasn't turned against the little mite then. Babies have a way of bringing people together. I guess we'll just have to wait and see."

Several days had slipped by since Aiden's revelation. In spite of what he'd done, it was hard for Abigail to simply stop loving her husband. True, he'd lost her trust, and she was still furious, but Aiden was her husband. She knew him well enough to know that he was genuinely distraught and desperately sorry for what he'd done.

In his favour, he was gentle and attentive to her at all times, and clearly adored Tiffany.

Perhaps time would heal her hurt.

Aiden came into the room.

"Good news! I've just been talking on the phone to the company. They're still thrilled about the contract being secured. I suggested that in future, I work more from home, and only go up to London for meetings. My boss was quite happy with that idea."

Abigail looked at him.

"That means I'll be home much more. I can help you, and be with you and Tiffany. Only if you'd like that, of course."

Abigail paused before speaking.

"Yes, I think I'd like that," she said at last.

Aiden stooped to drop a kiss on his daughter's head and, with a new spring in his step, headed back to the room he had converted into an office.

On the front doormat, something brightly coloured caught his eye. He picked up a postcard and stared at the picture before turning it over to read. It was a New York city skyline, instantly recognisable by the Empire State building and Twin Towers. His heart lurched. He knew only one person in New York. Turning it over, he read the message.

I'm beginning to have second thoughts about giving up the brat.

Oh no! What did it mean? Was Martha going to become a nuisance? She'd made it very clear that she didn't want to be saddled with a baby and he'd paid her handsomely. What was she playing at?

What to do?

Nothing, he decided. Except to phone the telephone company to get her calls blocked, just in case. Perhaps this was just another of Martha's malicious games.

———

Time is a great healer, and slowly, slowly, as the days passed, Abigail's broken heart began to mend itself. She brooded about Aiden's betrayal a little less each day and her time was taken up with the joy of raising Tiffany.

Together, she and Aiden set up Tiffany's nursery and established a routine. Any outsider might have thought they were the perfect little family.

Aiden dared to hope that one day, Abigail would forgive him.

The only fly in the ointment was Martha. The woman was so spiteful and unpredictable. Every day he listened for the postman's footsteps on the gravel drive and made sure he was the first to pick up the mail.

The next postcard showed the Statue of Liberty against a clear blue cloudless sky. Little boats dotted the island around it. The message was terse.

Blocking phone calls from me won't work because I know where you live.

Aiden's heart went cold. Could she take Tiffany back? Or was this just another ploy for more money? Should he tell Abigail?

No, he decided, it would destroy her.

Weeks passed and things were going well between them. No more postcards arrived and Abigail seemed to be warming to him a little more each day. Next week was her birthday and he had made big plans to surprise her.

On the morning of her birthday, a timid tap on the bedroom door woke Abigail.

"Come in..."

"Happy birthday, Abs."

"You remembered."

"Of course."

Aiden came in, carrying a beautifully arranged breakfast tray complete with a tiny vase of primroses.

Abigail sat up sleepily.

"Gosh, that looks wonderful! Thank you."

"And I have something for you."

He reached into his pocket and pulled out a tiny gift-wrapped box and placed it on the tray.

"What's this?"

"Open it."

Abigail tore off the paper and opened the box. It was an exquisite Tiffany eternity ring. She gasped and looked at Aiden.

"It's beautiful."

"I had it engraved, although the writing is so tiny you may need a magnifying glass to read it. It says 'You are my world - A'. I want you to know how sorry I am and that I will love you and Tiffany forever. I want you to think of that whenever you see the ring."

"That was a lovely thought," she said, slipping it on her finger with her engagement ring and wedding band.

Aiden smiled down at his wife. She smiled back.

"Now go and get another plate," she said. "Help me eat this lovely breakfast. There's far too much for one, and hurry up because Tiff will be yelling for her breakfast in a minute."

Abigail never forgot that birthday. It was a beautiful day, and they went for a walk along the lane. Aiden pushed the pram and Abigail held Sam's lead. The grass verges were lush and green, and wild flowers peeped at the little family as they passed.

Archie Draper saw them go by from a distance and smiled, making a mental note to tell Emily that all seemed well with the Martins.

Aiden cooked a romantic meal for two that evening. He poured sparkling champagne into glasses.

"To us, and the future," he said.

"To us," said Abigail, raising her glass.

Their eyes locked.

That night they shared a bed for the first time in months.

16

When no more postcards plopped onto the doormat during the following weeks, Aiden dared to hope that Martha had lost interest and would no longer harass him.

Life was good. Tiffany was thriving, and Abigail was beginning to regain her sparkle. The wound that Aiden had inflicted was deep, but she was healing.

Then one dark day, another postcard landed on the mat. A garish photo of Times Square stared up at him. Aiden picked it up, shuddering, and read the message on the back. This time it was a little longer.

I've made my decision. I'm coming to collect the brat. Be warned, no court in the US or UK would come between a baby and its real mother.

Aiden's face was ashen. The thought of losing his baby daughter was unbearable. Should he warn Abigail and risk breaking her heart again? With a trembling hand, he placed the postcard with the others, hidden in his desk drawer.

Next day, another arrived, a picture of Brooklyn Bridge on the front.

I've booked the flight. I'll hire a car at Gatwick and drive down to Ten Cent Dump. See ya!

Aiden needed advice and made a decision. He dialled Stan Cooper's number at the police station.

"Morning, Stan. Aiden Martin here. I wonder whether I could pop down and see you for a chat? Something's come up and I would really appreciate your advice."

"Morning Mr Martin. Of course! Is it official business, or just friendly advice? I only ask because if it's informal, instead of going to the police station, knock on our kitchen door and Sally will make us a cuppa. Sometimes three heads are better than two."

"It's just friendly advice I need, and a cup of tea would be nice, thank you. It's about Tiffany."

Plucking the postcards from his drawer, he slipped them into his inside jacket pocket and called to Abigail who was upstairs with Tiffany.

"Abs, I'm going to walk down to the village to post a letter. Do you want anything?"

"No, thanks, don't think so. I'm going to try to have a tidy up here, otherwise Hilary will be very shocked when she comes back to start cleaning again next week. We'll see you later."

Aiden sat at the kitchen table with Stan and Sally Cooper.

"I took the liberty of filling Sally in on all the details," said Stan. "I hope you don't mind."

Aiden shook his head.

"How is that little baby of yours?" asked Sally, smiling.

"She's gorgeous, thank you, growing fast. Abigail is a fantastic mother. But the reason I've come is this..."

He drew out the postcards and handed them to Stan one by one, in the order in which they had arrived.

"They're from Martha, of course. Tiffany's real mother."

Stan looked at each card, front and back, then passed them to his wife, who gasped.

"You see, I don't know if she's telling the truth, or just trying to frighten me to get more money out of me."

"She certainly doesn't sound very motherly," remarked Sally.

Stan laid the postcards in a row, end to end, and sat quietly thinking.

"But can she really take Tiffany away?" asked Aiden.

"Surely she can't," said Sally. "Can she, Stan?"

Stan took a deep breath.

"Here's what I think, for what it's worth. I think Martha is probably trying to scare you into offering her more money. If that's the case, you mustn't pay her because it'll never stop. She'll always be asking you for more money."

Sally and Aiden nodded.

"However, let's say that, after all, she's genuinely decided she wants to be a mother and take Tiffany back. I'm afraid it's possible that she *could* claim the baby. But she can't just turn up and knock on your door and expect you to hand over the baby. These things take time and have to be done officially. There'll be DNA checks and paperwork to complete. Maybe even a court case."

"You did well keeping these postcards," said Sally, tapping the cards on the table. "They may be used as evidence later."

"I suggest this," continued Stan. "Keep me informed of everything. If any more postcards arrive, tell me straight away. And if she turns up, *don't* let her in, just call me immediately."

"Should I tell Abigail, do you think?"

"Judging by these postcards, Martha is very unstable. If she writes again, yes, I think you should tell Abigail. I think it's only fair to warn her," said Sally.

Stan nodded in agreement.

"With any luck, Martha will just give up, and you won't hear any more," he said.

The next day, the sky was black and storm clouds rolled in. Torrential rain fell, leaving great puddles in the lane.

In spite of the terrible weather, the postman crunched up the drive to deliver the mail. A picture postcard dropped on the mat. It showed a picture of Big Ben, and bore an English first class stamp. Aiden's pulse raced as he picked it up.

Cooeee! I'm here! Gotten myself a car and should reach Ten Cent Dump tomorrow. Make sure the brat is ready.

Aiden checked the postmark. Yesterday! That meant that Martha could arrive at any minute!

He raced to the phone and read the latest message out loud to Stan.

"Right," said Stan. "Make sure all your doors are locked. If anything happens, and I mean *anything,* inform me. And I think you should tell Mrs Martin."

Outside, the storm raged. Giant raindrops pounded the windows and lightning flashed in the sky. Aiden walked into the kitchen where Abigail was rocking Tiffany to sleep.

"Can you believe this weather?" she asked, staring through the window.

"Abs, I need to tell you something. I didn't want to, but it's important."

Abigail caught the urgency in his tone and looked up, concerned.

"What is it?"

So Aiden told her about the postcards, and his visit to Stan. He showed her the cards and saw her face blanche. He handed her the final postcard.

"The postmark means she's on her way now," he said.

Abigail's hand covered her mouth in shock.

"What shall we do?"

"Stan says we should lock all the doors. She can't take Tiffany, and we're not going to let her into the house. If she turns up, we phone the police."

Abigail's face was white, but her jaw had a determined set to it. She nodded, clutching Tiffany closer to her.

"I think you should take Tiffany upstairs, and I'll keep watch downstairs."

As he spoke, the sky flashed white, followed by a terrific clap of thunder that shook the house.

All the lights went out.

iden grabbed the flashlight from the drawer. Rain lashed the windows.

"Quick! Grab everything you might need and take Tiffany upstairs. I'll help you get settled then I'm going to wait down here. If that madwoman turns up, I'll be ready, storm or no storm. Let's hope the electricity comes back on soon."

When Abigail and Tiffany were safely installed upstairs, Aiden took up his station by the window, watching the rain bounce as it hit the ground. It was going to be a long day and night.

The hours ticked past and there was no sign of Martha. The rain never eased and the black clouds remained knitted together, blocking out any glimpse of the night sky. At around 3:00am, Aiden could keep his eyes open no longer. He slept fitfully in the chair by the window, but even as he slept he was listening for a car or footsteps on the gravel.

The electricity stayed off until morning. The ground was soaked and puddles glimmered under the grey sky, but the rain had stopped. Aiden tensed when he saw a figure approaching. He relaxed when he saw it was the postman who dropped two bills through the letterbox. No postcards.

Abigail came downstairs. She looked exhausted.

"Do you think Martha was lying?" she asked.

"I don't know…"

The phone rang and they both jumped.

"Stan here. Nothing to report?"

"No, nothing. I stayed on watch all night."

"Well, perhaps it was an empty threat. I suggest you get some rest, but keep your doors locked for the moment, just in case. I've got my work cut out because of this storm, it's created havoc in the village. But I'll be here if you need me."

Aiden and Abigail tried hard to relax, but found it difficult. They talked endlessly about the possibility of Martha turning up, their eyes forever flicking to the window, their ears tuned in to the sound of any approaching car. To Aiden's relief, Abigail and he were united, utterly determined that Martha would never claim Tiffany.

Already worn out from being awake all night, every new noise alarmed them. They stared questioningly at each other, silently attempting to analyse the source of the sound. Their nerves jangled. When the paper boy wheeled his bike up the drive, they both nearly jumped out of their skins.

The phone rang again and Aiden picked it up.

"Hello?"

"Mr Martin? Stan Cooper here again. Have you had the Yewbridge Gazette yet?"

"Yes, it's just been delivered, this very minute. Why?"

"Do you have it there in front of you? Look at the main story. I think you have nothing further to worry about." Stan rang off.

Aiden picked up the paper and smoothed it out. The whole of the front page was devoted to last night's storm.

Aiden stared at the main photo which showed the wreckage of a white car.

"Abigail! Look at this!"

"Oh my…"

STORM CLAIMS LIFE OF US TOURIST

Police have confirmed that the violent storms of yesterday have claimed the life of an American tourist. The driver appears to have lost control on a sharp bend between Yewbridge and Sixpenny Cross. There were no witnesses.

A police spokesman said, "The accident was reported by a motorist at 4:00pm yesterday. The car must have swerved off the road in the bad weather and hit a tree. The driver was pronounced dead on arrival at Yewbridge Hospital. Our enquiries show that the car was hired at Gatwick Airport by a Miss Martha Guttman. A passport has been found and a positive identification has been made.

Miss Guttman's family in New York have been informed. Miss Guttman was not married and leaves no children."

Police have asked the public to continue to be aware of dangerous driving conditions caused by the storm.

"Abs, it's over… It's finally over."

Husband and wife fell into each other's arms. They stood entwined for a long time.

The next day, the sun shone on the village of Sixpenny Cross. The pond on the village green was fuller than anybody remembered it. The ducks' nest had been washed away, but the eggs had already hatched and the ducklings were safe and well. A tree had been struck by lightning in Sixpenny Woods, and the church had lost a few slates. Branches and debris needed to be cleared. Apart from that, there was not too much damage.

That evening, Aiden smiled into his wife's eyes across the restaurant table in Yewbridge. They must have passed the spot where Martha had spun off the road, but they hadn't looked for it.

"Well, this is a nice surprise," said Abigail. "I can't remember when we last went out to dinner together! It was good of Daisy to babysit at such short notice."

"I thought we should celebrate. I know we didn't wish Martha dead, but it's wonderful to know that nobody can ever take Tiffany away from us now."

The tiny diamonds in Abigail's eternity ring sparkled in the candlelight as she put her hand over his.

"Yes," she said, looking directly into his eyes, unblinking. "Especially since Tiffany is going to have a little brother or sister in a few months."

Aiden's eyes widened.

"Really?" he breathed.

"Yes, really."

Stan Cooper was enjoying a quiet pint in the Dew Drop. Actually, it was his second but he felt he deserved it. The Captain and his friend sat in their usual corner, and Bella Tait occupied another table, reading the Yewbridge Gazette and stroking Scout, the pub cat.

"Terrible storm, wasn't it?" said Angus, buffing up the beer taps and making conversation from behind the bar. "That poor American woman who crashed her car! What bad luck. I wonder where she was heading?"

"Dunno," said Stan, shaking his head.

"And I hear that nice Martin couple are keeping that baby that was found in the woods?"

"Yes, I heard that too," said Stan, and took a long sip of his beer.

18

*S*o you see, my dear, Abigail's story had a happy ending. She and Aiden went on to have lots more children. Abigail always wanted to fill that house in Sixpenny Lane with children, and over the years, that's exactly what she did. There wasn't one room in that house that wasn't bursting at the seams with kids, toys and laughter.

Of course, the children soon rubbed off the house's 'designer shine' and it began to look much more like a home, and less like a photo from *Country Estates* magazine. It began to look rather like the Drapers' farmhouse, cosy and rather worn round the edges. And Abigail and Aiden were very comfortable with that.

Aiden worked from home most of the time, and wore jeans with holes in them, only changing into his tailored suit when he had to go up to London on business. Money was not important to either him or Abigail. They lived for their children.

The children went to the village school across the green, which is where you will go when you're bigger. You'll like it there, and your teacher will take you on nature study trips across the green, and you'll catch little creatures with your net in the pond.

Perhaps if Martha had been a nicer person, none of this would have happened. Nobody wanted her dead, of course, but she kind of brought it on herself.

Just one little thing puzzled me and Jayne Fairweather, the postmistress, about Martha Guttman's death. You see, Jayne was the motorist who reported the accident to the police, so she was probably the first one on the scene.

She was driving back from Yewbridge to Sixpenny Cross, and she said the rain was bucketing down so hard she could scarcely see the road ahead. When she rounded the bend and caught sight of Martha's car wrapped round a tree, she stopped straight away, and rolled down her window. She realised it was extremely serious, but as she prepared to drive away to report the incident, a movement caught her eye.

She thought she saw two figures melting into the trees.

She told me it looked like an old lady with a shawl over her head, holding the hand of a small pale-faced child.

When she looked again, they'd gone, so she probably imagined it.

It's good to see you fast asleep with not a care in the world, little one. Next time I'm asked to watch over you, I'll tell you another story. Sixpenny Cross is bursting with stories.

I know you love animals, so I'm going to tell you all about Bella Tait.

Yes, _B is for Bella_. And Bella Tait's love of animals, big and small, scaly or fluffy, was a joy to behold.

But kind, loving, generous Bella didn't know she had a mortal enemy.

ABIGAIL MARTIN'S CARROT CAKE

"Abigail, sorry to be a pest, but can you give me that carrot cake recipe again, please? I can't find it and I've searched everywhere."

INGREDIENTS

- Olive oil, to grease
- 2 (about 300g) carrots
- 1 cup (150g) self-raising flour
- ½ cup (75g) plain flour
- 1 teaspoon bicarbonate of soda
- ½ teaspoon ground cinnamon
- ½ cup (80g) brown sugar
- ¾ cup (185ml) olive oil
- ½ cup (125ml) golden syrup
- 3 eggs
- 1 teaspoon vanilla essence
- 250g (8oz) spreadable cream cheese
- ½ cup (80g) icing sugar
- ½ teaspoon vanilla essence

METHOD

- Preheat oven to 170C or 150C fan-assisted, or 340F.

- Grease a 20cm (8in) round cake pan lightly with oil, and line with
  non-stick baking paper.
- Peel and grate the carrots, and set aside.
- Sift the flours, bicarbonate of soda and cinnamon into a large bowl.
- Put the brown sugar, oil, golden syrup, eggs and vanilla in a
  separate bowl. Use a balloon whisk to mix until combined.
- Pour the oil mixture into the dry ingredients. Use a wooden spoon
  to stir gently until just combined. Stir in the grated carrot.
- Pour the mixture into the pan and bake for 1 hour. Set aside for 5
  minutes, before turning out onto a wire rack to cool completely.

TO MAKE THE ICING

- Place the cream cheese, icing sugar and vanilla in a bowl. Use a
  wooden spoon to mix until well combined.
- Spread the icing over the cake.

B IS FOR BELLA

SIXPENNY CROSS 2

When two babies are born within weeks of each other in the village of Sixpenny Cross, one would expect the pair to become friends as they grow up.

But nothing could be further from the truth.

1

When I was younger, I used to amuse myself in the evenings by sewing patchwork quilts. That quilt you are sleeping under now was made for your mother. Sometimes I blink when I see you curled up in that crib because you, my dear, are the spitting image of her.

Now I have arthritis in my hands, and I can scarcely hold a needle in my crooked fingers. My poor old eyes can't see the stitches either, so I'll sew no more patchwork quilts. Heaven allowing, I'll teach you, little one, when you're older.

My own mother used to make patchwork quilts, as did her mother before her. Our quilts were washed so often that they became faded and threadbare. But we never threw them away, even when holes began to appear.

No.

Everybody knew who would be grateful for them.

Bella Tait.

Sweet Bella Tait couldn't bear to see any animal in need and cared for so many creatures that she needed all the old towels, quilts and bedding she could lay her hands on.

Yes, B is for Bella.

I'll tell you the rather unusual story of Bella Tait while you sleep, little one. It'll keep my mind busy, now that I have no quilting projects on my lap.

You see, Bella Tait and Christine Dayton were born within weeks of each other. And though they were almost neighbours, they were *never* friends.

2

In the heart of Sixpenny Woods is a curious rock. Nobody knows how old it is, or how it got there. Some say it's made of granite, but there are no traces of natural granite in that part of Dorset. How and why that huge rock came to be resting in the woods is a mystery.

Plenty of guesses have been hazarded. Some suggest that it is the remnant of some giant rock that struck our planet countless years ago. Some say it was transported by Druids, to serve as an altar. Others whisper that aliens were responsible for the appearance of a rock so out of character with its surroundings. Gypsies camp around the rock, believing in its magical qualities.

Whatever their opinions, most agree that the rock possesses supernatural powers, and since time immemorial, the inhabitants of Sixpenny Cross have called it the Wishing Rock.

The rock is nearly as tall as some of the trees around it. It is weathered and smooth, with little holes and crevices, inviting one to climb it. Ivy fights to take hold, its tendrils creeping over the surface.

In 1954, Bill Haley & His Comets recorded *Rock Around the Clock,* and Roger Bannister ran the first under four minute mile in Oxford.

That same year, a married couple were enjoying a Sunday walk through the dappled light of Sixpenny Woods.

"Hey, I'd forgotten all about the Wishing Rock!" exclaimed the young man, running up to it and pulling away the ivy to reveal the dark stone beneath. "Why don't we climb it?"

"Don't be silly, Don, it's far too hot for climbing. You climb it if you want to."

"Oh, come on! We should climb it and sit on the top, then we can both make wishes."

"Knowing me, I'll fall and break a leg."

"No, you won't, I'll help you."

They scrambled up and sat close together on the narrow summit, legs dangling. Don draped an arm around his wife's shoulders. The trees were green, thick and silent around them.

"Go on, then. Make a wish," said Don.

"You know what I'm going to wish for," June answered, a faraway look in her eyes.

"Yes, I do, but don't tell me or your wish won't come true."

June squeezed her eyes shut.

Please, Wishing Rock, no more miscarriages, no more stillbirths. Let me have a healthy baby. I don't mind what it's like, a boy or a girl, fat or thin, ugly or pretty… Just one healthy child.

Beside her, Don was also wishing.

Please help me to take June to Italy to see her grandmother's village. I'd give my life to see her exploring the place where her family came from.

On the other side of Sixpenny Cross, another husband and wife stayed indoors, oblivious to the beautiful day and the sunshine streaming through their dirty windows.

"You stupid woman! You're pregnant again? For gawd's sake, what do we need another brat for?" The man leaned forward, eyes narrowed to slits, his finger stabbing her shoulder. "Get rid of it! Did you 'ear me? I said *get rid of it*."

His wife stared at him as he emptied a beer bottle down his throat.

Maybe I will get rid of this one, she thought bitterly.

He belched.

Or maybe I won't. That would teach Mr 'igh and Mighty.

She raised her own beer to her lips and drank deeply.

Months passed. It was April the 5th, 1955, and Britain was shocked, but not surprised, to hear the following radio announcement.

"The Right Honorable Sir Winston Churchill had an audience with the Queen this evening and tendered his resignation as Prime Minister and First Lord of the Treasury, which Her Majesty was graciously pleased to accept."

The man who had led Britain throughout the war was eighty years old and his health was failing.

Down in the south of England, in the Tait household in the village of Sixpenny Cross, nobody heard the announcement. The radio wasn't even switched on.

A new life was beginning. And from the second that June and Donald Tait's newborn baby took her first gasp of air and yelled, she was adored.

"It's a girl!" said the midwife. "A beautiful baby girl with an excellent set of lungs. Let me just give her a little wash, and then I'll pass her to you and call your husband upstairs before he wears out the linoleum with his pacing up and down."

June lay exhausted but numb with happiness. After all the miscarriages and two heartbreaking stillbirths, they finally had a perfect, healthy baby.

"Do you know what you're going to call her?" asked the midwife.

"Yes. She'll be named Bella. After my Italian grandmother. Bella means 'beautiful' in Italian, you know."

"A lovely name," said the midwife. "A beautiful name for a beautiful baby."

To be fair, only a midwife or the baby's parents would have

described this baby as beautiful. Little Bella's face was scarlet, screwed up and furious.

Donald had heard the cry and didn't need calling; he raced up the stairs and charged into the bedroom. Standing at his wife's side, he clutched her hand.

"Is the baby okay?" he asked the midwife.

"Bless you, she's perfect! Here you are, I've wrapped her up. Meet your brand new little daughter."

Oh so carefully, Donald took the precious bundle from the midwife and sat down slowly on the edge of the bed. He gazed at his daughter's angry little red face, her toothless mouth wide open in a howl.

"Hello Bella," he whispered, "I'm your daddy. How beautiful you are! Believe me, whatever you want or need, for the rest of my life, I'll move heaven and earth to get it for you."

Baby Bella stopped crying and fell asleep. The midwife smiled.

On the other side of Sixpenny Cross, another baby was crying. The man slurped the last of his beer and dropped the bottle on the floor.

"Oh, for gawd's sake shut that brat up!"

"I can't help it if she cries all the time," his wife protested. "I 'aven't got time to see to her every minute."

"I told you, you shouldn't have 'ad it."

"Too late now."

"Well, call Mary then. I swear if that brat don't stop bawling, I'm outta here."

"Mary! Mary! Go and see what your baby sister wants, I'm tryin' to get your dad's dinner ready."

"But Mum, why does it always 'ave to be me?"

"Because I said so. Rock the pram a bit, see if she'll go to sleep. If she doesn't, dip 'er dummy in a drop of your dad's whiskey. Then just shut the door on 'er so we don't 'ave to listen to her bawling. And get me another bottle of stout from the cellar when you've done that. I'm parched."

Mary stamped out and they heard her speaking to the baby.

"For gawd's sake, what's the matter with you? Why are you always crying? When I'm older, I ain't going to 'ave kids, they're too much work. And I ain't going to live in Sixpenny Cross. I'd rather be back in Yewbridge, this place is a dump!"

She rocked the pram for a while, but the baby didn't stop crying.

3

"Perhaps you'd like to pass her back to your wife and we'll see if Bella will take her first feed?"

June Tait smiled into her husband's eyes and took her baby daughter, holding her close. Still half asleep, Bella latched on immediately and the room fell silent as everyone watched her suckle.

"Well, she certainly likes her food!" laughed the midwife.

That was true, and Bella never lost her love of food. When she was tiny, June and Donald marvelled at her appetite but delighted in giving her the food she so enjoyed. If anything upset her, they'd placate her with a slice of pizza or a few spoons of homemade *gelato*. She was a smiling baby who grew into a chubby, happy toddler, enveloped in the adoration of her parents.

Bella loved everything and everybody. If anybody asked her what she loved most, food and animals came high on the list. Only her parents topped them.

One day, when June was cooking macaroni in the kitchen, Bella toddled outside into the backyard. June caught sight of her daughter through the window. She was squatting on the path.

"Donald, are you there? Bella is in the garden doing something.

Could you check on her, please, and bring her in? I'm just about to serve the macaroni."

Donald strolled outside and crouched down beside his little daughter.

"What are you doing, *la mia bella* Bella?"

"Worm!" said Bella, holding up a large, wriggling earthworm for her father to admire.

Donald recoiled a fraction, then smiled at his earnest little daughter.

"Oh! He's a beauty, isn't he? Shall we put him down and go inside and have some macaroni?"

"No!"

"Willy the worm likes to dig in the garden. He doesn't want to be inside with us."

To his consternation, the little girl burst into tears.

"Want worm, want worm!"

Donald thought quickly.

"Don't cry, *la mia bella* Bella. I'll tell you what, we'll find a jam jar. We can fill it with soil and put Willy the worm in there, and take him inside to watch us eat our dinner."

The tears stopped, and serious brown eyes regarded him.

"Well, *la mia bella* Bella, what do think? Shall we do that?"

The little girl nodded.

Father and daughter found a suitable jar in the shed. Donald punched holes in the lid and together they filled the jar with soil.

"Pop him in then," said Donald, and Bella dropped the worm into the jar.

Donald sprinkled some more soil on top, screwed the lid on tight, and the pair returned to the kitchen, just as June was pouring homemade tomato and basil sauce over the steaming macaroni. They put Willy the worm on the counter to watch them eat.

Later, Willy came with them to the bathroom to see Bella have her bath. Willy listened to the bedtime story that June read to her daughter, and he stayed on the shelf when Donald turned off the light.

"I'm not sure about Bella keeping a worm in a jar," said June later. "It might not survive and Bella will be so upset."

"I can fix that," said Donald.

He took an old shoelace from the kitchen junk drawer and snipped it to roughly the same length as Willy. Then he tiptoed into his sleeping daughter's room, collected Willy's jar and emptied the contents into the garden, giving Willy back his freedom.

Then he refilled the jar with soil, dropped in the shoelace, and added more soil.

When Bella woke up in the morning, her first thought was for Willy.

"Mummy, where's Willy?"

"He's in the jar, darling. He's dug right down but you can still see a little bit of him if you look carefully. He can see you, too. Do you want to bring him to the table to watch you eat breakfast?"

For the next few weeks, 'Willy' went everywhere with the little girl, and she never suspected that she was carrying part of a shoelace around.

Willy the worm was the first of Bella's pets but by no means the last. By her fourth birthday, she was the proud owner of several guinea pigs, two hamsters, a budgerigar and five white mice.

It was only a matter of time before she asked for a kitten, but actually, the kitten found her.

Visitors who drove through Sixpenny Cross couldn't help but admire the village green and the cottages with their neat front gardens. In summer, window boxes were crammed with scarlet geraniums, and the Dew Drop Inn was decorated with hanging baskets stuffed with multi-coloured petunias.

These visitors probably wouldn't have noticed one particular street at the edge of the village. Springfield Road was a cul-de-sac flanked by new redbrick semi-detached council houses. Each one was identical in structure to the next. Some were well cared for, others not so much.

The villagers had fought Yewbridge Council when it was announced that these homes were to be built, and that the new residents would be 'difficult' families rehoused from Yewbridge council estates. But to no avail. The houses were completed and the 'problem' families moved in.

At the police station, PC Arthur Cooper groaned when he heard the news. He was close to retirement and looking forward to the day when he could hand over all duties to his son, Stan, who was following in his father's footsteps.

"Let's hope these new families don't bring trouble with them," he said to his wife.

Arthur changed the route of his beat to take in Springfield Road, just in case. He decided that a police presence couldn't do any harm.

To be fair, the new families hadn't really caused any problems yet. When Arthur cycled up the street every day, some of the residents even greeted him. But already the front gardens looked untidy, particularly the Dayton family's. The grass was overgrown and weed-filled. An old fridge lay on its side, and broken toys and a threadbare sofa sat in the drive.

Young Christine Dayton was often around. Arthur guessed that she'd been told to play outside, and he smiled at her. She stared at him, her ratty little face devoid of expression. Then she poked her tongue out, and turned her back on him.

Charming, thought Arthur and pedalled away.

He didn't see what Christine was doing. She'd found a green cricket in the long grass, and she was pulling its legs off, one by one.

The Tait's cottage in Sixpenny Cross was quite near the village green. One afternoon, June and four-year-old Bella walked over to the pond to feed the ducks. On their way home, Bella tugged at her mother's hand.

"What's that?" she asked, pointing at something in the gutter.

"Oh no," said June. "Don't look. I do believe it's a tiny kitten. I think it must have been hit by a car."

Bella froze, wide-eyed, then burst into tears.

"We have to help it!"

"I think it's too late, darling," said her mother. "I don't think it's alive."

Before June could stop her, Bella wrenched her chubby hand out of her mother's and crouched down. She lifted the mangled body of the kitten out of the dirt. A green eye cracked opened and gazed at her.

"Mummy! We have to help it!"

June jumped into action. She tugged the knitted woollen hat from her head and held it out.

"Quick, put it in there, that'll keep it warm. We'll go home and ask Daddy to take us to the Animal Hospital in Yewbridge."

Mother and daughter raced home, trying hard not to jolt the kitten nestled in the hat.

"Daddy! Daddy!"

"What's the matter, *la mia bella* Bella?"

"We got a kitty wot's been in a accident!"

The urgency in his daughter's voice stopped him correcting her English.

"We have to take it to the hostibal!"

Donald peered at the scrap of fur in his wife's hat and immediately grabbed his car keys.

"Quick, I don't think we have any time to waste."

Donald's car ate the few miles to Yewbridge in record time. They ran into the building and were immediately attended to by one of the vets. She carefully lifted the broken little body out of the hat.

"Please make her better," begged Bella.

"The vet will do her best, *la mia bella* Bella," said her father, "but that's a very sick kitten."

"I think you should go home," said the vet. "Leave her with me. I'll take a good look at her, and then I'll phone you."

The Tait family left their details at the desk and drove home.

"What will be, will be," said June.

4

*L*ater that evening, June tucked her daughter into bed.

"You know the kitty is very poorly, don't you?" she said, stroking her daughter's head.

Bella nodded, a giant tear squeezing from the corner of her dark eye.

"The hostibal will make her better."

"The hospital will do the very best they can. Now snuggle down, and we'll know more in the morning."

A little later, the phone rang.

"Hello, it's Sandra, the vet at the Animal Hospital. I have good and bad news for you," she said. "Your kitten is seriously injured. She has two broken legs and was concussed. The good news is that she has no internal injuries. I think we can fix her, but it'll be very expensive."

She named a figure and June gasped. They agreed that June should first talk with Donald and then get back to the hospital quickly with a decision.

"We can't afford this," said June sadly.

"I know," replied Donald, "but how can we allow the poor little thing to be put down? Bella will be devastated."

"Do we have the money?"

Donald took his wife's hand and gazed into her face.

"You know our Italy money? We could use that."

June looked back at her husband and finally nodded her head.

"Yes, let's use the Italy money."

The Taits had been putting aside a little money whenever they could. June's dream was to visit Italy and see the village where her grandmother had been born and raised. She wanted to feel the same sunshine that had warmed her grandmother's face, and smell the same Italian scents. She wanted to see the sapphire-blue Ionian sea, and taste the grapes and olives, just as her grandmother had.

It was hard saving up the money for the holiday. Donald didn't earn very much as a mechanic and it wasn't the first time they'd needed to raid the Italy fund. A couple of years ago, the stairs in their cottage had needed re-carpeting. Another time they had to replace the engine in the car.

This time they dipped into it for the sake of their beloved little daughter and a kitten they'd never seen before that afternoon.

"We'll get to Italy one day," promised Donald, and June nodded.

"Who knows?" she said. "Perhaps some day we'll win the football pools."

It was a nice dream.

"*La mia bella* Bella, we have good news for you," said Donald the next morning. "The hospital is going to make your kitten better."

The smile on Bella's face was worth every penny of the Italy fund.

"Can we go and see my kitty?"

"Not today, but soon."

"I'm going to call her Hattie, because she was in Mummy's hat."

"That's a perfect name, Bella. When we visit her, we'll tell her."

Bella beamed, and her parents basked in her happiness.

At Yewbridge Animal Hospital, Donald and June were worried that the metalwork on the kitten's tiny legs might alarm Bella.

Nothing could be further from the truth. Bella was fascinated by the hospital and the treatment. Years later, Donald and June agreed that visit to Yewbridge Animal Hospital marked the day that little Bella Tait decided her future.

The vet was patient, taking time to explain in simple terms why Hattie had metal pins in her back leg, and how the splint and plaster cast on her front leg would keep the bone straight while it healed.

"When you take Hattie home, you'll need to keep her in a little crate. She mustn't move around much. It's very important that she keeps as still as possible while her legs mend."

Bella absorbed the vet's words and nodded.

At last they were allowed to take Hattie home, and Bella took on most of the nursing duties. She fed the kitten by hand, and stroked her head until she purred. She sat with her, making sure she wasn't lonely and didn't move too much.

When Hattie's treatment was over, she was as lively and agile as any kitten could be. Apart from a slight limp, she was as good as new.

"Mum, can I 'ave some money?"

"What for?"

"Sweets."

"What d'you think I am? Made of bloomin' money?"

"It's not fair!" Christine kicked the wall in temper.

"I'll tell you what I *will* give you, though. A smack round the chops, that's what I'll give you."

Her hand shot out. The slap was sharp and spiteful.

Christine gasped. But she didn't cry.

Bella's first day at the village school in Sixpenny Cross was harrowing for both mother and daughter.

When the school bell rang, they followed the other mothers and children inside. Bella's new school uniform swamped her, and her leather satchel and lace-up shoes squeaked with newness.

Another mother dragged her daughter into the cloakroom. The child was thin and pasty, with a ratty face and small, hard eyes like marbles that stared at the world defiantly. Her school uniform was crumpled, stained and clearly secondhand.

"Christine, get a move on," snapped the mother. "I 'aven't got all day."

June and Bella found the peg labelled 'Bella Tait' in the cloakroom. Christine Dayton's peg was next to it.

"Right, so 'ere's your peg," said Christine's mother, hanging her daughter's coat on it. "Now, I'm off. Get yourself into the classroom, and *behave*. I don't want to 'ear no stories from your teacher that you been playin' 'er up."

Christine said nothing and showed no emotion on her pale, pinched face. Flat eyes stared at Bella and her mother. She didn't even say goodbye to the departing figure of her own mother.

June was finding it hard to leave.

"I have to go, darling," she said at last, gently detaching Bella's arms from around her legs. "I'll pick you up later, and we'll have spaghetti for dinner, shall we?"

Bella wasn't used to other children or the noise. She wanted to be home with her mother and Hattie and all the animals. She opened her mouth and howled. Christine Dayton stared on in fascination.

"Hello Bella," said the teacher, crouching down to her level. "Mummy will be back to pick you up this afternoon. Now, I wonder if you could do something for me? Our goldfish needs feeding. Can you help? And then after that, do you think you could draw me a picture of all your family?"

Bella stopped crying.

Christine needed no consoling. She flitted from one activity to the next, quickly tiring of each before moving on. If another child had what she wanted, she snatched it away or pushed them off. Christine's name was the one that the teacher used the most.

"Christine, dear, we don't push each other like that."

"Christine, please don't do that, you could hurt somebody."

"Christine, wait for your turn."

But Christine pleased herself. She stopped to watch Bella hard at work on her picture. She picked up a paintbrush, dipped it into a paint pot and deliberately swiped it across Bella's picture. The blue paint ran down Bella's picture, saturating the paper.

Christine waited, expecting a reaction, but although Bella stared at the blue paint, she didn't complain.

Christine clenched her fists. Bella was supposed to cry. Christine wandered off to cause trouble elsewhere, but she kept looking over her shoulder at Bella.

A little later, the teacher went to see how Bella was getting on with her picture. Bella was still working hard, oblivious to the children milling around her, her tongue clenched between her teeth in concentration.

"You've been busy," her teacher said. "What a lovely picture and what a lovely blue sky. Tell me who you've drawn."

So Bella explained about her mother and father, Willy the worm, Hattie the cat with the limp, the rabbits, guinea pigs, mice, rats and budgerigars.

"Gosh," said her teacher. "What a lot of animals you have! When you've finished that beautiful picture, do you think you could sort out the box of farm animals for me?"

Bella nodded.

"Then tomorrow, we're going to make animals out of plasticine."

Bella rarely cried at school again.

When the mayor of Yewbridge visited Sixpenny Cross village school, he toured the classrooms. He was ushered into Bella and Christine's class, and smiled at the children. Christine Dayton narrowed her eyes, already aware that this was an authority figure, the type of person her parents had taught her to hate. Bella was standing close by, fascinated by the important visitor with the shiny gold mayoral chain around his neck.

"Hello, little girl," he said, patting Bella on the head and ignoring Christine. "Would you like to be a mayor when you grow up?"

"No thank you," said Bella. "I'm going to be a vet."

Nobody was surprised.

Sometimes it seemed as though the Tait family was dogged by bad luck. It was always a struggle to pay the mortgage on the cottage, but other events occurred over the years, each one making it necessary to raid the Italy fund again and again.

"We'll get there one day," Donald said to his wife when their ancient boiler broke down and no amount of tinkering would fix it.

"I know," smiled June sadly, "but we need to buy a new boiler first, there's no question about that. Italy will have to wait."

"Well, I've just filled out this week's football coupon. Perhaps we'll get lucky this time and win the pools!"

But bad luck was always waiting around the corner.

With Bella at school, June took on a part-time job which certainly helped bolster the family finances. For a few hours a week, she helped Jayne Fairweather in the village shop and Post Office, and the Italy fund slowly began to swell again.

"Oh, I can almost smell the lemon groves," said June as she helped Jayne stack cereal packets on the shelf. "And I can imagine the sea, with little boats bobbing about. My grandmother came from a fishing village, you know."

"It sounds just wonderful," said Jayne, leaving to answer the phone.

She came back white-faced. June straightened up and stared at her.

"Jayne? Whatever's the matter?"

5

*J*ayne Fairweather reached out and grabbed June's hand.

"It's Yewbridge Hospital. They want to speak to you about Donald."

The colour drained from June's face. She flew to the telephone. She heard a woman's voice answer when she spoke into the receiver.

"Am I speaking to Mrs Tait?"

"Yes," June replied, her heart pounding.

"This is Sister MacArdle at Yewbridge Hospital. Your husband, Donald, had an accident at work but it's nothing to be alarmed about. A car he was working under fell on him and broke his leg. We're putting his leg in plaster before sending him home."

June breathed a huge sigh of relief. It could so easily have been a lot worse than just a broken leg.

An ambulance brought Donald home when his leg had been set in plaster. The hospital lent him a wheelchair and a pair of crutches. Bella was the first to scrawl her name on her father's cast, and then set to work drawing all the animals in the house.

"Does your leg hurt, Daddy?"

"No, *la mia bella* Bella, it doesn't hurt now, but it feels a bit itchy. They showed me the x-ray, and it was quite a clean break. They made sure that the bones were in the correct position, then they set it in plaster to stop it moving about."

"Just like Hattie's cast?" Bella was fascinated by anything medical.

"Exactly like Hattie's cast."

"Will you have a limp like Hattie?"

"I don't think so. But I'm going to have to stay at home for a long time. I can't go to work until the cast comes off."

Bella was delighted and didn't catch the worry in her father's eyes. Seeing more of her father was very good news. But Donald knew no work meant no pay, and life was going to be tough for a while, even if they claimed unemployment benefits.

As father and daughter chatted, they didn't see the small, pale face hovering at the window, spying on them.

Donald's leg didn't heal well, and weeks, then months, passed and the bills piled up. Once again, June and Donald were forced to dip into the Italy fund.

Christine couldn't remember her father ever having a job. She knew he got something called 'Benefits' and she knew that their money came from 'the Social'.

"Mary, and you, Christine, if anybody ever asks about your dad's back, you tell 'em it's really bad," their mother frequently told them.

"Why?" asked Christine. "Dad ain't even got a bad back, 'as he?"

"'Course he has! That's why he can't work. If the Social don't believe us, we'll lose our benefits. So you make sure you tell 'em about how bad his back is."

So their father continued to loaf around the house, usually with a beer in his hand. He rarely went out, unless it was to the pub.

Christine, young as she was, was left to her own devices. Bored, she discovered she could sneak out of the house and go wherever she pleased. Nobody noticed her absence and nobody ever missed her.

Small for her age, and light on her feet, she developed the knack of blending into the shadows, unseen and unheard. She peeped into homes. She spied on her father drinking in the Dew Drop Inn. And she watched the vicar through the vicarage windows.

But most of all, Christine followed the movements of Bella Tait and her family.

And the more she stared through the windows of Bella's cottage, the more her eyes narrowed and her heart hardened.

Eventually, Bella's father was pronounced fit and he returned to work. Both he and June sighed with relief, as it meant he was earning again.

Around that time, Bella found a tiny fledgling in the garden. She knew that one should never interfere with fledglings because their parents were usually close by, feeding them and teaching them how to fend for themselves.

Bella shut Hattie into the house, and watched from a distance. No parent bird turned up and the tiny fledgling didn't move. Occasionally it cheeped, and its beak gaped, but no mother came to feed it.

Bella approached it, but the baby bird didn't hop away. She stooped down and carefully picked it up.

"Oh, you poor little thing! You've got a broken leg!"

It was so light in her hand she felt nothing at all except the tiny beating heart.

"Don't be frightened," she said, "I know exactly what to do. Hattie had a broken leg, and so did Daddy. We have to make sure your leg is very straight, then put on a splint to keep it like that until it mends."

She took the little bird inside and showed it to her mother. Together they made a miniature splint from a matchstick, but it was Bella's deft, confident fingers that straightened the leg, applied the splint and fixed it in place with sticky tape.

She had successfully treated her first patient.

"Good job, *la mia bella* Bella!" said her father, admiring her handiwork. "Good job!"

Christine, at the window, watched and her hands balled into fists.

Christine hardly heard the shouting matches between her mother and father any more. They happened so frequently, they were almost a nightly affair. It often ended with her mother being slapped about. But that's what husbands did, didn't they? Then her father would collapse into his favourite chair in front of the TV, a bottle of beer at his elbow, and shout abuse at her mother who was preparing his dinner in the kitchen.

But one particular night it ended differently.

Her father swayed up their path, then hammered on the front door with his fist.

"Where are you, woman?" he bawled, "let me in!"

"Eh, 'old your horses! You're 'ome early, ain't you? Did you drink the Dew Drop dry?" asked her mother, opening the door.

"Woman, you won't believe what's 'appened," he said, standing unsteadily over her in the hallway.

"What?"

"They barred me! I ain't allowed to drink in there no more!"

"Really?"

"Yes, really. They've barred me from the Dew Drop!"

"Well, perhaps that ain't such a bad thing…"

Upstairs, the listening child held her breath. It wasn't wise to cross her father when he came back from the pub. Everybody knew that. Booze always made him angry. Christine crept out of her bedroom, knelt down and peered through the bannister at her parents below.

"*What* did you say?" he asked, menace in his voice.

"I just meant we'd 'ave more money perhaps if…"

"*What?*"

"I just meant that you don't need to go to the pub every night…"

But her mother had gone too far.

Her husband's hands were already balled. He swung back and slammed a hard fist into her stomach. Christine heard a little "ouf" as her mother exhaled and crumpled into a pile on the floor, her head hitting the hall stand as she went down.

"You stupid woman," he slurred, kicking her unconscious body. "I ain't staying around 'ere. I should 'ave stayed in Yewbridge. This place is like a bleedin' morgue."

He slammed the front door behind him and staggered back down their path.

It was the last time Christine saw her father in Sixpenny Cross.

6

Christine's stomach was growling. She was hungry, and there was nothing in the pantry. Her sister, Mary, was out somewhere, and her mother was snoring on the couch, her mouth hanging open.

"Mum! Wake up, I'm hungry! Can I go and buy some bread?"

Her mother slowly opened her eyes and groped for the cigarettes next to the overflowing ashtray. Coughing, she pulled one out of the pack and stuck it between her lips, reaching for the matchbox with a shaking hand.

"I need money to buy some food," said Christine.

"Do you think I'm made of money? For gawd's sake, we ain't got any, and that's that. You can blame your stinking father for leaving us."

She blew a smoke ring into the air and closed her eyes. As Christine left the room, she heard the glug of liquid being poured into a glass. Her mother was on the sherry again, and there was no point talking to her when she was drunk.

Christine's stomach growled again.

I'll just have to do what I usually do. Steal some food.

It was easy really. Nobody in the village of Sixpenny Cross locked their back doors. All Christine had to do was watch and wait until a kitchen was empty, then she'd sneak in and help herself to whatever was on the table or in the fridge.

She almost drooled at the memory of the pie she had stolen from the pub pantry, and the freshly baked scones she'd snatched from the policeman's house. Haha! Very satisfying stealing from the police. And it was very funny when the policeman's wife blamed first her husband, and then blamed Stan, their grown up son.

Christine knew where she was guaranteed to find food.

Bella Tait's house! Mrs Tait is always cooking that Italian stuff for Fat Belly Bella and 'er dad. No wonder Bella's so fat! Why, I'd be doing her a favour if I stole some of Bella's food!

The row of terraced cottages that Bella lived in backed onto fields. Hugging the hedges, Christine made her way towards Bella's cottage, then hopped over the low fence. Success. She entered the backyard, crept past Donald's shed and up to the kitchen window. Even before she peeped inside, the delicious cooking smells made her stomach flip.

The kitchen was brightly lit, and June Tait hummed to herself as she drained spaghetti. She gave the sauce a final stir with a wooden spoon. Steam and the scent of herbs and tomatoes filled the little kitchen.

"Don, Bella, tea's ready! Sit up, I'm bringing it in."

She heaped steaming spaghetti onto three plates, then spooned the sauce over.

"Tut, tut, I've made too much again," she muttered and carried the laden tray out of the kitchen to her waiting family.

Christine quietly opened the back door and let herself in. There was plenty of spaghetti and sauce left. All she had to do was help herself. Quickly. She grabbed a bowl from the side and began ladling spaghetti.

"Christine?"

Christine spun round, hunger gnawing at her insides, furious at being caught.

Bella's eyes flicked from Christine to the food.

"Here," she whispered, "use this plastic bowl, it won't be missed. Take as much as you like, but hurry up!"

"Bella, did you find the parmesan?" June's voice sailed in from the next room. "It's just on the side."

"Got it!"

Bella and Christine evacuated the kitchen at the same time, Bella with the parmesan, Christine with her spoils. She closed the back door quietly behind her.

As she sat in the bus shelter, using her fingers to devour the delicious food, she seethed with embarrassment. She was mortified that Bella, of all people, had not only caught her stealing, but had given her food.

Who did that fat Bella think she was? Miss 'igh and Mighty would probably snitch on her, tell her parents, which meant another visit from that stupid policeman.

But Bella didn't breathe a word about Christine's clandestine visit to her parents, or anybody else.

Was Christine grateful?

She was not.

Instead, the humiliation of being discovered by Bella festered in her soul. If she disliked Bella before, she *hated* her now.

Why should Bella have everything? It's so unfair!

"I'm going to teach that fat lump a lesson," she vowed.

"Miss, my mum put a piece of chocolate cake in my satchel, and now it's gone. I saw Bella eating chocolate cake at break time, I bet she was eating mine."

The teacher looked at Christine in surprise.

"Are you sure?"

"Oh yes, Miss, quite sure."

"Bella, come here a minute," called the teacher, beckoning to Bella who was busily working at her desk. "Did you take some cake out of Christine's satchel?"

Bella's mouth dropped open in astonishment. She stared at Christine, who refused to make eye contact. There was a long pause before she spoke.

"I'm sorry, Miss. I'm sorry, Christine. I shouldn't have taken it, and I won't do it again."

If Bella thought she was doing Christine a favour, she was mistaken. Christine ground her teeth and redoubled her efforts to make Bella's life difficult.

If Bella's homework was lost, or her pencils broken, or her work messy, Christine was usually responsible. But Bella never retaliated or complained.

England went crazy when their team won the football World Cup in 1966. That year the Beatles released their album, *Revolver*, and both Bella and Christine celebrated their eleventh birthdays. It was time to move on from the homely environment of Sixpenny Cross village school.

Bella had done well. The teachers were kind, and the classes small, so Bella felt secure. She didn't make friends easily, but that didn't concern her. She was content with just her father, mother and her pets.

Next term she'd catch the bus to Yewbridge High School, with the other Sixpenny Cross kids. But today had been the last day at the village school and she bid her sad farewells.

"Goodbye, Bella," said her teacher, handing over her end of term report. "Good luck at Yewbridge High."

"I'm so proud of you, *la mia bella* Bella," said her father when he read the report. "With results like these, you'll be accepted into a university to train as a vet one day."

Bella radiated happiness.

That evening, June served one of Bella's favourite dishes, homemade ravioli, as a treat to celebrate her school report. Bella had three helpings.

In the council house on Springfield Road, Christine tore open the brown envelope containing her school report. She scowled as she read it.

Huh! It was her worst report yet, but it didn't matter. Her mother would never think to ask for it, so she'd never see it. Christine was accustomed to forging her mother's signature. No problem.

That September, when school began again, everything changed.

From inside the Post Office, Jayne Fairweather watched with interest as the kids began to gather at the school bus stop outside. She knew them all.

She saw skinny, defiant little Christine Dayton who lived with her mum and sister in Springfield Road. Christine's mum was a regular visitor to the shop. She cashed in her weekly welfare cheque at the Post Office counter and then spent a good proportion of her money on beer or cheap sherry. Her husband had vanished a long time ago. It was little wonder that young Christine was allowed to run wild. And, if the rumours were to be believed, Christine's big sister, Mary, was pregnant, and had moved back to Yewbridge.

Jayne's favourite was Bella Tait. A sweet child, well-mannered and earnest. A real animal lover, too. Shame that June was such a good cook really, because Bella would be stunning if she wasn't so plump. With that dark Italian skin, brown eyes and glossy black hair, she would be a beauty if she shed a few pounds.

Bella stood a little apart from the other children. She wasn't being unfriendly. If approached, she would have chatted with anyone, but she was shy and unable to join in the easy-going banter of the other children.

The bus appeared and young faces lined the windows, staring down at the waiting children. Bella was nervous. The bus doors swept open and Christine Dayton elbowed her way on first. Then the other children climbed aboard with Bella bringing up the rear.

Jayne waved cheerily but Bella didn't see her. She was on the bus and searching for an empty seat. She found one, sat down, and stared out of the window as the bus drew away.

"Hope Fatty isn't in our class," she heard Christine hiss from the seat behind her.

When they arrived, waiting teachers consulted lists and each student was sent to his or her classroom. Bella and Christine found themselves in the same one.

High School was very different from the village school where she'd been surrounded by children she'd known for years. Here, nearly every face was strange, and where there were never more than sixteen children in a class at Sixpenny Cross, now there were thirty-two. Each time the bell rang, Bella had to change classrooms and found herself amongst more new hostile faces in the corridors.

Unlike Bella, Christine Dayton was quite enjoying High School. It didn't take her long to form a gang, and appoint herself as the leader. Now, when she hurled spite at Bella, her gang was there to applaud her.

"It's Fat Belly Bella!" Christine would crow. "What did you have for breakfast today, an elephant?"

She snorted with laughter and her friends followed suit.

Bella pretended not to hear, and chose a desk as far away from her taunters as possible. She laid out her books and began to study, switching off the conversation around her.

"Fat Belly Bella, will you be goalkeeper when we play hockey this afternoon? No balls would get past *you!*"

"Hey, Fat Belly, wouldn't like to be near you if you ever explode..."

The bullying was relentless. Every day there were new insults. A few class-mates tried to put a stop to it, but they were only half-hearted attempts. The truth was that while Bella was the target, the focus was off them. Nobody told the teachers, and they were too busy and overworked to notice.

Physical Education lessons were the worst. Bella had to wear terrible grey shorts and short-sleeved white blouses that accentuated her dimpled flesh, providing additional opportunities for Christine and her gang to torment her. And if ever Bella was in trouble, you could be sure Christine was behind it.

Bella never breathed a word of her troubles to her parents.

"The thing is," she confided to Hattie, her cat, "that if I tell Mum and Dad, it'll really upset them. And if I tell the teachers, I think Christine and her gang will get worse. So I've decided to put up with the bullying and just ignore it if I can."

Hattie purred and rolled onto her back to have her tummy rubbed, all four paws blissfully paddling the air.

Meanwhile, Christine had one aim in her rotten life, and that was to make Bella's life as miserable as possible.

7

"How was school today?" asked June, ladling out a generous helping of pasta onto Bella's plate.

"Good," Bella replied. "We're doing equations in maths, and learning about onomatopoeia in English."

"Oh my!" said June, profoundly impressed and immensely proud of her daughter.

"We're so pleased that you like your new school," said her father, his mouth full of pasta. "But don't you work too hard, *la mia bella* Bella."

Bella smiled at him.

But Bella wasn't the only one keeping a secret. After dinner, when she went up to her bedroom to study, Donald closed the kitchen door and quietened his voice.

"I don't want Bella to hear this. I don't want to worry her."

June sighed. She knew what was coming.

"I'm so sorry, June, but I think we'll need to raid the Italy fund again."

June nodded, resigned.

"For the tax, you mean?"

"Yes. I'm so sorry."

Donald worked as a mechanic but because he was self-employed, he had to file his own tax returns. He'd got himself into a mess this year, and ended up owing the Inland Revenue a large sum of money.

"Of course," said June. "Don't worry, I know we'll get there someday. Italy and my grandmother's village will always be there, waiting for us. When the time is right, we'll go."

When Bella walked into the classroom, she was always prepared to close her ears, duck her head, and quietly make her way to her desk. But today was different. Today she didn't need to. Today Christine Dayton and her gang had found another victim to torment.

"Who set your head on fire?"

Bella quietly sat down, then dared to look up through long lashes.

An unfamiliar boy was standing at the front of the class. His skin was extremely fair, with a generous sprinkling of freckles scattered across his nose. He was very thin, and his shock of red hair stood on end. Bella couldn't help smiling to herself, thinking that he resembled a lit match.

The object of Christine's bullying had flushed a vivid scarlet. Later, Bella would learn that it wasn't fear or embarrassment that caused him to change colour, it was anger.

Their teacher marched in and put her heavy bag down on the desk. The class fell silent.

"Good morning, class. Today we welcome a new boy into our midst. This is Ryan Jenkins. Now, do we have a spare desk anywhere for Ryan?"

"Next to Bella Tait!" Christine shouted, and sniggered.

From anyone else, this may have sounded like a helpful suggestion, but Christine made it sound hostile and unwelcoming.

The teacher ignored Christine and smiled at Bella.

"Is it okay if Ryan sits next to you, Bella?"

Bella nodded, and Ryan picked his way between the desks and sat down.

The teacher began to call out the names in the register and Ryan and Bella stole shy glances at each other. Pale blue eyes fringed by almost white eyelashes looked into deep brown ones, the lashes thick and dark. Each picked up friendly signals. They smiled at each other and knew that they would be friends.

"Hello Ryan, I'm Bella," she whispered.

"I know, the teacher said. Nobody calls me Ryan, I'm Red."

"Hi, Red."

"Hi, Bella. Are you Italian?"

Bella glowed.

"No, but my great-grandmother was Italian. How did you know?"

"Your name, and your looks."

Bella smiled, and Red smiled right back.

"We're doing percentages today, have you done them before?" she asked.

"Yep."

"Good. You can help me."

"*Nessun problema*. No problem."

"Can you speak Italian?"

"No, I just like to pick up odd phrases from different languages, you never know when they may come in useful. You see? That one already did!"

Neither of them noticed Christine watching them, her eyes narrowed, her lips set in a thin line.

Bella and Red sat together whenever they could, happy and relaxed in each other's company. No longer did Bella dread school.

They were a strange couple. Bella's plumpness, olive skin and brown eyes contrasted sharply with Red's bony frame, white skin and pale eyes, all topped with flame-red hair. The pair were teased relentlessly, but they didn't care. Their friendship made them strong and the taunts bounced off.

"Here come Laurel and Hardy," Christine would scoff.

Disappointingly, her jibes had little effect. Anger caused her hands to clench into such tight fists that her fingernails pressed crescent shapes into her palms.

Red was an exceptionally bright student. His photographic memory allowed his brain to take a snapshot of whatever he read, permanently capturing information to regurgitate later. Bella didn't find her studies so easy, but she worked hard, and when she struggled, Red helped.

"You've put the decimal point in the wrong place, that's all," he would say when she'd nearly chewed off the end of her pencil trying to solve a problem.

"Ah, now it works, thanks!"

"*Nessun problema.*"

Red was a natural achiever, but his heart wasn't in it. His school results were good but he didn't enjoy lessons. What Red liked more than anything was working with his hands. It didn't matter what: woodwork, metalwork or later on, helping Bella's father install central heating into their cottage.

Bella and Red became inseparable. At weekends, Red sometimes caught the bus from Yewbridge and came to Sixpenny Cross so that he and Bella could study together. They sat at the dining room table, while June brought them drinks and snacks, and Hattie purred on Bella's lap.

"What does your father do?" Donald asked him one day.

"He's a scientist," Red replied. "He lectures at the university."

"And what do you want to do when you leave school?"

Red sighed.

"That's the trouble," he said. "I'm not like Bella who knows she wants to be a vet. My dad wants me to be a scientist, like him, and work in research or become a lecturer. I don't really want to do either of those things, but I don't know what I *do* want."

"Never mind, you've got plenty of time," said June, bringing in a plate of cake.

Nobody saw Christine Dayton watching through the window. And nobody saw her angrily plucking off the heads of the marigolds in June's flower beds.

8

*I*t was a beautiful day in March. Christine woke late and, bleary-eyed, she stumbled downstairs. She suddenly remembered it was her birthday.

I'm thirteen today!

She hoped that her dad would visit, but that was hardly likely. He hadn't bothered to turn up for any other birthdays, and if he did, her mum wouldn't let him into the house anyway. Chances were he was in prison.

Her sister, Mary, hadn't remembered either, probably too busy with her baby. In fact Christine wasn't even sure her mother had remembered. She found her, as usual, sprawled on the couch, a bottle of sherry close by.

"Mum, it's my birthday, did you get me a present?"

"What do you think I am, made of money? I paid for you to get your ears pierced last month, didn't I? Gawd knows you been nagging me about it enough."

Christine rolled her eyes. Her mother's answer didn't surprise her.

"Right, I'll 'elp meself and party on me own then," she muttered.

She returned to her bedroom and pulled on a pair of jeans and a sweater and planned her next moves.

Downstairs, she stole cigarettes from the pack on the table then raided the fridge, slipping two cans of beer into a bag.

"Just going out for a bit," she called over her shoulder, but expected no response.

The front door slammed behind her and her mood was black as she headed towards the privacy of Sixpenny Woods. Okay, she'd spend her birthday alone. Perhaps she'd climb the Wishing Rock and make a wish. Or maybe carve her initials again into the trunk of a tree. Somehow, gouging living bark with her penknife gave her a sense of satisfaction.

Over the years, the Wishing Rock had lost its battle with the ivy that smothered it. Although the boulder was enormous, it looked like a natural feature, blending in with its surroundings. Unless one knew that it was supposed to possess magical powers to grant wishes, one wouldn't look at it twice.

Christine carefully set her bag on the ground beneath the stone, then began to climb, her hands grabbing at the ivy and her feet seeking out footholds.

At the top, her head was level with high tree branches. She sat down to rest, swinging her legs. She pulled out a cigarette from her pocket and lit it with the lighter she always carried.

Might as well make a wish while I'm 'ere, she thought, inhaling the smoke. *I wish, I wish Bella Tait would find out what it's like to be really miserable, like me. Why should she 'ave everything? I want her to suffer. I don't even care if she dies...*

The delicious notion of Bella Tait suffering gave her renewed energy. She finished her cigarette and climbed down the stone, eager to drink the beer she had stashed. But the cheerfulness didn't last. By the time she'd downed the last drops and hurled the cans into the undergrowth, the blackness had returned. Even carving her initials into a tree only lightened her mood momentarily. It didn't last and her spirits sank to their usual low level. She headed home.

When Christine unlocked the front door, she sensed immediately that something was wrong.

"Mum? Mum? I'm 'ome!"

No reply.

She walked from room to room, but the house was empty. Something caught her eye on the kitchen table. A note.

Sorry Christine im fed up and ive gone away for a bit theres some food in the fridge. make sure you go to scool and Ill see you when I see you. Mum

Christine read the note through three times before she threw it on the table in disgust.

It was the icing on her birthday cake.

Well, she wasn't going to tell the school or the Social that her mum had gone again. If she needed anything before her mum came back, she'd steal it. Easy-peasy, lemon squeezy.

But she couldn't help wondering… How would Bella Tait spend her birthday?

To celebrate Bella's thirteenth birthday, June baked a cake and prepared a birthday tea with crustless sandwiches, *biscotti* and fairy cakes. It was a quiet affair, with just five around the table. Bella didn't want a fuss and apart from Red, and Jayne Fairweather, who was such a good friend that Bella called her 'Auntie', no other guests had been invited.

Christine hadn't been invited, but she was there, nevertheless. Had the Taits or Jayne or Red looked up, they'd have seen her small, angry face at the window. But they didn't, and savoured June's delicious cake and enjoyed each other's company.

In the background, the radio played the English entry for that year's Eurovision Song Contest, *Congratulations,* by Cliff Richard.

"Congratulations and happy birthday to you, *la mia bella* Bella," said her father smiling. "And here's to many more birthdays."

"I made this for you," said Red, passing Bella a wrapped gift.

"Oh! Whatever is it?"

"Open it and find out," said Red, smiling.

The white face at the window glared at the cosy scene and rolled its eyes.

Bella tore off the paper and revealed an exquisitely constructed small wooden box. It had been lovingly put together using dovetail joints, and then lacquered to a high sheen. But the eye was drawn to the highly decorated oval brass plaque set into the lid. Bella's initials were intertwined with green leaves and pink and white flowers. Tiny, intricate, coloured butterflies settled on delicate petals.

Bella gasped.

"BMT! Bella Maria Tait! Oh, Red, I love it! Thank you so much, I've never seen anything like that! How did you engrave it so beautifully, and in so many colours?"

"You didn't make that at school, did you?" asked Jayne, admiring the lovely box and running her fingertips over the glossy surface.

"No, I made it at home. I've been tinkering about in my shed," Red explained, "and I made a sort of tool. It isn't perfect yet, but it holds different coloured inks and engraves at the same time."

"That sounds ingenious," said Donald. "You're very clever with your hands, Red."

"I think my box is just beautiful," said Bella, tracing the letters with one fingertip. "Thank you. I shall always keep my treasures in it."

At the window, Christine was incandescent with jealousy. She backed away into the night, passing Donald's car parked in the street.

Christine picked up a rock and scored a deep groove in the paintwork, all the way down one side.

The next year, Red made an announcement.

"We're moving," he told Bella, gloomily.

"Where to?" asked Bella, horrified.

"Scotland. Dad's got a job at Aberdeen University. He's really excited about it. Nothing's going to change his mind. We leave at the end of this school term."

"I can't believe it!"

"I can hardly believe it either, but it's true."

"It won't be the same without you." Her eyes misted.

"Bella, we'll always be friends, don't worry."

Bella nodded miserably.

"I'll miss you so much, Red."

"And I'll miss you. But listen, if ever you are in trouble, I will drop everything and come and help you."

"I know. Will you write to me?"

"Of course! *Nessun problema.*"

But it *was* a problem. Red was her best and only friend. Every moment together was precious but the time spent in each other's company evaporated like dewdrops in the morning sun.

A small part of Bella's soul died with Red's departure. She made no attempt to befriend anyone else, but school without Red was dull. Sighing, she threw herself into her studies and worked tirelessly.

Donald and June were concerned.

"You mustn't work too hard, Bella," said her mother, bringing her a plate of chocolate muffins.

"I have to if I'm going to be a vet!" said Bella, chewing.

Christine Dayton left school. Everybody knew she would leave when she turned fifteen, the current legal age, although it would be raised to sixteen in a few years time. In fact, Christine wasn't yet fifteen when she stopped attending school, but the anti-truancy team and teachers didn't fight too hard to bring her back.

Christine's mother eventually returned briefly to the house in Springfield Road. Whether she felt guilty leaving Christine alone in the house or whether she needed to retrieve her welfare benefits was not certain. Rumour had it that she had a new boyfriend in Yewbridge. Soon after, Christine's mother moved back to Yewbridge, taking Christine with her.

A new family moved into the Dayton's house in Springfield Road. The fresh young police constable, Stan Cooper, continued to include Springfield Road on his beat, just as his father had done, but the new family gave him no trouble.

Although Christine no longer lived in Sixpenny Cross, Jayne

Fairweather was sure she sometimes caught glimpses of her in the village or lurking in the bushes. Once, when her back was turned, somebody had helped themselves to cash from the till. When she'd looked down the road, she thought she saw Christine Dayton melting into the shadows, but by the time she'd called PC Cooper, the figure had vanished.

That same evening, Donald Tait's car tyres were slashed and Bella's bicycle went missing.

"Who could have done such dreadful things?" asked June, wringing her hands.

Donald shook his head. Bella stared at her feet. She thought she knew who it may have been but she held her tongue.

9

Christine couldn't help herself. She was drawn back to Sixpenny Cross as though by an invisible thread that tugged ever tighter the further she went.

Very early one spring morning, just before the church clock struck two, Christine was back again. She skulked in the shadows, heading for Bella Tait's house. In the light of a street lamp, Christine glanced down at the flick knife in her hand. She flicked it open as she approached Donald Tait's car. She paused and stared at the Tait's house with its dark rooms behind drawn curtains. Nothing and nobody stirred in the street. Not even PC Stan Cooper was awake at that time of the morning.

Kev, her latest boyfriend, was an expert car thief and had taught her a lot. She knew how to break into a car and how to jump-start it but that wasn't why she was standing beside Donald Tait's car that night.

"What if I want the driver to have an accident?" Christine had asked Kev. "What could I do to make that happen?"

Kev had stared at her.

"Why would you want to do that?"

"Just interested, is all. So 'ow'd you do it?"

"Best way is to do the brakes. You have to get under the car."

Kev had pointed to one of the hydraulic tubes.

"See that rubber tube?" he had said, as they lay beneath his car, and Christine had nodded.

"Well, if you cut it, the driver ain't got no brakes after a while."

"After a while? What yer mean, after a while?"

Kev had shrugged but Christine seemed satisfied. She smiled to herself, a plan developing in her mind. That plan was the reason why she now found herself standing next to Bella's father's car.

Christine smiled. Now, with Kev's directions clear in her mind, she checked the windows in the street for one last time. Curtains tightly drawn. All clear.

Although the car was parked under a street light, nobody saw her slide on her back underneath, and, using her lighter to see, deftly slice the brake line with her blade.

Her work was done. Silently, she left the scene and disappeared into the inky darkness.

Next morning dawned bright. As the birds in the hedgerows greeted the day, Jayne Fairweather was putting the key in the lock of the Post Office. A family of ducks crossed the road, intent on reaching the pond on the village green.

"It all happened in slow motion," Jayne said later to PC Cooper, who was taking notes. "Don Tait was driving down the road as he always does that time in the morning. I was raising my arm to wave to him when I saw the ducks crossing the road. Don must have seen them at exactly the same time, but instead of slowing down and stopping, he swerved to miss them and drove straight into the village pond! I tell you, I couldn't believe my eyes!"

Stan Cooper was tempted to chuckle but restrained himself. Donald Tait hadn't been injured and neither had the ducks. No harm done. Except Mr Tait claimed that his brake cable had been severed. Now that wasn't the sort of thing that happened in Sixpenny Cross, and it wasn't funny.

It hadn't taken long for Archie Draper to arrive in his tractor and pull the car out of the pond. Strangely, Bella Tait's missing bicycle was found at the same time.

In Yewbridge, Christine listened to the local news on the radio. Nothing. No mention of deaths or cars spinning out of control. Her eyes narrowed into slits and she was filled with rage.

In 1973, Pink Floyd released *Dark Side of the Moon* and Princess Anne announced her engagement to Captain Mark Phillips.

Bella Tait had the world at her feet.

She read the letter from Bristol University for the umpteenth time.

...We are therefore pleased to offer you a place studying Veterinary Sciences...

"I can't believe it," said June, shaking her head. "Our little Bella going off to university to train to be a vet!"

"*La mia bella* Bella, we're so proud of you!"

"Thanks, Dad!"

"We're going to miss you, Bella," her mother said. "Make some space on the table, I've made a plate of hazelnut *biscotti* to celebrate."

"I wonder how Red is doing?" Bella wondered, nibbling on *biscotti*.

"Oh, he'll be starting university somewhere as well, I expect," said June. "Such a bright boy, he'll do well."

They'd promised each other to keep in touch, but the long-distance relationship was hard to sustain and they exchanged letters less and less often. One day, Bella's letter to Red was returned, unopened, marked *unknown at this address*. She didn't write again.

They say good luck breeds more good luck, and that may be true because, apart from Bella being offered a university place, another piece of welcome news arrived within the week.

"We've done it! We've finally done it!" yelled Donald.

He had the Yewbridge Gazette spread open before him on the dining room table, and was comparing it with his Littlewoods Pools coupon.

"Done what?" asked June, coming in, flour on her hands.

"We've won the pools!" said Donald. "Well, not the big prize, but if I've done my sums right, there'll be enough money to get Bella all set up at university. And there'll be enough to do repairs on the house. We can fix those loose tiles on the roof, for instance. Best of all, there'll still be enough for us to book a holiday to Italy! We're going to see your grandmother's village at last!"

June sat down heavily, her floury hands clutching her heart.

"Oh, Donald, are we? Are you sure? Are we really?"

"Yes! We're really going to Italy!"

"What's this?" asked Bella coming into the room. "What's happened?"

"We've won some money on the football pools! Enough to give us a holiday in Italy and set you up for university!"

Bella gaped at him.

"That's fantastic," she said at last. "Really good, but I don't think I'll come with you to Italy, if you don't mind."

"Oh Bella, why ever not? We can afford it," said June.

"It's not that, it's just that I only have a few short weeks before uni starts, and they've sent me a long reading list. I'd like to do some studying in advance, and I need time to get packed up, too. You go without me this time, I'm sure there'll be other chances."

"You're right *la mia bella* Bella, your future is more important at the moment. There will always be another time. But we won't go until you are settled at university."

The next weeks were filled with packing and anticipation. The whole family went to Yewbridge and bought suitcases.

"Going away, are you?" asked the girl at the sales counter.

"My husband and I are going to Italy to see the village my grandmother was born in," said June, her eyes dancing.

"Oh, that'll be nice," said the assistant. "Room for me in that suitcase, by any chance? Brrr, I can feel winter arriving here already. Bet it's lovely and the sun is shining in Italy."

June beamed, already feeling the Italian sun on her skin in her imagination.

For Bella, they bought bedding, clothes, stationery, a kettle, mugs and various other bits and pieces. Never had the Taits splashed out on so many items on one single occasion. It was a happy day, finished off by Donald treating them all to a meal at an Italian restaurant.

"To get us in the mood," he said.

"Just think!" said June excitedly. "Next month we'll be eating real Italian food in Italy!"

"Let's raise our glasses to Bella's future and our Italian holiday!" said Donald.

As the ruby chianti sparkled in the candlelight, all three members of the Tait family clinked glasses and sipped.

Bella had ordered all her text books, and when they arrived, she began studying like never before. She was determined to shine at university.

June was permanently pink with excitement and could talk about nothing but the coming trip to Italy.

"We've booked one of those newfangled package holidays," she told Jayne Fairweather. "When we arrive, the holiday company will take us to our hotel. On the first morning there's a welcome meeting and we can book excursions if we want. I want to see *everything*. Donald says we should hire a car for a few days too, then we can visit my grandmother's village."

"Sounds heavenly," said Jayne, dusting off a row of canned beans. "I could do with a holiday myself."

"Thank you so much for looking after Bella's pets while we're away," said June. "That is really kind of you."

"Just you concentrate on having a good holiday," said Jayne. "You deserve it."

"Bye, darling," said June, hugging her daughter. "We'll see you in a few weeks."

Taking leave of her daughter at university was just as hard as that day, years ago, when she had left Bella in the classroom on her first day of school. She looked around the student room, with its two beds, two wardrobes and two desks. It seemed stark and unhomely.

"I'll be fine, honestly," said Bella, reading her mother's mind. "Once I've unpacked and put my own bits and pieces around, it'll be just like home. Don't worry about me, I want you to have a wonderful holiday. I can't wait to hear all about it, so make sure you send me some postcards!"

"*Ciao, la mia bella* Bella," said her father and enveloped her in his arms. "Enjoy yourself, don't work too hard, and remember, we're so proud of you!"

When they'd gone, the first item Bella unpacked was the wooden box that Red had made for her.

"That's pretty," said Susan, Bella's roommate. "Are those your initials?"

"Yes, a friend made it for me."

Bella finished putting her books in the bookcase, filled her new kettle with water and plugged it into the socket.

"Would you like a cup of tea?"

"Yes, please," said Susan, serious eyes regarding Bella. "It all feels so strange, doesn't it? Have you ever been away from home before?"

"No," said Bella, popping a tea bag into each cup.

Had she been at home, her mother would never have used tea bags. She'd have used a teapot, with proper tea leaves, and she'd have left it for a few minutes to 'brew'. A pang of homesickness clutched at Bella's heart.

"Me neither," said Susan. "Everybody seems nice though. And we can always go home at weekends."

"My parents are going on holiday to Italy, so I'll wait until they come back."

"Oh, lucky them!"

"Do you take sugar in your tea?"

"No, thank you."

Bella passed the mug to Susan, then ladled three heaped spoons into her own and stirred until a whirlpool formed in the centre.

She watched the whirlpool slow, then cease altogether.

I mustn't keep thinking about Mum and Dad, and the animals, and Sixpenny Cross, she thought. *I want to be a vet. That's all that matters.*

It was excellent advice, but then Bella didn't know what would happen next.

10

"Bella, I've brought the post. Looks like you've got a postcard from Italy!" said Susan, handing over a few letters to her roommate.

"Thanks!"

Bella ignored the other letters and stared at the picture on the postcard. The scene was of a donkey with panniers strapped to its back. An old man was leading it through a sun-drenched vineyard.

She turned it over, and read the words in her mother's familiar handwriting.

Darling Bella, Italy is just heavenly as I knew it would be. Hotel is nice, food lovely and weather very warm. Missing you of course. Hiring car tomorrow. Daddy sends love and lots of xxx

Bella smiled. She could picture her mother in her new sunhat, basking in the Italian sunshine, revelling in the fact that she was finally visiting the country where her ancestors had lived.

"Looks like they are having a fantastic time," she said to Susan.

She stared at the picture for a long time, reading the words over and over again before finally slipping the postcard into her polished wooden box along with her other treasures.

University life and the many lectures and activities kept Bella very busy. The overwhelming homesickness she suffered in the first days retreated. She and Susan became good friends, the first friendship Bella had forged since Red left.

A few days later, while Bella was working at her desk, Susan came in with more mail.

"Looks like another postcard from Italy," she said, dropping the card on Bella's desk.

This time it was written in her father's scrawly hand, the characters small in order to fit more words in the space provided.

La mia bella Bella, having a wonderful time. We found the village and it's just how we imagined. Made friends with a fisherman who knew your grandmother's family. He's taking us on his boat tomorrow! Miss you, but will see you soon and tell all! Don't work too hard. Love you, Dad xxx

The picture showed white frothy waves lapping at a sandy beach. On the horizon, tiny sailing boats dotted the turquoise ocean.

Bella popped the postcard into her box and hugged herself. She'd be seeing them this weekend!

The plan was that on Saturday she would catch an early train to Yewbridge. Her father would pick her up from the railway station and take her home to Sixpenny Cross.

Her mother would have coffee and cakes waiting on the table and she imagined the feel of her father's arms around her. She couldn't wait to hear all about their holiday and to tell them about her course and university life.

In Sixpenny Cross, Jayne Fairweather turned the key in the lock and opened the Taits' front door. Her daily visit to water the plants and feed the animals had taught Hattie to listen for the key in the door, knowing she was about to be fed.

"Hello, Hattie," said Jayne, bending down to smooth the purring cat. "Pleased to see me, are you?"

Jayne hummed as she did her usual rounds. First she went into the kitchen and fed Hattie. The little cat wound around her ankles until she set the bowl down. Jayne washed her hands at the sink, running her eye along June's shelf of cookbooks. *Pasta like Mama Makes, 100 Italian Recipes, Italian Farmhouse Kitchen.* The titles made her feel quite hungry.

Next she fed the hamsters, the guinea pigs and put birdseed in the budgie's cage.

I'll give the plants one last drop of water, she thought. *June and Donald will be back tomorrow.*

As the water splashed into the watering can, the doorbell rang.

Whoever could that be?

Jayne turned off the tap and went to open the door.

PC Stan Cooper stood before her, his policeman's helmet held in both hands. A lady wearing navy blue uniform and a jaunty hat stood beside him.

"Stan!" exclaimed Jayne. "Don and June are away in Italy until tomorrow."

"I know," said Stan. His knuckles were white. "I wasn't sure if Miss Tait was here or not. I'm accompanying Miss Travis."

The lady took this as her cue and stepped forward.

"Forgive me," she said, "am I correct in saying that this is the Taits' house?"

"Yes, that's right," said Jayne, and Stan nodded. "I'm afraid they are away at the moment, can I help?"

"I'm representing Mr and Mrs Tait's travel company. May I ask who you are?"

"I'm Jayne Fairweather, I own Sixpenny Cross shop and Post Office. I'm a family friend, just feeding the animals and watering the plants."

"May we come in?" Miss Travis asked.

Dumbly, Jayne opened the door wider, and let Stan and the lady in, then showed them to the sitting room. Miss Travis sat down, but Stan remained standing, rocking on his heels, still clutching his policeman's helmet before him.

"PC Cooper tells me that Mr and Mrs Tait's next of kin is their daughter, Bella?" the lady began. She was sitting very upright, her briefcase on her knees.

"Yes. She's at Bristol University. She's studying to be a vet."

"I will need to see her in person. Do you know where she is exactly?"

"Yes, I have her student hall address. Listen, what's this all about? Can you not just tell me?"

The woman paused, unsure what to say next.

"I'm afraid it's against company rules."

"Oh for goodness' sake! Has something happened to June and Donald?"

The woman stared at Jayne for a moment, then glanced up at Stan. He nodded, giving her permission to continue.

"I'm sorry to have to tell you that Mr and Mrs Tait were reported drowned yesterday. We believe they were in a fishing boat when a sudden squall arose and the boat capsized. Nobody survived and the boat and bodies have been recovered."

Jayne's heart pounded and her mouth went dry.

"No. There must be some mistake."

"I'm so sorry."

"They were due home tomorrow."

"Yes."

Jayne stared at the stranger opposite her, then at Stan. His eyes were downcast. June's clock ticked on the mantlepiece.

"Are you sure it was them?" she said at last. "There must be lots of tourists…" Her voice trailed away.

"I'm so sorry. The fisherman was identified and hotel staff verified that the bodies were those of June and Donald Tait."

Jayne sat still, trying to absorb the information and accept the fact that she'd never see her friends again.

"What about Bella?"

"If you could give me Bella's contact details, I'll drive over to Bristol immediately and inform her."

"No! Bella adores her parents, she can't hear this from a stranger!"

"Perhaps you could accompany me?"

This was a nightmare. A complete nightmare.

Jayne closed her eyes, breathed deeply and nodded.

Bella. How was the poor girl going to take the news?

"We should go now," she said. "This is not something that we can delay."

11

J ayne Fairweather read the label.

Room 64, Susan Brown, Bella Tait.

She tapped on the door.

"Come in!" called Susan.

Jayne opened the door and stepped inside, her uniformed companion close behind. Bella looked up and could hardly believe her eyes.

"Auntie Jayne! Wow! What a lovely surprise!"

She leaped up and flew across the room to give her a hug. Susan smiled and wondered who the accompanying lady in uniform was.

"Bella…"

"Did you come especially to see me? How lovely! How's Hattie? Has she been missing Mum and Dad? And the hamsters? And the guinea pigs?"

"Bella…"

"Did you get a postcard from Italy? Look, I got two."

Bella's wooden box was open on the desk and she reached for the postcards to show Jayne. Jayne stopped her hand.

"Bella," she said, pulling her down to sit beside her on the bed, not letting go of her hand.

Susan and the lady in uniform watched. Something icy gripped Susan's heart. This was not a normal visit.

"What's the matter?" asked Bella, suddenly aware that the atmosphere was all wrong. She looked deep into Jayne's eyes and all colour drained from her face. A glance at the uniformed lady confirmed her fears.

"It's something to do with Mum and Dad, isn't it? Something terrible has happened!"

Jayne tried, but her throat had closed up and she couldn't speak. Huge tears filled her eyes and ran unchecked down her cheeks.

Miss Travis stepped forward.

"I'm so sorry," she said, "I'm afraid we have very bad news."

The university was sympathetic and helpful. Bella's tutors agreed to extend their deadlines and save lecture notes for her return.

They needn't have bothered. Bella's passion for her studies died the day she was told that her parents had drowned.

"Bella, you should think about going back to university," said Jayne, two months after the tragic event.

Bella shook her head.

"I'm not ready," she said, burying her face in Hattie's soft fur.

Hattie was an elderly cat now. No longer was she a threat to birds, and her days were spent sleeping in sun puddles, only moving when the sun swung round.

Jayne sighed. The last weeks had been tough. The bodies had been flown back, and their funeral was attended by the whole shocked village. Bella's parents had been buried side by side in the churchyard, a single gravestone marking their final resting place. Across its dark surface, chiselled in letters of gold, the inscription read:

My wonderful, beloved parents,

June and Donald Tait.
You were tragically lost at sea
but never from my heart.
Your adoring daughter, Bella.

Thankfully, Donald had taken out travel insurance and the payout covered all expenses. Her parents had also insured their lives so Bella would never need to find money to pay the mortgage on the house. There was a sizable lump sum too, and if Bella was careful, it would keep her for a long time. At least until she finished training and started her career.

But Bella could scarcely get up in the morning, let alone plan her career. The only reason she rose at all was to care for the animals, and she only dressed when she needed to go out for supplies.

Jayne was desperately worried. Bella refused to open the curtains which had been drawn since her parents died. She wouldn't touch June and Donald's bedroom, or clear anything in the cottage. Her mother's cookbooks were set out exactly as she had left them. The novel she was halfway through lay open on her bedside table. Her father's spare spectacles were still on the coffee table. The house was a shrine to their memory.

"Let me help you sort through their things," Jayne suggested gently.

"No, I'm not ready."

Bella's eyes were dull and lifeless, and her voice had taken on a monotonous quality. The house was growing more and more disordered and Bella made no attempt to tidy or clean it.

Bella's lost interest in everything, Jayne thought as she walked home. *And I don't know what I can do to help her.*

Jayne lived alone a few doors down from Bella, just a short walk away. She was so deep in thought, she almost didn't notice the heap on her doorstep.

A shivering, dirty, brown and white dog looked up at her from under heavy lids.

"Good gracious, where did *you* come from?" she said.

The dog wagged its tail weakly, but didn't seem capable of more.

Jayne opened her front door and let herself in. The dog questioned her with sad eyes, then got to its feet and followed her in, before collapsing again in the hall.

"You wait there," said Jayne. "I'll see what I can find for you."

The dog looked too exhausted to move, so Jayne filled a bowl with water, and another with the leftover chicken she was planning to eat for her supper that night.

"Here you are, Sad Eyes," she said. "Let's see if this makes you feel any better."

As the dog ate and drank, Jayne thought about her new problem. She couldn't keep a dog. She worked at the Post Office every day and the shop sold food. Animals, apart from guide dogs, were not allowed in food stores. No, the dog would have to find another home.

It suddenly dawned on her that she knew exactly who might want this mangy heap of fur. Bella! With luck, the dog might bring a sparkle back to the girl's eyes.

She dialled Bella's number.

Bella was standing in the kitchen. She should eat, but her appetite had left her the moment she heard of her parents' tragic death.

She'd recently caught sight of herself in the bathroom mirror and had been surprised.

Is that really me? she asked her reflection.

The weight was dropping off, which wasn't a bad thing, but where did those dark rings round her eyes come from? And had her hair always been so lank and dull? Surely it used to shine with health?

On the counter in front of her was her polished box. She ran her fingertips over its smooth surface then over the wonderful, elaborate engraving of her initials. She opened the box, gazing at her treasures.

There was the old photograph of her Italian great-grandmother, dressed in black, leaning on a walking stick. The elderly lady looked sad.

I wonder if she approved of her daughter marrying an Englishman, she thought. *I wish I'd known her.*

She picked up her mother's wedding ring and stroked her cheek with it. The gold felt warm, as though it been recently worn. Then she picked up the precious postcards.

La mia bella Bella…

She could almost hear her father's gentle voice. She imagined him choosing this particular postcard, knowing they were going out on a boat trip.

Tears streamed down her cheeks, blurring the image of the little boats bobbing on the Ionian sea.

Why did you have to go out in that fishing boat that day? Why, why, why?

The phone rang.

Bella considered ignoring it, but she wiped her tears away on her sleeve, walked into the living room and reluctantly picked up the receiver.

12

"Hello Bella, it's me again."

"Auntie Jayne? Did you forget something?"

So Jayne told Bella all about Sad Eyes.

"Of course, I can't keep a dog," she said. "So I wondered whether you may like to look after it? Perhaps when it's cleaned up a bit, and given a few good meals, we could find someone to adopt it."

"Of course! Do you want to bring the dog round now?"

For the first time in weeks, Jayne sensed a little animation in Bella's voice.

"No, I'll pop round in the morning. It's had a good feed and it looks exhausted, so I'm going to shut it in the hall for the night."

Bella suddenly had a purpose. When she went to bed that night, she was actually looking forward to the next day. And that hadn't happened for weeks.

The next morning, before heading to the Post Office, Jayne led Sad Eyes to Bella's house using a makeshift leash and collar.

"She's a little more perky today," she said to Bella. "And I discovered she's already been trained to walk with a leash. Poor thing must be lost."

Bella crouched down to examine the dog.

"I can see why you call her Sad Eyes," she said. "And you're quite right, it's a girl. She's so hairy I can't see if she has an injury. I don't think she has fleas though. I'll keep her under observation for twenty-four hours and let her settle in, then I'll examine her properly tomorrow."

"Good. I'll pop some dog food round from the shop later. And I'll put up a card in the Post Office in case anybody has lost a dog, though I don't remember ever seeing this one in Sixpenny Cross."

Not only did Sad Eyes know how to walk on a leash, she also knew all about cats. When Hattie walked into the room and saw Sad Eyes, she froze, her fur standing on end, her tail twice its usual size. Sad Eyes wagged her tail briefly, then ignored her. Hattie, although still wide-eyed, decided that the newcomer was not a threat. She jumped up to the windowsill, chose a spot, then walked round in circles before curling up for a nap in the sun.

"You really are a very nice, polite dog," said Bella. "And I shan't call you Sad Eyes, although it fits. I shall call you Sadie."

Sadie twitched her tail in acknowledgement.

Bella watched Sadie carefully all day. Sadie ate hungrily and drank water, but she seemed to lack energy.

That night Bella made her a comfortable bed in the kitchen, but Sadie wouldn't settle. She preferred to lie under the stairs, so Bella moved the bedding to Sadie's chosen spot.

"Good night," she said. "Tomorrow I'll examine you properly and maybe even give you a bath."

She climbed the stairs to her bedroom, averting her eyes as she passed her parents' room. Hattie was already fast asleep on her bed.

Bella slept, and for the first time in weeks she was not tortured by terrifying nightmares of tiny boats battered by wild waves, or cries for help drowned by the wind.

The next morning, she scampered downstairs to see how Sadie was doing in the cupboard under the stairs. Hattie followed at a more dignified pace.

"Sadie?"

Sadie didn't get up to greet her, but briefly thumped her tail. Bella sensed something was different. She snapped on the light then gaped at the dog at her feet.

Sadie was lying on her side. Firmly attached to her were seven tiny, squirming, newborn puppies.

"Oh my!" breathed Bella, crouching down.

Sadie's wet nose nudged her hand. She looked at Bella and twitched her tail a few times, as if to say, *hey, I did a good job, didn't I?*

The card Jayne Fairweather pinned up in the Post Office attracted no response except interest.

Found

Medium-sized brown and white, long-haired mongrel dog. Friendly and well-trained.

Please apply within.

"Oh," said PC Stan Cooper, "I see a dog has been found? Who's looking after it?"

"Bella Tait," said Jayne. "Actually, I was just going to take down that card and rewrite it a little. Bella phoned me a few minutes ago and it seems that the poor dog was not only homeless, but pregnant. She just gave birth to seven puppies under Bella's stairs."

"Oh my goodness," said Stan as he tried to pull on his leather policemen's gloves.

It was December, and the wind was cold. Wearing gloves when riding a bike in such cold was a necessity. A few minutes earlier his gloves had fitted him perfectly but now they were proving to be a struggle to pull on.

"I think you've got your gloves on the wrong hands," observed Jayne.

Stan Cooper's clumsiness was legendary amongst the residents of Sixpenny Cross. Like his father before him, he was an excellent policeman and well suited to the village where crime was rare and an understanding of the locals essential. He was liked by all, and his clumsiness was regarded with affection and accepted.

"Thanks," said Stan, switching the gloves over and successfully pulling them on. "Please wish Miss Tait well with those pups. I may even take one off her hands later if she's looking to find homes for them."

He put his policeman's helmet back on, and left the shop.

Jayne rewrote the card.

Found

Very pregnant, medium-sized brown and white, long-haired mongrel dog. Friendly and well-trained.

Please apply within.

The cell doors clanged shut. The prison warder's rubber-soled shoes squeaked as she walked along the corridor. The lights would be dimmed soon and the inmates were expected to sleep. Judging by the shouting and banging on the bars, few of the women were tired.

Christine Dayton wasn't happy, but then she seldom was. The Young Offenders' Institution they put her in first had been awful, but it had been a walk in the park compared with Her Majesty's Women's Prison, Holloway.

"You will be detained until you have learned that theft is not acceptable in our society," the magistrate had declared.

Sitting on the bed in her shared cell, she gnawed on her nails, trying to shut out the shouting of the inmates as they communicated with each other.

London had seemed so attractive compared with Yewbridge. Of course she knew the streets wouldn't be paved with gold but she thought finding a job and making a living would be easy in such a large city. Unfortunately, her poor attitude and lack of respect for those in authority ensured that she never kept a job for more than a few days.

Sleeping under the arches with the other homeless people and runaways wasn't so bad. She'd always been able to look after herself.

And learning how to break into people's houses and help herself to their possessions wasn't difficult either. She'd had plenty of practice in Sixpenny Cross. It was easy if you were careful.

She'd become an expert burglar and accomplished shoplifter. Then, when she'd been caught and sent to the Young Offenders' Institution, she'd mixed with others just like herself and honed her skills.

She learned how to jostle someone to distract them, whilst relieving them of their wallet.

She learned how to target householders and memorise their routines. She'd watch for the best time to break in, like when a mother was collecting kids from school.

She learned how to spy and take note where people hid their house keys. Amazing how many idiots hid keys under a flowerpot or doormat. Or left their doors open.

She learned how to find the blind spots in a store, where the security cameras didn't reach. And how to try on clothes in a changing room, and put one's own clothes back on top. Then walk out, bold as brass.

But her luck had run out, and now here she was in Holloway for a stretch. Caught again. And it was a lot worse than the Young Offenders' unit.

I wonder what that spoilt Fat Belly Bella is doin' now? That's if she ain't exploded. I bet she's at some stupid university, and that quarter-Italian mother of hers is still fillin' her up with pasta. And I bet her dad phones her every day. Loser!

When I get out of here, I might just leave London and take myself back to Yewbridge and the countryside. Lots of villages. All ripe for the picking. Might even pay smug lil Fat Belly and her parents a visit.

When they've gone out.

13

*B*ella was distracted for the first time since she'd lost her parents. Helping animals was what she lived for and what she did best, allowing little time for brooding.

Sadie was an excellent mother. She washed and fed her babies continually, and watched that they didn't stray too far. Bella loved looking after Sadie, and she loved watching the puppies grow.

"Those pups are going to open their eyes soon. And it won't be two minutes before they'll be under our feet and all over the place," observed Jayne on one of her regular visits. "Shall I help you have a bit of a tidy up? This pile of newspapers, and this empty box, for instance. Shall I take them outside and pop them in the bin?"

"No," said Bella. "No, thank you. Those newspapers could be useful for the pups when I'm house-training them. And I have plans for that box."

"Well, what about these empty cans?"

"No."

"Bella, you have to throw *some* things away. It's getting pretty cluttered in here. What about this empty bottle?"

"No, I'm going to use that."

Jayne gave up.

Apart from the untidy house, Jayne was pleased with Bella's progress. Sadie's arrival had given Bella a purpose, and Jayne hoped that when the pups and Sadie left for new homes, Bella might return to university and pick up her studies.

But Jayne would be disappointed because it didn't work out at all like that.

Christmas came and went, and the weeks slipped by. It was 1974 and Britain was in the grip of the coal miners' strike. The numerous power stations that depended on coal to generate electricity were forced to shut down and a three-day week was introduced in an effort to conserve energy. A general election was called, resulting in Edward Heath's resignation and Harold Wilson becoming Prime Minister.

By March, Sadie's pups were ready for new homes. Jayne was concerned that Bella had made no attempt to have the puppies adopted, and the cottage was filled with the yaps of seven young dogs and beginning to look the worse for wear.

"Bella, shall I put a postcard up in the Post Office and see if we can't get these pups adopted?" she asked. "Hey, stop that!"

This remark was directed to a pup whose sharp little teeth were sunk into the hem of her skirt, playing tug of war.

"There's no hurry," said Bella. "They're doing well here."

"Are those puppies of Miss Tait's ready for adoption yet?" asked PC Cooper a day later, popping his head round the Post Office door.

"Well, yes, and no," replied Jayne. "They are old enough now, but whether you can persuade Bella to part with them is another matter."

"I'll have a go," he said, grinning. "I'll pay her a visit."

He walked up Bella Tait's path and tapped on the peeling front door. Her father had been planning to sand down the door and revarnish it in spring.

His knock set off a chorus of yaps from within.

"Hold on, I'll just shut the puppies away," Bella called, then opened the door, her face blanching when she saw PC Cooper on her doorstep.

"It's okay, Miss Tait," said Stan hurriedly. "I'm not here on police business. I heard you had some puppies and wondered whether I might see them."

"Of course!" said Bella, suddenly more cheerful. "Please come in."

Stan stepped inside, and his shiny leather boot landed in a pile of puppy poo that should have been cleared up.

Bella opened the door to the kitchen and seven fat, hairy, brown and white pups tumbled out. In the lead was one with a patch over one eye and hair that stuck up at all angles.

Stan crouched down and the puppy stopped tugging at his shoelaces long enough to smother the policeman's face with wet licks.

"Hey, Tufty, good to meet you!" said Stan, picking up the wriggling, affectionate puppy.

"I think you've made a friend there!" said Bella.

"Are they ready to leave their mother yet?"

"No," Bella said quickly, almost snatching the puppy from his arms, "not nearly ready yet."

"I'd love to adopt young Tufty here, would that be okay? He'd live at the police house with me, not far away at all. Perhaps I could call back for him in a couple of weeks?"

"Well, I don't know... I'll contact you when I feel they are ready to go."

Stan had to be satisfied with that.

Weeks turned into months and the puppies grew. Bella turned away PC Cooper and all prospective owners. Jayne Fairweather worried more and more about the state of Bella's home and her health. It was only a small house, and the puppies and other animals filled it.

Word had trickled round the village that Bella rescued animals. Jayne Fairweather was partly responsible for this because, in an effort to help Bella, she'd put up a postcard in the Post Office saying:

Wanted.

*Old towels, blankets or quilts to be used for animal rescue. Please drop them here
or at Bella Tait's house.
Thank you!*

People brought their old blankets and quilts, but they also brought all manner of animals and wildlife for Bella to nurse and care for. The house began to fill up with rescued and injured animals and Bella needed to make space to accommodate them all.

The living room was mainly given over to Sadie and her puppies. The pups had grown big and their boisterous behaviour was ruining the furniture and carpet. Sharp puppy teeth had shredded the curtains and chewed the upholstery. A window was broken, and roughly boarded up. Bella dragged one big chair into the front garden, uncertain what to do with it next. And in spite of her efforts, the room smelled of urine and puppy poo. Hattie sought peace on the mantlepiece.

Her mother's dining room was now unrecognisable. Chair legs were chewed, crates sat on top of each other, some with occupants, others empty but not cleaned out. Those that were occupied contained a pigeon with a broken wing, other injured birds, and even a barn owl that had flown into a power line. There were rabbits, both wild and domesticated, white rats that bred alarmingly, and guinea pigs, either abandoned or injured. There were hedgehogs, a ferret and mice.

The crates spilled over into the kitchen leaving just enough space for Bella to prepare the animals' food. A small area was set aside for a pair of scales to weigh her patients and keep notes on their progress.

Henrietta, the chicken, marched in and out of the house as she pleased. In the front garden, her mother's carefully tended flowers were neglected and the weeds allowed to take over. The easy chair from the living room sat rotting. The once neat picket fence had slats missing and leaned drunkenly.

Bella shared her bedroom with an assortment of rescued cats and two litters of kittens. Apart from her late parents' bedroom, which remained untouched with the door firmly closed, the house was full to bursting.

There wasn't a label for the condition in those days, but Bella had become an animal hoarder. Her whole life was taken up by caring for the animals.

Bella threw herself into the job of nursing her patients and tending the orphaned and abandoned creatures.

At least I have no time to think about Mum and Dad, she thought as she ladled dog food into bowls. *These animals depend on me.*

Mr Dodd, the bank manager, was not so sympathetic. His expression was severe as he stared at Bella over the top of his horn-rimmed spectacles.

"Miss Tait, you must curb your spending. If you carry on at this rate, you'll use up all your inheritance in no time."

Bella stared back at him.

"But I have to feed the animals," she said.

Mr Dodd blinked.

"Miss Tait, there'll be no money to feed *yourself* if you don't cut back."

"Sign here," said the prison warder.

Christine scrawled her name on the dotted line.

The warder handed her a plastic bag containing an opened packet of cigarettes, a lighter and some small change, Christine's belongings before she had been admitted to Holloway.

"You know that you must report to your probation officer? If you don't, you'll be straight back in here."

"Yes, I know."

As if I'm gonna bother with that!

"Right," said the warder wearily, "here's your allowance, a gift from Her Majesty the Queen. And here's your probation officer's phone number, and the address of the halfway house. They're expecting you." She unlocked the metal door and pushed it open. A blast of cold air swirled in. "Off you go then, good luck."

Christine stepped out into the street and sucked the grey London air into her lungs. The prison gate clanged shut behind her. There was nobody to meet her but she didn't care.

Freedom! At last!

With a spring in her step she walked down the street, heading for the bus stop. The money in her pocket wasn't going to last long so she'd better top it up. And where was a sure-fire place to acquire some? On the platforms of the good old London underground, of course.

A bus approached just as she reached the bus stop.

"Where you goin', Miss?" asked the conductor.

"Caledonian Road, please," she said.

Yes, just one underground stop away from King's Cross, on the Piccadilly line. A nice busy platform. Perfect!

14

*B*ella sat hunched on the doorstep of her cottage with her head buried in her hands. Behind the closed front door she could hear thumps and yaps from inside. The puppies, adorable as they were, had become adolescent wreckers. The inside of the cottage was ruined, even Bella acknowledged that. Her mother would turn in her grave if she could see how her cottage looked now.

Tears trickled from Bella's eyes. She was so tired. Worrying kept her awake most of the night and even when she slept, nightmares tormented her.

How had it got so bad?

The event that Mr Dodd, the bank manager, had predicted, was nearly upon her. She had almost run out of money.

Who will look after the animals if I can't? They'll starve!

Fresh tears sprang from her eyes. She shuddered and sobbed into her hands, shoulders heaving.

"Bella?"

Bella was too wrapped in her own misery to hear the voice or see the figure in front of her.

"Bella? Is that you? Whatever is the matter?"

Bella paused. Choking back a sob, she tilted her head slightly and peeped through her fingers. Who was this tall, slim man with a thatch of deep auburn hair? He was a stranger, yet he looked familiar. She gasped, and her hands fell away from her pale, tear-streaked face.

"Red?"

Red smiled into her bloodshot eyes.

"Yup! It's me all right! I think I came back just in time, didn't I?" He plonked himself down on the doorstep beside her and draped his arm around her shoulders. "I'm here to help."

Bella gaped at him.

"Now, before you tell me what the tears are all about, explain to me what's causing the thumping and barking behind us in the house. Has a circus moved in?"

"It's the puppies," wailed Bella and, burying her face into his chest, renewed her sobbing.

Red held her and stared over her head, waiting for her to quieten. He didn't show it, but he was shocked to see the tumbledown fence and the unkempt front garden. But only when Bella's sobs turned to hiccups did he speak.

"Bella, before you tell me everything, I want to tell you some stuff you need to know."

Bella was silent, listening. Only an occasional hiccup escaped her.

"When my family moved to Scotland all those years ago, I was miserable. I'd lost my best friend and nobody could take your place, Bella. I used to watch the postman like a hawk, in case he brought me a letter from you. Then one day, it struck me. If you felt the same as I did, you would be miserable, too. So I forced myself to write less and less often. I was trying to help you to move on, you understand? Then, one black day I wrote *unknown at this address* on your envelope and posted it back to you."

Bella stared at him.

"I never wrote again after that," she whispered.

"I know," he sighed. "I thought I'd done it for the best."

"Did you go to university?" asked Bella.

"No. My parents wanted me to, but I fought it. I'm afraid I became a rebellious teenager and got myself into a lot of trouble. I started drinking."

Bella drew away from him in order to stare into his face.

"Are you serious?"

"Yes, absolutely serious. I found it was a good way to hide from life. I started drinking because I wanted to escape, and now I drink because I need to."

"You… You're an alcoholic?"

"I believe I am. Then, a couple of days ago, I was sitting drinking, and I thought of you. And I felt as though you were in trouble. The impression just wouldn't leave me. I tried drowning the feeling but the whiskey tasted horrible on my tongue. Eventually, I lost patience. I decided I had to travel down and see you for myself, put my mind at rest."

"Two days ago?"

Bella recalled the fitful night she'd had two nights ago, robbed of sleep by worry. *Help me!* she'd sobbed into her pillow, not knowing who she was calling upon.

"Yes. I stopped fighting the feeling and packed up my worldly goods. They are in that holdall over there by the gate. I told my landlord that I wouldn't be coming back, and I caught a train to London, then another to Yewbridge. Then I walked from Yewbridge to Sixpenny Cross. And here I am, at your service, ma'am."

Bella stared at him anew, still shocked to the core.

"It's your turn," he said gently. "I've told you all my secrets."

Bella swallowed. She had no idea where to start.

"How are your parents?" asked Red, trying to be helpful.

Bella's face crumpled.

"They're dead!" she whispered, "They drowned in Italy."

Christine was in her element, the adrenalin rushing. It was five o'clock on the Piccadilly line, and the underground platform was crowded.

Lights flashed and the dull, distant rumble of an approaching train grew in volume. The train slid to a halt by the platform and its doors whooshed open. The crowds surged forward, jostling and pushing, and Christine was in the thick of it.

Nobody noticed Christine's skinny arm snake out and dip first into a commuter's pocket, then into a shopper's bag. In a split second, light fingers found what they sought: a wallet and a purse.

The doors closed and the train rolled away leaving nobody on the platform but Christine and new passengers just arriving.

Christine locked herself into a public toilet and stripped the wallet and purse of cash.

Lovely! Enough money for a nice meal, a bottle of wine and a decent room in a hotel.

She threw away the plundered wallet and purse and stuffed pound notes into her pocket.

Too easy!

She was enjoying herself. She'd get some more money together, then, when she felt like it, she'd head south to Sixpenny Cross and look up a few old 'friends'.

Christine hummed to herself as she tipped the lavatory attendant and returned to the platform to target more victims.

The sun dipped behind Sixpenny Woods and bats flitted round the street lamps snatching dizzy moths. Bella and Red were oblivious to the world as they talked.

"And now I have all these animals to look after…"

"What animals?"

"Well, there's Hattie of course. And the mice and guinea pigs. But…I…I seem to have set up a kind of animal rescue centre."

Red stared at her, waiting.

"I have dogs, a whole litter of puppies! Stray cats and their kittens, wildlife like hedgehogs and birds… I even have a chicken. And a ferret."

"That's a lot of animals, Bella."

"I know! And I can't cope. I've run out of money, but if I don't look after the animals, who will?"

The light from the street lamp blanched her face, drawing all colour from it. Her cheekbones, invisible behind plump cheeks for so many years, were now high and pronounced.

"*Nessun problema.* I told you, I'm here to help."

Bella smiled into his eyes, then stopped.

"But you have your own problems. What about the drinking?"

"I told you, I haven't had a drink for two days. I know it's not going to be easy for either of us, but I want you to help me stop."

"*Nessun problema.*"

"It's a deal then. May I stay? I can sleep on the couch."

"Of course. But I'm afraid it's covered in dog hair. And cages… Perhaps you'd be more comfortable in my parents' room."

Suddenly, it didn't seem so important to keep her parents' room exactly as they'd left it before they took that fateful trip to Italy.

They stood up and Red picked up his holdall. Bella found herself shaking as she opened the front door. For the first time, she was seeing the state of the cottage through somebody else's eyes. The last time Red had been here, the house was clean and tidy, smelling of furniture polish and fresh Italian cooking.

What now lay behind the front door would shock anybody.

15

*I*f the stench of dogs, cats and urine shocked Red, he didn't allow himself to show it. Neither did he flinch when Sadie's puppies hurled themselves at him in exuberant welcome.

"Hey! Down guys!"

His eyes darted around, missing nothing. He drank in the broken furniture, the cages, boxes and crates stacked on top of each other, some with occupants that either slept or regarded him with frightened eyes.

"It's bad, isn't it?" said Bella, as she scooped up a passing kitten and hugged it to herself. "I'm afraid these are only some of my cases. There are more in the kitchen and wherever I could find space."

"Yes, I'm not going to lie to you, it's bad. But, like I keep saying, I'm here to help. Now, what needs doing tonight? Tomorrow is a brand new day and I'll have stopped drinking for three whole days. I give you my word, Bella, I'm going to help you sort everything."

That night, Bella slept soundly, and no little boats on turquoise seas sailed into her dreams.

Restoring the cottage to its former self was not going to be easy. Alone in Bella's parents' room, Red made plans for the renovations in an effort to chase away his own demons. He forced himself not to imagine tipping a bottle and watching the contents splash into a glass before raising it to his lips and drinking himself into sweet oblivion. Instead, he thought about mending fences and reglazing windows.

At last, he slept.

It was lucky that Red was so good with his hands. He took over Bella's father's workshop which had remained untouched since his death, with the tools hanging in neat rows and timber stacked in the rafters. Now the sound of hammering and sawing could be heard once more. When Bella heard it, a little ripple of happiness washed through her.

Red's first job was to fence off an enclosure for Sadie's puppies in the backyard which successfully removed them from the overcrowded cottage. Bella brought him out a mug of tea and admired his handiwork.

"Red, may I ask you something?" she asked, looking at him sideways.

"Fire away! Anything."

"I know you said you're going to help me, and I'm really grateful, but what about money? You don't have a job, and neither do I…"

"Ah! There's something I didn't tell you."

Bella raised her eyebrows in question, surprised to see Red smiling.

"You remember that box I made you for your fourteenth birthday?"

"Of course! I still have it."

"Well, do you remember that I invented a kind of engraving tool which I used to write your initials on the lid?"

Bella nodded. Red's eyes were dancing now.

"Well, I patented it, and a big company in Scotland bought the rights to manufacture and sell it. They pay me a percentage of the sales."

"Wow! That's fantastic!"

"I know! And if I invent anything else, they want first refusal on it."

Bella was still gaping at him when they both heard the doorbell.

"That'll be Auntie Jayne," said Bella. "She said she might pop round. Come with me, she'll be so surprised to see you!"

Red followed as she ran through the house to open the door.

"Morning, Auntie Jayne, I have a surprise for you! Look who's here!" she stepped aside to reveal a grinning Red.

"Hello, Mrs Fairweather."

"Oh my goodness! Red, is that you? I haven't seen you since…" Jayne trailed off, her brow creasing as she attempted to calculate the years.

"Years and years," said Red, shaking her hand. "How are you, Mrs Fairweather? Do you still have the Post Office?"

"I certainly do. Are you here on a visit, Red?"

"Yes, a long one, I hope. If Bella will have me."

Bella's blush told Jayne all she needed to know.

"Will you stay for a cup of tea?" asked Bella. "I've just made some."

"I don't have time for tea, but I'll come in for a moment," said Jayne, entering and catching sight of Red's backyard project through the window. "I see you've made an enclosure for the puppies. That's wonderful! "

Bella nodded reluctantly.

Jayne's mind raced. Perhaps Red would help bring Bella to her senses and succeed where she had failed.

"Bella's place was getting rather cramped with all those pups hurtling around," she said to Red. "Wasn't it, Bella?"

"Well…" Bella started.

Red was a clever young man, and he knew that he and Jayne had a common goal, and that he had an ally in Jayne Fairweather.

"I promised Bella I'd help sort the animal situation," he said brightly. "I think we'll need to find homes for those pups. Really good homes, of course. In fact they aren't really puppies any more, isn't that right, Bella?"

"Well, no, but…"

"You weren't thinking of keeping all those dogs, were you? I know you'd only consider letting them go to really good homes," he added quickly, before Bella had time to speak.

"I…" she began.

"Mrs Fairweather, do you know of anybody looking for a dog to adopt?" he asked, before Bella had time to say anything else.

"Funnily enough, yes! I do!"

Bella closed her mouth and stared at her friends.

"PC Stan Cooper took a real shine to that pup with a patch over his eye. The scruffy-looking one with hair that sticks up in all directions," said Jayne.

"Good! He'll have a great life at the police house, won't he, Bella? Mrs Fairweather, would you mind asking PC Cooper if he's still interested?"

Bella opened her mouth again, but then snapped it shut, allowing Red to call the shots. Deep inside, she realised she was enjoying having somebody else making decisions for her for a change.

"No problem at all," said Jayne, beaming.

"Poor Bella's had a lot on her plate," said Red. "I intend to help her get things running as smoothly as possible again."

Bella glowed. The pain in her heart caused by the thought of losing Tufty and the other pups and animals was eased a little by the knowledge that Red was there to help her cope.

"Well, I'll be off then," said Jayne. "Welcome back, Red, it's really good to see you again."

Waving goodbye to the couple, she walked away up the street. A car rounded the corner, swerving briefly to avoid Henrietta who was pecking at something in the gutter.

"I think mending the front fence will be my next job," declared Red, "or Henrietta will end up as flat as an omelette. Incidentally, how did she come to be here?"

"I was at the Drapers' farm, and Henrietta had been attacked by a fox. She was injured and they were going to wring her neck and eat her because she stopped laying eggs. I said I'd treat her injuries then take her back to the farm when she was well."

"Well, she looks very healthy now. Has she started to lay eggs again?"

"Yes." Bella said, hanging her head, knowing what was coming next.

"Don't you think she'd be happier back with her flock?" Red's voice was gentle.

"I suppose so…"

As the weeks rolled by, Jayne was delighted to see big changes taking place. Red replaced the picket fence at the front of the house, and gave the rusty old gate a lick of paint. He varnished the peeling front door and replaced the broken window panes and repainted the frames. He cleared the front garden, removed the rabbit cages and built better ones in the backyard. Best of all, he fixed Don's shed and erected another, so the small animals and wildlife now had new homes outside.

With Bella's reluctant permission, Jayne pinned another notice on the Post Office noticeboard.

Free to Good Homes

Can you give a good home to any of the following animals? We have puppies, kittens, hamsters, guinea pigs, a ferret, white rabbits and rats. Apply within if you are interested.

Thank you!

The response was excellent. PC Stan Cooper had already claimed Tufty and the other pups soon found good homes. Bella shed a tear each time a puppy left with its new owner, but Red's reassuring arm round her shoulders told her she was doing the right thing.

"I'm so proud of you, Bella," he said, and her heart melted.

"And I'm so proud of you, Red. I've lost count of how many days you've gone without a drink."

"It'll be five months soon. It gets a little easier every day."

"I know what you mean. What happened to Mum and Dad hurts a tiny bit less each day. I guess we are all starting new lives. You, me and the animals."

They smiled at each other.

The kittens gradually found new homes, too. One was adopted by the landlord of the Dew Drop Inn, Angus McDonald. He named it Scout, and the kitten fast became a favourite with the regulars.

Another two kittens, with their mother, went to live on the Drapers' farm where they spent their days chasing rats and mice in the barns, or snoozing on the hay bales. The Drapers welcomed the ferret, too, and Henrietta rejoined her flock.

The rabbits and small animals were claimed by village children, each of whom faithfully promised their parents that they'd look after their new pet forever. They probably didn't keep their promises, but Jayne and Bella knew the families well enough to be confident that no pet would ever be neglected.

Even without much formal training, Bella had worked wonders nursing the sick, injured and abandoned wildlife, bringing them back to health. Together, she and Red decided which animals and birds were strong enough to be released.

One evening, they stood together in the field behind the cottage.

"Open the box," said Bella at last, and Red did so.

The barn owl peered around the edge of the box, then waddled a few steps forward.

"Come on, Barney, we're setting you free."

Barney stood tall, lifted his shoulders, then launched himself, flapping on silent wings across the twilit sky to settle on a tree branch, silhouetted black against the pink backdrop.

"You've done a wonderful job with these animals," said Red.

Bella smiled. She was enjoying watching her former patients being set free, knowing they had a natural life ahead of them, and that she'd probably saved their lives.

Mission accomplished, they strolled back to the cottage leaving two trails of down-trodden grass, very close together.

If anybody had asked Christine, she probably wouldn't have been able to explain exactly what kept drawing her back to Sixpenny Cross. Time had blurred Bella's memories of Christine and she rarely thought about her, but Christine's obsession with Bella never waned. Regular clandestine visits to Sixpenny Cross and spying on Bella was like a fix to an addict for her. She craved them, and the overwhelming need to find an opportunity to harm Bella had to be satisfied.

Christine was unaware that she had developed an involuntary spasm. It was subconscious and only occurred when powerful emotions enveloped her. Now, as she sat on the train bound for Yewbridge, the thought of Bella Tait set her eyelid twitching.

Without the cages and hutches squatting in every space, Red could address himself to the task of restoring the house back to how it had looked when Donald and June were alive. He tackled each room in turn, mending furniture or buying new. Bella helped by painting walls and sewing new curtains. She hummed as her needle flew along the hems.

Bella had never looked more lovely. Her olive skin was clear and as soft as thistledown. Her hair gleamed in the lamplight, and her dark eyes were bright and fringed with charcoal lashes unaided by cosmetics.

"Bella?"

Bella looked up.

"Bella… There's something I want to ask you."

16

$\mathcal{B}$ella waited, the sewing still on her lap. Red walked over to her and looked into her face, his eyes serious.

"I promised myself I'd wait, not rush things, but... Well, I just don't have the patience."

"Red?"

"You don't have to answer yet, just listen."

"Red, you're scaring me..."

Red knelt in front of her whilst slipping something small out of his pocket.

Bella stopped breathing.

"Bella, I think I loved you from the first day we sat together at school. I can't imagine life without you and I think we are good for each other. I want to look after you forever, have children together, grow old together. I love you, Bella."

Bella gasped.

"Bella, will you marry me? Will you wear this ring on your finger?" Red took her limp hand and straightened the fingers. "It's a sapphire, like your mother's engagement ring, and I used my engraving tool to write something inside. Look!"

Bella read the tiny delicate script. Tears coursed down her cheek.

La mia bella Bella.

"Bella? Do you like it?"

"I love it, Red," she whispered. "And I love you. Of course I'll marry you."

The sewing fell to the floor in a crumpled heap as Red leant down and kissed her passionately for the first time.

Neither of them saw the pale face pressed to the window, flinty eyes boring into the room, one eyelid twitching.

Christine waited her turn in the queue at the ticket kiosk. She'd walked from Sixpenny Cross back to Yewbridge station, and now she'd catch a train home.

Home? Where was home?

London. Nobody would miss her if she didn't go back, but London was where she earned a living dipping into the pockets of unsuspecting commuters. It was where she broke into people's houses to steal their valuables. It was where she squatted in empty houses or slept beneath the arches when she was homeless.

Her mother and father had long since disappeared from her life. For all she knew, they and her sister were still in Yewbridge but it had been years since she had seen them. As for looking for them, that was the last thing on her mind.

She still couldn't believe what she'd seen with her own eyes. Fat Belly Bella *kissing*? Fat Belly with a *ring* on her finger? And where was the fat belly? Gone! Bella looked slender and beautiful, with her almost black, glossy hair cascading down her back.

And who was the man she was kissing? He looked familiar somehow...

Having torn herself away from Bella Tait's window, Christine paid the Post Office a visit. Jayne Fairweather recognised her immediately.

"Christine Dayton, is that you? Long time no see."

"I've been livin' in London," said Christine. "Just came back to see a few old friends."

Jayne raised her eyebrows a fraction. As far as she knew, Christine had never had any friends in Sixpenny Cross.

"Seen Bella Tait lately?" Christine asked lightly. "I ain't seen 'er for years, 'ow is she?"

"Ah, you probably didn't hear about Bella's parents…"

"What about 'em?"

"It was very sad. They died in a tragic accident abroad."

"Really?"

Christine was surprised. She tried hard not to smirk, then remembered. *So who was that man in Bella's house?*

"So Bella's all alone now?" she said casually.

"Well, not quite. Red Jenkins came back…"

Jayne checked herself but Christine had heard enough. Of course! That's who it was! She remembered Red Jenkins from school, Bella's dorky little pal. His hair was more orange then, and he had been skinnier, but she was certain it was the same Red.

Instead of sympathy, rage consumed Christine. Any good fortune that Bella might enjoy was fuel for the powerful envy that Christine nursed within herself.

How come Bella has a man and is in love, when nobody cares a fig for me? It ain't fair, she thought. *No, it ain't fair at all.*

"Where you goin', miss?" asked the ticket vendor.

"Waterloo station," she replied, jerking herself out of her thoughts.

"Single or return?"

Christine was silent.

"Miss, are you coming back?"

"Nope, I ain't coming back. Well, not yet, anyway."

1978 was an interesting year. Pope Paul VI died, and was replaced by Pope John Paul I, who also died after just 34 days in office. At Wimbledon, Martina Navratilova defeated Chris Evert, and Bjorn Borg was declared the men's champion for the third successive year. Sony introduced the Walkman, the first portable stereo, and the Yorkshire Ripper was being hunted in England.

In June, no church bells rang at Bella and Red's wedding. They'd elected to marry at Yewbridge Registry Office, a quiet affair attended only by the happy couple, Jayne Fairweather and Bella's old teacher from the village school. But it was a joyous day. After the ceremony, Red and Bella posed for photographs in the grounds outside. The air was heavy with the scent of freshly mown grass and roses and Bella's white shoes sank into a fragrant carpet of daisies and clover.

No newlywed couple could have been happier, and nobody could have been more delighted for them than Jayne Fairweather.

Months passed, and the cottage was almost completely restored. Donald and June's old bedroom sported a new carpet, new furniture and Bella had sewn curtains with a matching bedcover. It looked fresh and clean, and she loved it.

Apart from Sadie and Hattie, no animals were housed inside. The remaining birds and animals that still needed Bella's attention were now cared for outside in the shed.

Yes, married life suited both Red and Bella, and as Red began to tinker with more inventions, the future looked rosy.

Christine watched the fields, hedges and farms flash past without really seeing them. She inhaled deeply and blew smoke out of the window.

It's high time I paid Fat Belly another visit.

She crushed her cigarette stub underfoot and sank into her favourite daydream, the one where she poisoned Fat Belly's pasta.

She'd caught the train on a whim, a spur of the moment decision. Train stations and undergrounds were her place of work, where she helped herself to distracted travellers' possessions. She was so skilled and light-fingered, she hardly ever went on burglary jaunts any more, unless she was bored and needed to pump up the adrenalin. When she'd heard the station announcer mention Yewbridge, she'd nipped back to her gloomy little bedsit and stuffed a few clothes in a bag. Then she hopped on board the next train to Yewbridge.

What's Fat Belly doing now? she wondered. *Did she marry that dork, Red? I 'ope they make each other miserable. What's she ever done to deserve 'appiness?*

Christine's eyelid twitched. The mere thought of Bella made jealousy, hatred and revenge course through her veins. She dismissed the fact that Bella had lost her parents in tragic circumstances, and that Bella, in the past, had actually prevented Christine from getting into serious trouble by not telling tales. In fact, it only made matters worse because she resented being in Bella's debt. Christine was deaf and blind to reason.

She had no plan, but she knew Yewbridge was not her final destination. She was drawn to Sixpenny Cross like a fox to a rabbit hole. And Sixpenny Cross was just a short bus ride away from Yewbridge.

From the Post Office, Jayne Fairweather saw Christine alight from the bus and watched her walk up the street to the Dew Drop Inn. She didn't see her come out again.

Christine sat on the bed and smirked to herself. Here she was staying at the Dew Drop, the very place whose kitchen she had robbed continually as a child. Would the landlord have welcomed her so warmly had he known?

She'd eat in the pub lounge later, then maybe, when night fell, she'd go for a little walk…

She was prepared to wait. She lit another cigarette, and amused herself by singeing loose threads along the edge of the blanket.

17

*B*ella pushed her bare feet into her slippers and tiptoed towards the bedroom door, careful not to wake Red.

"Bella?"

"Oh, I'm sorry - did I wake you?"

"No, I just sensed you weren't there. What time is it?"

"Three o'clock. Go back to sleep, I'm just popping down to the shed to feed the baby rabbits."

"Okay, don't be long."

"I won't be, keep the bed warm for me."

She smiled as Red buried his face into the pillow and knew he would be asleep before she reached the foot of the stairs.

Bella didn't need to turn on lights. Faithful Sadie trotted behind her, well used to this nightly vigil and not wanting to be left out.

With a shiver, she crossed the yard, a stiff breeze making her clutch her robe more tightly about her. She entered the shed, closing the door behind herself and Sadie to keep the warmth in. Sadie flopped down as Bella switched on the lamp and drew some milk substitute up in a dropper.

She was looking after two sets of rabbits. One set was almost ready to release into the wild, but the newborns needed her care. Very gently, she plucked the rabbit babies out of their nest and encouraged them to lick the dropper, carefully massaging each afterwards to encourage it to defecate, just as their mother would have done. So engrossed was she that she hardly noticed Sadie sit up and give a low growl.

"Settle down, Sadie. I have three more little rabbits to do, then we're finished and we can go back to bed."

The streets of Sixpenny Cross were deserted as Christine made her way towards Bella's house. She glanced at her watch. Three o'clock. Nothing stirred apart from fallen autumn leaves caught by gusts of wind.

The Dew Drop Inn was silent, both staff and guests in their beds. In her house, Jayne Fairweather had been asleep for hours as she needed to be up to sort the early morning newspapers. She passed the silent police house. Inside, PC Stan Cooper snored in his bed, while Tufty twitched and dreamed on the floor beside him.

Christine smirked. *The police are such idiots.*

She glanced up and down, then pushed open Bella's newly oiled gate and walked silently up the path. She still had no plan, just a terrible need to spy on her enemy and, if she could, cause her harm.

She pressed herself against the wall, merging into the shadows, and peered through the lounge window. She could see nothing inside but automatically tested the window with the tips of her gloved hand. It no longer surprised her that so many people didn't lock their windows at night and, once again, she wasn't disappointed. The window yielded and she quietly pushed it fully open. She paused to consider her options.

Shall I climb in? It'd be easy...

Then she had a better idea.

Reaching through the window, she grabbed a handful of Bella's new curtain and pulled it outside. She inspected the fabric, appreciating its quality before she flicked her cigarette lighter.

Flame met fabric.

At first the curtain only smouldered a little, but then a small flame grew. She watched the fire slowly take hold, the flickering light reflected in her small eyes, bright with excitement, and her thin lips twisted in a smile.

She replaced the curtain but didn't move. She was not a natural arsonist but the growing fire fascinated her. She stared as the yellow flames began to light up the room showing the comfortable and tastefully arranged furnishings. She opened the window a little more, allowing the autumn breeze to fan the flames.

Whoosh!

Now all the curtains were alight and the flames were spreading fast.

It satisfied Christine that she was destroying Bella's possessions. That Bella might be in danger meant nothing, if she died it would be the icing on the cake.

Christine turned away from the house and walked back to the Dew Drop Inn. Once, a pair of headlights approached, but she slunk into the shadows and nobody saw her come or go.

***

In the shed in the backyard, Bella was finishing off.

"That's the last bunny fed, then," she said as she placed the baby rabbit next to its siblings. "Time for bed, Sadie."

Together they crossed the yard, but as Bella pushed the kitchen door open, Sadie hung back.

"What's the matter, girl?"

Bella smelled the smoke before she saw it. Grey curls were wafting into the kitchen and the orange flicker of flames could be seen beyond.

"Red!" she screamed. "RED! Wake up!"

There was no answer.

No time to lose.

Grabbing a towel from the counter, she quickly wet it and pressed it to her face. She headed for the source of the fire, the living room. Through the thick smoke, Bella saw that two chairs were already on fire and the wallpaper and carpet were smoking. She briefly noted that the living room window was wide open but now was not the time to think about such things. Flames licked the walls and the telephone was now out of reach. Smoke had escaped out of the room and was floating up the stairs.

Bella slammed the door shut and flew up the stairs taking them two at a time.

"RED! FIRE!"

No answer.

The bedroom was already filled with smoke and Red was not moving.

"Red! Wake up! We have to get out! The house is on fire!"

With her free hand, Bella grabbed hold of Red's shoulder but no amount of shaking would wake him.

Bella flung open the bedroom window, lowering the wet cloth to shout an alarm.

"Help! HELP ME! Fire!" she screamed.

She turned back, ever mindful that, at any moment, the fire could block her exit at the bottom of the stairs. Now she needed both hands and so transferred the wet cloth to Red's unconscious face. Coughing, she grabbed him under the armpits and, using all her strength, dragged his inert body out of the bedroom to the top of the stairs.

"Red! You have to wake up! We've got to get out of the house!"

But Red was in another place and her pleas went unheard. The crackling of flames was growing ever louder and smoke continued to seep from under the living room door. Bella knew the flames could explode through the door at any second.

Somehow, she manoeuvered him down the stairs, cruelly bumping his body on every step. At the foot of the stairs the heat was intense. But Bella had reached her limit.

"Don't let him die," she croaked. "Don't let him die."

Coughing and sobbing, she crawled on her hands and knees, up the hall, away from Red's lifeless body, desperate to find help. She didn't get far. Smoke inhalation had taken its deadly toll. Bella slumped, unconscious.

18

*P*C Stan Cooper was so deep in thought that he absentmindedly stirred his tea with his biro. Both Red and Bella Jenkins had nearly lost their lives that night. There was no doubt that they were minutes from death and owed everything to the quick-acting van driver who raised the alarm. The driver had hammered on the door of the police house, raising not only Stan Cooper, but several neighbours.

The van driver arriving just then was nothing short of a miracle, he mused. *If I was a believer, I'd think Mr and Mrs Tait were watching over their daughter that night.*

Somebody phoned the Fire Brigade, while others rushed to the house to find both Bella and Red unconscious. As they were dragged out, the Fire Brigade arrived and took charge. The fire was put out before it could spread.

Outside, Bella gasped fresh air and regained consciousness immediately, but Red took longer. An ambulance arrived from Yewbridge and both were taken away for treatment.

PC Cooper had just finished speaking with Yewbridge Fire Department and their findings were puzzling. Their investigation concluded that the fire at Bella Jenkins' home had begun in the corner of the living room, but no trace of fire accelerant had been found. That made arson seem unlikely. However, there was also no evidence of faulty electrical wiring, or, indeed, any other cause.

So how did the fire start?

Not everybody appreciated that Stan's amiable, clumsy exterior hid a sharp detective brain. Also, having been born in the village, he was familiar with all the residents and privy to many village secrets. His forehead furrowed in thought as he applied himself to the mystery.

Did Red and Bella Jenkins have any enemies?

He knew that Bella Jenkins and Christine Dayton had never been friends, but were they mortal enemies? He couldn't imagine Bella being unkind to anybody, but what about Christine?

Stan cast his mind back to the time when Jayne Fairweather had reported a theft from the till in the Post Office. Mrs Fairweather had thought she'd seen Christine Dayton skulking in the shadows. That same night, somebody stole Bella's bicycle and slashed her father's car tyres. Coincidence? Probably not. He knew Christine had spent time in prison for theft and she was more than capable of slashing tyres.

And then there was that strange incident of Donald Tait's severed brake cable. Had Christine Dayton been behind that? But nobody had seen her in the village at that time, so he'd kept his suspicions to himself.

So what happened the night of the fire?

Two facts kept niggling him. Bella had said that she'd noticed that the lounge window was open. When he questioned her, she didn't remember opening it, and she didn't think Red had either. It was a cold autumn night and they would have kept the windows and curtains closed.

"Was the window locked?" Stan had asked.

"Probably not," Bella had admitted.

The second fact bothered him, too. Was it coincidence that Christine Dayton had been staying at the Dew Drop Inn that very night? Angus McDonald, the landlord, had seen nothing. Neither had any of the guests staying there at the time. Everybody in the village, including Christine Dayton, had declared they were fast asleep in their beds.

To imagine that Christine had left her warm bed and crept out in the early hours of the morning to set fire to Bella's house seemed highly unlikely.

Or was it?

Jayne Fairweather set the tray on the bedside table, and poured tea into the two awaiting cups. On the rug, Sadie sat up and wagged her tail. Jayne patted her absently then turned to the bed.

"Morning! How are you feeling, my dear?" she asked her guest.

"My throat's still sore, but otherwise not too bad, thanks, Auntie Jayne."

"Here, drink this tea. It'll help. The doctor said to drink plenty of fluids."

Jayne sat on Bella's bed and they sipped their tea, both lost in their own thoughts.

"Just imagine if the newspaper delivery van hadn't driven past just then. And what if the driver hadn't noticed the smoke and flames?" Bella asked for the hundredth time.

"It doesn't bear thinking about," said Jayne, shaking her head. "And if you hadn't been outside, feeding those baby rabbits in the shed, you'd both be…"

Bella shuddered. Death had been close.

"If you're feeling okay, we'll drive over to Yewbridge Hospital and see Red later, shall we?"

"Yes, thank you," said Bella.

"I was talking to Stan Cooper," said Jayne. "He told me that it's still a mystery how the fire started."

"Yes, I know. I'm positive we didn't leave anything electrical on. Maybe it was a loose wire somewhere."

"I'm sure they'll find out eventually." Jayne said, then remembered something. "Hey, you'll never guess who's staying at the Dew Drop for a few days."

Bella waited.

"Christine Dayton! She can't seem to stay away from Sixpenny Cross, although the Lord only knows why she keeps coming back."

"I haven't seen Christine for years," said Bella. "I wonder what she's been up to?"

Until the house was repaired, Bella and Sadie would be staying with Jayne Fairweather. Thanks to the quick actions of the Fire Brigade, the destruction was limited to the living room, which had been gutted, while the rest of the house suffered from smoke damage.

With Jayne busy at the Post Office, much of Bella's time was spent alone. Red was getting stronger every day and would soon be discharged from hospital, but for now, she had time on her hands.

She made daily visits to the shed in her backyard. The baby rabbits were doing well, and no longer needed their nightly feed. The older rabbits were now six weeks old and ready to be set free.

Bella dusted out the pet carrier, lined it with newspaper and popped the two rabbits inside. She decided that the open fields might not be a safe place to release them, and, leaving Sadie at home, she headed instead for Sixpenny Woods. It was a chilly day, and the track was deserted.

"Bella."

The voice stopped Bella in her tracks.

"Christine, how are you? I haven't seen you in a long time." she said. "I heard you're staying at the Dew Drop."

"Yeah, just for a few days."

"I'm just looking for a spot to let these young rabbits go, they're big enough to fend for themselves now. Want to join me?"

"Yeah, why not."

Christine fell into step with Bella and the pair of them walked together into the woods.

"So where are you living now?" asked Bella.

"London. I got a great job, pays really well."

"That's good."

"I 'eard about your 'ouse nearly burning down and all," said Christine. "Do they know what 'appened?"

"No, they've no idea what started the fire. My husband, Red, could have died. Well, we both could have. Luckily we were rescued in time and he's going to be all right."

They walked on, and the tree branches met above them, blocking out much of the light.

"Spooky place, this, isn't it?" remarked Christine, her eyelid beginning to flicker. "You could die in 'ere and nobody would find you for ages."

"I'm heading for the clearing by the Wishing Rock," Bella said, ignoring the observation. "That'll be a perfect place to let the rabbits go."

"I used to come 'ere when I was young," Christine said. "I used to carve my name on the tree trunks with my knife. I've always carried a knife. Never know when you might need it. Look, 'ere it is."

Christine's hand darted to her pocket and emerged with a flick knife.

19

"That looks dangerous," Bella said nervously. "Put it away."

Christine hesitated for a moment, grinned, then slipped the knife back into her pocket.

When they reached the rock, Bella opened the carrier.

"This spot will do nicely," she said. "Come on, bunnies, I'm setting you free."

The two young rabbits sat on their haunches for a few seconds, testing the air with twitching noses. Then they bounded away into the thicket, white tails bobbing.

"I've been meaning to climb the Wishing Rock," said Bella. "I know it's probably a lot of superstitious nonsense, but my parents always said they believed it had special powers."

She looked directly at Christine for the first time.

"Do you fancy climbing the rock for old time's sake?"

"Yeah, okay."

Bella took the lead. She tugged at the ivy on the rock, testing it. Her toe found a foothold, and she began to climb. Christine scrambled up behind her. It wasn't an easy climb and neither young woman spoke as she concentrated on where next to place her hands and feet. Christine was quick and light, but Bella was stronger. At last they were both at the top, sitting side by side on the narrow outcrop, just like Donald and June Tait had done more than twenty years before.

Bella brushed the dirt from her hands.

"So here we are," she said brightly. "On top of the Wishing Rock."

For a while, they sat together, side by side, neither girl speaking. Bella was the first to break the silence. She took a deep breath.

"Christine, I know how the fire started in my house. I saw you that night."

Christine was caught off guard. Her head jerked round to face Bella, her eyes full of hatred.

"So what? You can't prove it!"

It was at that moment that Bella knew, without a shadow of a doubt, that Christine was responsible.

"Actually I didn't see you, Christine, I guessed. But now I *know* it was you."

Christine's hand flashed towards the knife in her pocket, but Bella was faster. She grabbed Christine's bony wrist, preventing her from reaching the weapon.

"Let go! You're hurting me!"

"That knife isn't going to help you now, Christine. You set fire to my house, and you nearly killed Red. I'll *never* forgive you for that. I've always thought you had something to do with my dad's accident, that brake cable in his car didn't cut itself. In fact, nearly every bad thing that has ever happened to me was caused by you. Let me see… My bike going missing, I bet that was you."

Christine tried again to pull free, but could not escape Bella's powerful grip.

"I bet you loved hearing about my parents' death, didn't you? But still you wouldn't leave me alone. You've stalked me for as long as I can remember. But it stops now."

Christine glared at her.

"I felt sorry for you when I was little," Bella continued. "I tried to help you, but it never made any difference. You hated me whatever I did. And you know what? I bet I know what you're wishing right now. You're wishing you'd never climbed this rock with me, aren't you?"

"Let go! You're gonna make us both fall off the bloody rock!" Christine hissed.

It was the last sentence she ever uttered.

"Not me," said Bella. "You."

One sharp push was all it took. Christine fell, and her head struck a rocky outcrop on the way down. She hit the ground with a dull thud and lay still, a trickle of blood seeping from her ear.

It was a full two minutes before Bella could even move.

What have I done?

She was terrified at what she'd see at the bottom and her legs shook uncontrollably as she clambered down the rock. Christine's lifeless corpse was heaped on the ground, one hand clutching an ivy tendril she had grabbed on her way down in a futile attempt to break the fall. Sightless eyes stared at nothing.

Bella stumbled out of the woods and back to the village. Instead of heading for Jayne's, she staggered to the police house and knocked on the door. Stan opened it. Tufty recognised her and hurled himself at her.

"Ah, Mrs Jenkins," said Stan, his mouth full of sandwich. "Excuse me, just having a snack."

"That's okay," said Bella, uncharacteristically ignoring the dog's welcome. Her face was pale and she held onto the door jamb for support. "I've just come from the woods. I... I think I've killed Christine Dayton."

Stan acted quickly. He guided Bella by the elbow, steering her inside.

"Mrs Jenkins, come in and sit down. When you're ready, you can tell me what's happened."

Bella sank into the chair he offered and sat silently staring at her feet for a long time. Then she spoke. There was no expression in her voice.

"I was going to Sixpenny Woods to set some young rabbits free, and I met up with Christine. I suggested we climb the Wishing Rock, for old time's sake, and so we did. When we were at the top, I pushed her. She fell, and I heard her head hit the rock on the way down."

PC Cooper stared at her, then grabbed his helmet from the rack.

"Are you sure she was dead?"

Bella nodded dumbly, her eyes devoid of expression.

Stan's mind raced.

"Mrs Jenkins, I need you to do something for me. I need you to stay here and don't move until I get back. Can you do that?"

Bella nodded again.

"I'll wait," she said, her hand on Tufty's head.

Stan leaned his bicycle against a tree and hurried to the Wishing Rock. A few autumn leaves had already settled on the body on the ground. He noted Bella's abandoned pet carrier set down close by.

It wasn't necessary, but duty made him lift Christine's wrist and check for a pulse. There was none. Without disturbing any possible evidence, he checked her pockets, finding nothing but a pack of cigarettes, a lighter, a flick knife and a train ticket stub.

He didn't hurry. He sat down on a tree stump and removed his policeman's helmet. A squirrel ran up a nearby tree, its tail twitching as though annoyed by the policeman's presence. But Stan didn't see it. As he cradled his helmet in his hands, he was thinking hard. He stayed in that position for a long time before he finally stood, replaced his helmet and picked up the pet carrier. With a last glance at the body, he marched over to his bicycle and climbed back on. Steering wasn't easy with the pet carrier held in one hand, but Stan wobbled his way back home without mishap.

Stan hung his helmet back on the rack and turned to face Bella in the chair. Her face was tear-streaked and almost as white as the corpse lying in the woods.

"Did you find her?"

"I did."

"Are you going to arrest me now?"

"No, Mrs Jenkins, I'm not."

Bella looked at him.

"Why not?" she whispered.

He sat down in the chair facing her and leaned forward, speaking quietly and deliberately.

"Here's what I think, Mrs Jenkins, and I don't want you to say anything. You see, I think I know what happened today. I've suspected it for a long time, but of course I had no proof. Christine Dayton was always jealous of you, wasn't she?"

Bella opened her mouth but Stan raised his palm.

"No need to answer, Mrs Jenkins. I think Christine was behind that business when your father's brake cable was cut, am I right? Don't answer… And she stole your bicycle, didn't she? I expect she carried out countless nasty deeds, but you never reported her. But then she went too far. Christine Dayton set fire to your house, Mrs Jenkins, didn't she?"

Bella buried her face in her hands. She was sobbing.

"I thought so," he said gently. "Today, as the pair of you sat on the top of the Wishing Rock, she told you what she'd done."

"She could have killed Red," Bella moaned. "I was so furious, I pushed her!"

"Now here's what I'm going to do," said Stan, ignoring her outburst. "I'm going to file a report. It will state that you were in the woods releasing young rabbits and found Christine dead at the bottom of the Wishing Rock, and that's all. It's obvious that she climbed the rock and fell from the top."

"But why would you do that?" Bella stammered through her tears.

"Because, Mrs Jenkins, if you hadn't pushed her, I believe she would have killed you. The world is probably a better place without Christine Dayton and what's done is done and can't be undone. That's my final word. I don't think we ever need to talk about what happened today again, Mrs Jenkins."

20

The people at the Fire Brigade carried out numerous tests, little one, but they never discovered the cause of the fire at Bella's house. Most people believed it must have been some kind of electrical fault.

Christine Dayton was dead, and the coroner declared it 'death by misadventure'. She was given a council funeral in Yewbridge. They couldn't trace her parents, or her older sister, Mary. Only four people attended the funeral, and I don't believe they did it out of any fondness for Christine.

PC Stan Cooper, Bella, Red, and my very good friend, Jayne Fairweather, listened as the priest said a few words and the coffin disappeared behind the curtains to be cremated.

Red was lucky the smoke inhalation hadn't done his lungs any permanent damage. He became a very respected inventor and earned a good living. The couple were able to rent a little house with a garden in Bristol where they stayed while Bella continued her studies at the university. Of course Sadie went with them. Hattie had passed away peacefully from old age a few months before.

When Bella qualified as a veterinary surgeon, she joined the team at the Animal Hospital in Yewbridge, the same one that had saved Hattie so many years before.

I'm pleased to say that Red stayed sober. Bella occasionally popped into the Dew Drop Inn, but only to stroke Scout, the cat that Angus McDonald had adopted from her.

As Scout lay on his back enjoying a tummy rub, two figures sat beside the fire, engrossed in a game of dominoes. They were regulars, almost part of the pub's fixtures and fittings.

They were known as the Captain and Sixpence, and the next time I watch over you, little one, I'll tell you their story.

Yes, C is for the Captain, but the story of the Captain and Sixpence isn't a pretty tale, my dear, so I'll wait until you're fast asleep before I begin.

JUNE TAIT'S CINNAMON HAZELNUT BISCOTTI

"We're going to miss you, Bella," her mother said. "Make some space on the table, I've made a plate of hazelnut *biscotti* to celebrate."

INGREDIENTS

- ¾ cup butter
- 1 cup white sugar
- 2 eggs
- 1½ teaspoons vanilla extract
- 2½ cups all-purpose flour
- 1 teaspoon ground cinnamon
- ¾ teaspoon baking powder
- ½ teaspoon salt
- I cup of roughly chopped hazelnuts

METHOD

- Preheat oven to 175°C or 350°F. Grease a cookie sheet or line with parchment paper.
- In a medium bowl, cream together butter and sugar until light and fluffy.
- Beat in eggs and vanilla.

- Sift together the flour, cinnamon, baking powder, and salt; mix into the egg mixture.
- Stir in the hazelnuts.
- Shape dough into two equal logs approximately 30cm or 12 inches long.
- Place logs on baking sheet, and flatten out to about ½ inch thickness.
- Bake for about 30 minutes in preheated oven, or until the edges are golden and the centre is firm.
- Remove from oven to cool.
- When the loaves are cool enough to handle, use a serrated knife to slice the loaves diagonally into ½ inch thick slices.
- Return the slices to the baking sheet.
- Bake for an additional 10 minutes, turning over once.
- Cool completely, and store in an airtight container at room temperature.

C IS FOR THE CAPTAIN

SIXPENNY CROSS 3

Ageing bachelors, the Captain and Sixpence, have always been inseparable. Then Babs, the new barmaid, begins work at the Dew Drop Inn.

1

*D*ream on, little one, and I'll put another log on the fire. I do so love to watch the orange flames flickering. Nothing is more welcoming than a real fire, so much nicer than those new-fangled electric things. It's a great pity, but nowadays not many people can be bothered with fireplaces in their homes.

If you asked me, I would say that the best fireplace in Sixpenny Cross is in the saloon of the Dew Drop Inn. I've seen the logs stacked up in the yard, higher than my shoulder. Everybody knows they can pop in and warm themselves by a blazing fire on a frosty winter's evening. The pub is hundreds of years old, and the fireplace has inglenooks on either side.

You are much too young to go in a pub, little one, and of course you won't know what an inglenook is. So I'll tell you. It's the space either side of the hearth, roomy enough for bench seats in the Dew Drop. Those seats are always occupied by regular customers. The same old faces, day after day, month after month, year after year.

Why am I telling you this? Well, I promised to tell you the story of the Captain and Sixpence, and they always sat by the fire playing dominoes, happy in each other's company. Greater friends I never saw.

Nobody in Sixpenny Cross could have guessed what would happen to those two gentlemen. It's a terrible story and I'm glad you are fast asleep, little one, so you'll hear none of it.

Yes, C is for the Captain.

But wherever the Captain was, Sixpence wasn't far behind.

2

Richard Edwards, heir to Sixpenny Manor, sat at his father's bedside. The old man's life was ebbing away and there was nothing his only son could do to prevent it. He cradled his father's gnarled old hand between his own.

"The war changed all our lives," quavered the old man. "Thank God, my boy, it ended without taking you away from us."

"Yes, Father. Rest now, and try not to worry about anything."

"You know that your mother and I are very proud of you. You came out of the army an officer, a captain. I'm quite sure you would have reached a higher rank had the war continued."

"Well, thank goodness it didn't. Too many lives were lost."

Father and son lapsed into silence. The old man closed his eyes while his son watched over him. Then the dying man's eyes opened again.

"Look after your mother, Richard, she's very frail," he said.

"Of course I will, Father."

"I wish we'd given you brothers and sisters, but it wasn't to be, I'm afraid. The responsibility now is all on your shoulders."

"Don't worry, Father. Just rest."

"Son, find yourself a good woman to marry."

Father and son smiled into each other's eyes.

"I will, Father, and we'll fill this house with babies and dogs!"

"Is that a promise?"

"It is!"

His father's hand twitched once, and the smile still played on his lips as his heart finally stopped and his eyes clouded over.

The son sat motionless beside the bed, still holding his father's hand, as the bedside clock ticked the minutes away. Eventually, even his loving clasp couldn't keep the hand warm. Tears rolled down his cheeks as he bid his father a final farewell.

His mother, unable to cope with the loss of her cherished husband, soon joined him in Sixpenny Cross churchyard. Husband and wife lay side by side under the sun and stars, while their son was left to continue alone in the manor house.

It was 1951, and the Captain was thirty-one years old. A shy man at the best of times, he was discovering that being in sole charge of the manor house was too big a burden to bear.

His gregarious parents had actively participated in village events but their introverted son had avoided the limelight, preferring his own company to that of the village children. The situation was made worse when he was sent to a private boarding school, alienating him even more from the villagers.

Now, as the new squire of the manor house, his only visitor was the vicar, Thomas Ridsdale, who, having officiated at the funerals of Richard's parents, hoped their son would continue where they had left off.

"Would you care to present the prizes at this year's village fête, Captain? I'm sure the villagers would appreciate the gesture."

"I think not, Vicar," said the Captain, and the vicar didn't ask again.

Richard's days in the army had taught him how to issue orders but he didn't understand the basics of running a large house. He was awkward with the servants, and although Mrs Anderson, the housekeeper, did her best, the house did not thrive.

His father was right. He needed a wife.

And he wasn't going to find one in Sixpenny Cross.

A year had slipped by since his parents had passed away. Apart from the few remaining servants, he'd been rattling around alone in the Manor House and things needed to change. Something had to be done before it was too late. Soon, a plan began to formulate in his head.

"Mrs Anderson, I wonder if you'd mind joining me in the library in an hour. I have something rather important I wish to discuss with you," he announced one day.

"Of course, Captain."

Mrs Anderson had worked in the manor house for decades, and had known Richard since the day of his birth. Then she had addressed him as Master Richard but now, with the death of his father and as a mark of respect, addressed him as Captain.

She too had mourned the passing of the old squire, whom she had loved dearly, and now she stood in front of her employer in the library, anxious to hear what he had to say.

"Do sit down, Mrs Anderson, this won't take long."

"Thank you, Captain." Mrs Anderson perched herself on the edge of a chair and smoothed her apron.

"How is your boy, Mrs Anderson?"

The Andersons' son was actually a couple of years older than the Captain.

"We don't hear from Peter very often, sir, thank you for asking, but he's fine. When the war ended, he took a long time to find a job but he's working up north now."

"Not married?"

"No, sir. Not yet..."

The fact that the Captain, too, had not married, hung uncomfortably in the air between them.

She paused, waiting for him to continue. The Captain took a breath and resumed.

"Mrs Anderson, I've come to a decision. I've decided to live in London. I'm going to move into the family apartment in Kensington and shut this house down for the time being."

Mrs Anderson gasped, a hand flying up to cover her mouth.

"Please don't worry, Mrs Anderson! Let me explain. When I go, I'd very much like you and Mr Anderson to carry on living in the estate cottage. Of course I won't need a housekeeper any longer, but I wondered if instead, you would take on the role of caretaker? The grounds will still need looking after, so I'll still require your husband's gardening skills. His job would hardly change."

Mrs Anderson's eyes had grown large as she absorbed this information.

"I... I..."

"Of course you and Mr Anderson must have some time to think about it," the Captain hurried on, "but I would be most grateful if you would accept."

———

"London?" asked Anderson, shock on his face.

"Yes! If you ask me, I reckon he's going to look for a wife. He's not going to find one round here, is he?"

"And we can just carry on livin' here?"

"Yes. He said we could stay in this cottage for as long as we want. I'm to keep an eye on the house, and you're to look after the grounds and gardens like you've always done. And if the work ever gets too much for us, he'll hire some help, and if something needs fixing or mending, he'll hire somebody from the village to do that."

"Well! That sounds very decent!"

"Yes, it certainly does!"

"And how's he goin' to look after himself in London?"

"He'll go to that Gentlemen's Club to eat, the one his father was a member of."

"No, I meant financially. Will he look for work in the city?"

"No! I know for a fact he'll never need to work, his parents left him very secure. Mark my words, he won't stay in London long. Some lady will snap him up and they'll be back down here, ready to open up the house and start a family."

"You could be right. It'll be good to hear a bit of life in the old manor house again. I bet he'll be back in no time."

3

*B*ut time marched relentlessly on.

If the Andersons thought the Captain would easily find a wife in London, they were mistaken. And if the Captain imagined he would slip effortlessly into London life, he was wrong.

The greyness of London depressed him. An all-pervading fog seemed to permanently cloak the streets, and he missed the clear air of Sixpenny Cross. He experienced the 'pea-souper' fogs he'd heard so much about and didn't enjoy them at all. Then, although the people of London were accustomed to thick fogs, worse was to come.

History was made in the December of 1952, following a spate of cold weather when folk burned more coal than usual to keep themselves warm. On a windless day, the pollution, combined with vehicle exhaust fumes, smoke from homes and industrial chimneys, was so bad, it blanketed the city.

The effects of the sulphur dioxide laden fog were deadly. At least 4,000 people died from respiratory problems, and 100,000 more were made ill. Traffic ground to a standstill because there was no visibility, and the Captain had to walk to his Club with outstretched hands, unable to see anything beyond a few feet ahead. The Great Smog of

London lasted for five days. Then the weather changed and breezes arrived which swept the pollution away.

The Captain was lucky and soon shook off the cough he had acquired but the event only made him more determined to quickly find a wife and return home. He found himself staring at all females that crossed his path, wondering if any might suit his needs.

As an only child at home, then educated in a boys' private boarding school, and finally joining the army, the Captain had had very little contact with the fairer sex. Ladies attended his parents' parties, but if any attempted to engage him in conversation, he was struck dumb with fright. He could converse well enough with male acquaintances in the Club, but as soon as they introduced him to their sisters, he became awkward and tongue-tied.

And so the years passed.

He had left the manor house entirely in the charge of Mr and Mrs Anderson, and now they were too old to do much more than potter around. When they retired to a tiny bungalow in Worthing, he paid a company to board up the manor, make it secure, and to check it regularly.

One day, he promised himself, he would go back to Sixpenny Cross. But the promise he had made to his father still ate at his soul.

It was 1964, and the Captain would soon be forty-five years old. The war had ended almost twenty years before and England was a very different place. The nation had gasped at the audacity of the Great Train Robbery, Beatlemania had swept across the country and mods and rockers were clashing at seaside resorts.

And still the Captain had not found a wife, although not for the want of trying. He'd never felt that deep emotion the Beatles sang about, the love that he knew had existed between his parents.

But he'd never stopped looking, and maybe, just maybe, he'd finally found the perfect woman in Margaret. He patted his pocket.

In his Kensington apartment, the Captain peered into the mirror, staring at his own face, trying to see it through Margaret's eyes. He wasn't a bad looking chap, he decided. Yes, his hair was beginning to silver at the temples, but nobody could call him unattractive. He turned away and pushed the curtain aside to peer out of the window onto the street below. His apartment was on the third floor, and if he craned his neck, he could see the street stretch away on either side.

Although residential, this was a busy road, vehicles travelling faster than they should. Two businessmen wearing long coats and bowler hats walked together. Each carried a rolled up newspaper and an umbrella. A beggar sat on the pavement, leaning against the railings. He lifted his hand hopefully, palm upwards, as the men approached, but he might as well have been invisible. The men hardly slowed their pace as they skirted round him.

A street cleaner trundled his cart up the road, and this time the beggar didn't even lift his head.

A black taxi cab rounded the corner, and the Captain's heart gave a little lurch.

Margaret!

The Captain bounded down the communal stairs and walked out into the street just as the cab driver drew up. The rear window was wound down, framing Margaret's pretty face.

"Richard!"

"Hello, Margaret, shall I hold the driver, or pay him off?"

"Oh, pay him, I think."

Margaret watched as the Captain paid her fare, then opened her door. She stepped out onto the pavement, and straightened. The taxi drew away to join the stream of traffic, leaving them alone.

"Margaret, you look wonderful, as usual."

"Thank you, Richard."

If her voice sounded a little flat, and her eyes avoided his, he didn't notice.

He kissed her proffered cheek, enjoying the scent of jasmine that always accompanied her.

"I thought I'd take you to a new restaurant for lunch. Are you hungry?"

"That sounds super, Richard, but do you think we could just go for a stroll?"

"Of course, shall we head towards the Gardens? We can always hail a cab to the restaurant from there."

"Good idea."

It wasn't far to the park and they walked together, side by side. Margaret was unusually quiet and the Captain couldn't think of a word to say. The little square ring box was burning a hole in his pocket as he silently rehearsed his script.

I'll ask her at the park, he thought, *when it feels right. Or perhaps I should wait until we get to the restaurant? I'll make sure we have the best table. Should I kneel? No! Perhaps I'll wait until we are quite alone, somewhere else, another day…*

The Captain used the busy road as an excuse to hold her arm as he found a safe gap between the passing traffic. He guided her across, but when they reached the other side, Margaret pulled away from his grasp.

Ah, she's such an independent soul, he thought to himself. *Father would approve of that.*

"It's a pity we didn't bring bread for the swans," said Margaret, breaking into the Captain's thoughts. "Shall we sit here at this bench, for a while?"

"Of course."

They sat side by side, facing the water, watching the swans dip their long necks into the water. Their view was interrupted for a moment by a mother pushing a high baby carriage in front of them. The infant seated in the pram regarded the pair on the bench without expression.

Shall I ask her now? he thought, and his hand started snaking towards his pocket. *Is now the right time?*

"Richard, I've been meaning to talk to you," said Margaret.

"Oh, Margaret, I've been meaning to talk to you, too!"

He reached for her hand, and she allowed him to hold it. The Captain took this as a good sign and his heart swelled.

"Oh dear, I'm afraid you may not like what I am about to say," said Margaret, looking into his face properly for the first time that day.

4

Something icy gripped the Captain's heart. He stared at the lady by his side, desperately trying to read her expression but failing miserably.

"I'm so sorry, Richard, but I don't think it's going to work."

A pair of mallards swam into view and a swan stretched up to flap its wings.

"What? What isn't going to work?" He gripped her hand tighter, but she pulled it free.

"Us, Richard. You and me. I'm terribly sorry. I care for you, of course, but I don't feel we were made to be together..."

The Captain felt cold, almost detached. This wasn't what he'd planned. This wasn't how it was supposed to be.

"But you care for me?" he said at last.

"Yes, but not in *that* way, if you know what I mean..."

"But perhaps you could, in the future..."

"No, Richard. I'm sorry. I didn't want to tell you, but I've met somebody else..."

He gaped at her.

"Richard, you must let me go. Please don't be sad, and I know you'll meet another nice girl very soon. I'm so sorry, but there was no easy way to tell you."

She was standing. She leaned down and patted his arm, then turned and swung away up the path.

"Margaret!"

But she didn't respond.

Numb, he watched her receding figure disappear behind some ornamental trees. When he lost sight of her, all hope died.

"I bought you a ring," he whispered, "I was going to ask you to marry me."

And then the world seemed to collapse around him. He stumbled to his feet and lurched back along the path the way they had come.

"Oy!" said a man jumping out of his way. "Watch out!"

But the Captain was blind to his surroundings.

Margaret doesn't want to be my wife.

Margaret has gone.

He staggered across the road, ignoring the honking from irate drivers.

"'Ere mate, look where yer bleedin' going!" yelled a taxi driver, shaking his fist.

But the Captain heard nothing. All he wanted to do was reach home, close the curtains and sit alone in the dark to lick his wounds. Miraculously, no vehicle mowed him down and he reached the other side safely.

Home was within sight, just one more street to cross.

Looking neither left nor right, he stepped into the road.

Kevin Stephens' knuckles were white as he gripped the steering wheel. He was late. He was supposed to pick up his wife from the corner of Kensington High Street twenty minutes ago, and Lynn Stephens didn't like being kept waiting. If Lynn was annoyed, she could sulk for England.

If he took a shortcut, and kept his foot heavy on the pedal, he might get away with it. He'd tell her that he'd been delayed because he'd been in a travel agency, looking at booking one of those new package holidays to Spain she was always harping on about. Or he'd suggest they go to the pictures, maybe see that new film, *A Hard Day's Night*, starring those long-haired layabouts she liked so much. Kevin glanced at his watch.

It all happened in a split second.

He never saw the man step out into the road in front of him.

Just as the Captain stepped forward, a small figure materialised from nowhere, grabbing the Captain's coat and yanking him backwards. The corner of the car's bumper made contact with the Captain's right leg as he fell back into the arms of his saviour.

Kevin slammed on his brakes and screeched to a stop. As the smartly-dressed man and the beggar slowly extricated themselves and stood up, he exhaled, realising that nobody was hurt.

"You bloody idiot!" he yelled at the Captain with a mixture of anger and fright, "I nearly ran you over! If it hadn't been for that bloke jumping in, you'd have been a goner!"

Shaking his head, a relieved Kevin drove off. At least now he had an excuse for Lynn. Perhaps he might embellish the story just a little bit...

The Captain gaped at the man who was still supporting him, guiding him back to the pavement and safety.

"You saved my life," he said.

"It was just luck," said the beggar. "I happened to see you walkin' down the street, and I could see you were a bit distracted, like. So when you walked out into the road, I only had to grab you. Are you hurt at all?"

"No, just bruised, I think..." The Captain rubbed his shin and looked ruefully at his torn trouser leg. "But if it hadn't been for you, it would have been much worse."

"Oh, it was just a bit of luck. Anyway, that driver was goin' much too fast."

"Well, I can't thank you enough. Let me shake your hand!"

The two men shook hands, one manicured, the other grimy with torn fingernails.

"If you hadn't grabbed me, I think I'd have died under the wheels of that motor. I live just over there, will you come in? I think we could both do with a drink to get over the shock."

"Well, sir, if you're sure…"

"Oh yes, I'm very sure! And I daresay I could rustle up something to eat, too, if you fancy it."

The beggar grinned from ear to ear.

"Just one thing, sir, would you mind if I asked you a question?"

"Of course not! Fire away!"

"Forgive me if I've got it wrong, sir, it's been a few years," said the beggar, "but is your name Richard, by any chance? Richard Edwards from Sixpenny Cross?"

The Captain gaped at the beggar, then stared closer at the slight figure in front of him. He looked past the ten-day stubble and the tattered scarf wound round the neck, past the unkempt hair and torn clothing.

"Good Lord!" he exclaimed, his mouth hanging open. "Mr and Mrs Anderson's boy!"

"Well, hardly a boy, sir," said the beggar, smiling. "I'm actually two years older than you. But yes, I was born in the cottage in the grounds of Sixpenny Manor."

"Well! Good gracious! What a coincidence! Come along, old man, let's drink to this! We've got a lot to talk about!"

The Captain clapped Peter Anderson on the back, and the pair made their way up to the Captain's apartment.

Much later, the street cleaner trundled his cart back down the road, when something in the gutter caught his eye. He bent down, squinting. It was a small, velvet-covered box, the kind used by jewellers to display rings. Looking left and right to check he wasn't being observed, he picked it up and cracked it open. A flash from the diamond inside was enough for him to slip the box quickly into his pocket and hurry away.

"Finders, keepers," he muttered.

It was his lucky day.

5

Upstairs in the Captain's apartment, the two men sat in armchairs, a decanter of whiskey on the table between them.

"It's Peter, isn't it?" asked the Captain, suddenly recalling their housekeeper and gardener's son's name.

"Yes, that's right, sir, but nobody calls me that."

"They don't? So what do they call you?"

"Well, don't laugh, sir, but everybody calls me Sixpence, on account of my size, and where I come from."

"Then I shall call you Sixpence, too," decided the Captain. "And nobody calls me Richard, either. They all know me as the Captain. A relic of the war, of course."

Peter Anderson had indeed begun life in the grounds of the manor house in Sixpenny Cross. His parents had met because his mother was employed as a maid, and his father worked in the gardens. The pair had married and a party was held in the servants' hall to celebrate. The happy couple were presented with an estate cottage, and two years later, Peter was born.

Mrs Anderson went on to become housekeeper, and Peter's father was promoted to chief groundsman. Peter, although not naturally academic, went to school in Sixpenny Cross, and later he attended a school in Yewbridge.

The housekeeper's son, Peter, and Richard Edwards, the squire's son, were similar in age, but their paths seldom crossed. They belonged to different social classes.

"So what did you do when you left school?" the Captain wanted to know. "I don't remember seeing you at Sixpenny Cross. And how did you come to be, er, on the streets of Kensington?" He had avoided the word 'begging' but they both knew that's what he meant. "I assume, Sixpence, that things lately haven't been too prosperous for you?"

"You could say that, sir."

"Have you been in contact with your parents? I understand that they are living in Worthing now."

Peter shifted uneasily in his armchair.

"I'd rather not, sir, seeing as how things have been with me. I don't want to worry them."

Sixpence had devoured a thick gentlemen's relish sandwich that the Captain had prepared for him, and the delicious taste of anchovies was still on his tongue. Now the whiskey warmed him, and he was ready to talk.

"When I left school, I became apprenticed to a builder in Yewbridge. Didn't like it much, to be honest. I was pretty happy to be accepted into the army when the war broke out."

"You were in the army, too?"

"I was. Only a Private."

"Did you see action?"

"I did." Sixpence smiled ruefully. "If I'd known how hard it was going to be, I doubt I'd have volunteered so quickly."

The Captain nodded. Life hadn't been easy for any soldiers in the second world war. But to have been a Private would have been very hard, compared with that of an officer like himself.

"And I wouldn't have lost my fingers."

Sixpence held his hand up, revealing three missing fingers, a fact that the Captain had failed to notice until now.

"What happened to them?"

"Blown away by a mine."

"And when the war ended, what did you do then?"

"Oh this and that. So many houses needed rebuildin' after the bombing, I thought I'd pick up work easy. But I couldn't go back to the buildin' trade, not with no fingers, nobody would employ me. So I had to think again. I was a caretaker in a school in north London for quite a few years until the council took over and changed things. I worked for a while as a petrol attendant and then I had a stroke of luck. I got chattin' with one of the regulars at the petrol station, and he offered me a live-in job as caretaker at his block of flats in Battersea. I jumped at that, I can tell you!"

"So what happened?"

"It was fine for a few years until the old boy, the owner of the flats, passed away. Soon as he was laid in the ground, his relatives were swarmin' all over the building, givin' tenants their notice and makin' plans about what they were goin' to do with the place. They couldn't give me my notice fast enough. I got into an argument about it, and they refused to give me a reference. Believe me, you can't get a job without a reference nowadays. So that's why I ended up on the streets."

The Captain shook his head in disbelief. How many times had he passed Sixpence, and never even really seen him, let alone offered any help?

"You never married?" he asked.

"No, sir. Never felt I found the right girl, and never felt I had anything to offer a wife, anyway. What about you, sir? Was that your wife I saw you with earlier today?"

The Captain started. He had forgotten all about the painful break up with Margaret. He patted his pocket, and was surprised to discover that the ring box was gone. Curiously, he felt no sense of loss.

"No, she was just, er, a friend," he said. "I never married."

"Righty-ho," said Sixpence, and took another sip of whiskey.

The Captain's leg was throbbing painfully reminding him how close his brush with death, or very serious injury, had been.

"I want to demonstrate my thanks to you for saving my life today," he said. "Would you accept a sum of money?"

Sixpence looked affronted.

"No, of course not, sir. I told you, it was just luck that I was there. Anybody would have done the same thing."

"Well, at least stay here in my apartment for a few days. As long as you like. Until you get back on your feet."

"That's very kind, sir, but I don't think so. It wouldn't be right. I wouldn't be comfortable doin' that."

"But I want to help you, old man. If it hadn't been for you, I'd be in Westminster hospital, or maybe even some morgue, by now."

Sixpence shrugged and took another sip of whiskey.

"Well, thank you, but I'm afraid the only thing I really need is a job," he said.

The two men sat in silence, Sixpence enjoying the rare comforts, while the Captain thought hard.

Suddenly, it came to him in a flash of clarity.

"I've got it!" he said, setting down his glass and almost spilling it in his haste. "How would you feel about going back to Sixpenny Cross?"

6

Sixpence stared at his companion.

"How do you mean, sir?"

"It just struck me that I've had enough of London, and I want to go home. I want to go back to Sixpenny Manor."

Sixpence was listening hard.

"Don't you see? The house has been shut for years. In fact it's boarded up. Your parents have retired to Worthing and I need you to help me get it all opened up again. Nobody has lived in it for years."

"A job?"

"Yes, we'll need to get the electricity and water connected again. And reconnect the telephone. The place will be frightfully dusty and will probably need to be cleaned thoroughly. We can get help from the village, of course."

"We'll have to check the roof tiles and windows for storm damage," said Sixpence, beginning to become infected by the Captain's enthusiasm. "And check the oak panellin' and furniture for woodworm."

"Exactly! And goodness knows what the grounds are like! You can see I'll need a man like yourself to help me straighten it all up."

Sixpence's eyes danced as he stared back at the Captain. Then he sobered.

"And when the house is comfortable again, what then?"

"Well, let's see how we rub along together," said the Captain. "We can discuss it more later, but I imagine I'll still need some help. If it all goes well, I think I'd like you to stay on as my companion, if you will. Can you cook at all, by any chance?"

"Yes, I enjoy cookin'. Just plain food, mind, not fancy stuff."

"Well, you saw what a mess I made of your sandwich earlier, and that's about the only thing I know how to prepare. I wouldn't expect you to do much, just a meal now and then."

Sixpence was beaming.

"So what do you say, old man, will you accept the job?"

"Thank you, sir, I will."

For the second time that day, the Captain shook Sixpence's hand.

Over the weeks that followed, the two men set to work breathing life back into the manor. The Captain visited Jayne Fairweather, the postmistress and owner of Sixpenny Cross's only general store, who provided him with the details of local tradesmen.

They employed painters and carpenters, glaziers and roofers. They replaced the ancient fridge in the kitchen, and added a new electric cooker, which soon became Sixpence's pride and joy. They had linoleum laid, as well as acres of new carpet. They bought a Persian rug and a black-and-white television set for the drawing room.

When the house was finished, they settled down to a quiet life, and soon fell into a comfortable routine that would continue for years. The Captain read his newspapers, wrote letters, paid bills and sometimes took a walk in the grounds. Sixpence carried out household duties. A keen gardener, he used any spare time to tend his beloved roses. The Captain employed outside help to look after the extensive grounds, but the roses and kitchen garden were Sixpence's domain.

Every evening, after dinner, the pair would walk to the Dew Drop Inn and sit in the inglenook. The pub landlord, Angus McDonald, always left the battered old box of dominoes on the table. The pair would play a few games, drink two pints of beer, then return home to retire to bed.

And so the years slipped by.

Neither man had found a wife to share his life, but they were content enough in each other's company.

Now it was March, 1985. The devastating, year-long miners' strike had just ended and a debate in the House of Lords had been televised for the first time.

The Captain smiled, remembering the black-and-white TV set he and Sixpence had purchased back in 1964, when they'd first returned from London with such enthusiasm to open Sixpenny Manor. His mind drifted back even further, to the 1950s, when the house had buzzed and he was a young man with his life ahead of him.

Visions of the manor house in the old days played in the Captain's head. When his parents had been alive, the house had throbbed with life. Servants, ruled by Mrs Anderson, the housekeeper, kept the rooms clean and tidy. The family had a resident cook then, and the kitchen smelled of baking bread and roast meat.

During those years after the war ended, the country was gripped by a kind of forced gaiety. The wireless was usually left switched on to the BBC's Light Entertainment Programme, and comedy shows like Max Bygraves's *Educating Archie* filled the drawing room with canned laughter.

His mother had held cocktail parties, soirées and seasonal balls. His father hosted shooting parties. On those days, the boot boy, the gardener and the gardener's boy were employed as beaters for the day. Their job was to scare the game birds out of the thickets and into the path of the huntsmen. The men returned, victoriously brandishing braces of pheasants that were thrown onto the kitchen table. Later, the pheasants, or trout from the river, would be served up on silver platters.

In those days they had labradors, dogs that slept under tables or in front of the fire, but barked when visitors' cars swept up the gravel drive.

The Captain gazed up at his father's portrait. His father leaned on a shooting stick, a slight smile on his healthy, sun-reddened face, the light catching his slightly bulbous nose, so like his son's. When the portrait was painted, his father must have been in his forties. His hair, already receding, was beginning to silver. The Captain had inherited the same trait. Now, in his sixties, the Captain's own hair was sparse and almost white.

What would Father say if he could see the manor house now? the Captain wondered.

"Well, I've given your old Dad a good dusting, Captain," said Sixpence, breaking into the Captain's thoughts. "Amazin' how these old portraits attract the dust."

"Thank you, Sixpence. You are a good man. I often wonder how I'd manage in this big old house without you."

"It's a pleasure, sir. You've given me a roof over my head for more years than I care to remember."

The Captain smiled and looked back at his newspaper.

When the Captain and Sixpence had first moved back to Sixpenny Cross, they'd thrown themselves into opening up the house again, but it was soon apparent that most of the rooms would never be used. They rarely had visitors, and the large, empty house proved too much for Sixpence to maintain.

Gradually, over the years, he and Sixpence had closed off unused rooms, covering the furniture with dust sheets. The dining hall that used to ring with witty conversation and the sound of laughter was locked and rarely visited. The library was shut, its books seldom read. Tapping heels no longer waltzed on the parquet dance floor, and the grand piano was silent. Most of the bedrooms were shrouded and dark, the heavy drapes remaining drawn year after year.

No chatter emanated from the kitchen, and the only dishes that ever cooled on the counters were plain fare prepared by Sixpence.

What need did two old men have for all those rooms? Apart from the kitchen, and a bedroom and bathroom each, they only required a room to sit in, to while away the long hours in each other's company. In summer and winter they sat in the overstuffed armchairs of the drawing room.

Long ago, the Captain had asked Sixpence to pack away most of the ornaments that decorated the side tables, mantlepiece and all available surfaces.

"We've no need for all those things," he had said, with a sweep of his arm, indicating the buddhas, carved antelopes and tigers his grandfather had brought back from India a lifetime ago.

"All of 'em, sir?" Sixpence had asked.

"Yes, they're just dust traps. No need for all that clutter."

"Well, I won't argue with that," Sixpence had replied.

"And get rid of the old wireless, it hasn't worked for years."

"Very good, sir."

"And I know my mother loved all that cut glass and crystal, but I've never been very fond of it. It can all be packed away, except perhaps the carved elephant on the hall stand. Mother said it brought the house luck."

"Right you are, sir."

"And leave a few vases? I do enjoy seeing the roses you grow, Sixpence."

Sixpence had beamed. He had inherited his love of gardening from his own father, and over the years, the manor's roses and kitchen garden had flourished under his care.

"Most of the paintings can go, too." The Captain's eyes had swept round the room, taking in the hunting scenes and seascapes that adorned the walls. "Just leave the portraits of my father and mother, either side of the fireplace, and maybe that Indian scimitar. I've always rather liked that."

When the paintings had been removed, rectangles marked the wallpaper where they had hung for decades.

"Well, I'm off to grill us a couple of nice pork chops," said Sixpence, snapping the Captain back to the present. "Dinner will be in about half an hour. Then we'll toddle off to the Dew Drop as usual, shall we?"

"Yes, thank you. Let me know if you need any help with the dinner."

"Ta, I will."

But they both knew Sixpence would never ask for the Captain's help. He prided himself in caring for his friend and benefactor.

The Captain gazed at his parents' portraits, then shut his eyes, dozing.

The lights blazed in the Dew Drop Inn even though the landlord, Angus McDonald, hadn't yet unlocked the doors. Opening time was in twenty minutes and there was still a lot to do.

7

ngus McDonald watched carefully as the woman pulled the handle slowly towards herself. Dark beer poured into the glass until it almost reached the rim. Before the white froth overflowed, she stopped, then looked at him sideways.

"Well?"

"Well, I must say, Barbara, you managed that pump with no trouble," he said. "That's a perfect pint you've pulled there. I can see you've had plenty of bar experience."

"Oh, I'd love a penny for every pint of ale I've drawn over the years! It's like second nature to me." She threw back her head and laughed. Then she looked at him coyly and winked. "And call me Babs, nobody ever calls me Barbara."

"Good! And you're quite happy handling the till?"

"Of course." She folded her arms confidently over her ample bosom.

"Right then, Babs, you familiarise yourself with the optics, and the different types of glasses. And could you check the Ladies' and Gents' rooms, please? I'm going to bring in some more wood and stoke up the fire. It's another cold night, and our regulars always expect a good fire to warm themselves."

Yes, he thought as he tended the fire. *I think I made a good choice with Babs. She's not in her first flush of youth, and she's a bit, er, loud, but she seems capable. She's an experienced barmaid and customers like to see a cheerful face behind the bar.*

When he'd placed the advertisement for bar staff in the Yewbridge Gazette, a handful of applicants had responded, but only Babs had worked in a bar before. He'd offered her the job, and he was pleased with his choice so far. True, everything about Babs seemed a little exaggerated. Her laugh was a little too loud, her skirt a little too short, especially for a lady her age, and her top was a little too plunging. But nothing too serious. She *was* a barmaid after all.

"Right, time to open up," he said, glancing at his watch.

He slid open the two bolts on the front door and returned to stand beside Babs behind the bar.

"Tell me about the regulars," she said. "Always good to know a bit about the clientele."

"Well, Stan Cooper often drops in for a pint after work. He's the village policeman."

"I bet there's not much crime here in Sixpenny Cross!"

"No, you're quite right. The Tait's cottage down the street burnt down a while ago, but that was an electrical fault, they think. Actually, you might meet Bella Tait. She pops in sometimes to see Scout here." He stroked the cat curled up on the counter. "I adopted him from her when she used to rescue animals."

"Anyone else?"

"There's Archie Draper, he's got the farm near Sixpenny Woods. And Simon and Daisy Granger. Oh, and of course there's the Captain and Sixpence…"

Babs went off into a peal of laughter.

"Who? The Captain and Sixpence?"

"Yes. The Captain owns Sixpenny Manor. Sixpence is his companion and lives with him. They come in every evening and sit by the fire and play dominoes."

"They're not married?"

"No, they live alone. The Captain is a simple sort, but Sixpence looks after him. Ssh, here they are."

The pub door was pushed open, and two men entered, one tall and well-built, the other short and angular.

"Evening, Captain, evening, Sixpence," called Angus. "Cold out there tonight, isn't it?"

"It is," agreed the Captain, as he and Sixpence hung their hats and scarves on the rack beside the door.

"Never mind, spring is comin'," said Sixpence cheerfully. "The daffodils are ready to open and warmer weather will soon be here."

"Can't wait! I'm tired of these winter clothes," said Babs, laughing as though she had made a joke.

Both the Captain and Sixpence swung round, noticing the owner of the voice for the first time. Sixpence gave Babs an easy smile, while the Captain's eyebrows shot up in surprise.

"This is Babs Mason, my new barmaid," said Angus. "I'll send her over with a pint of your usual in just a moment, and you can meet her properly."

The Captain and Sixpence settled down in their customary corner, without speaking. Sixpence overturned the waiting wooden box and spilled the dominoes onto the table in readiness for a game.

"Good fire tonight," he remarked.

But the Captain didn't hear him. He was staring over Sixpence's shoulder, his gaze drawn to the buxom woman behind the bar as she loaded a tray with two pints of beer. She probably sensed his eyes upon her and looked up from her task. One of her heavily painted eyelids lowered and rewarded the Captain with an exaggerated wink.

The Captain shivered very slightly, and Sixpence caught the movement.

"You alright, sir?" he asked.

"Yes, yes. Perfectly okay thank you."

Babs had reached the table with her tray.

"Here you are, gentlemen," she said, a broad smile on her face. She placed a pint in front of each man, bending low enough for both men to view her ample cleavage.

"Thank you, and very pleased to meet you," said Sixpence extending his hand to shake. "They call me Sixpence."

"Oh!" said Babs, seizing his hand, "and what did they call you when you were a nipper, Threepence?" She threw her head back and laughed at her own joke.

"Very good," said Sixpence, smiling politely and reclaiming his hand.

Babs turned to his companion.

"And you must be the Captain."

But the Captain had been struck completely dumb.

"My name's Babs, but you know that already." Another peal of laughter. "Well, good to make your acquaintance, gentlemen. Just let me know when you're ready for another pint and I'll be right over."

She made her way back to the bar as Sixpence laid all the dominoes face down on the table. He selected seven of them for himself. Although appearing to be busy, he was very aware that the Captain was unsettled. He waited.

"What a creature…" said the Captain, shaking his head.

"Babs? Oh, typical barmaid type, I'd say."

"Do you think so?"

"Yes, I think she'll be a real asset to the Dew Drop, probably cheer the place up."

The Captain said no more and selected his own seven dominoes.

The door swung open, admitting more thirsty customers. Angus and Babs were kept busy pouring drinks as the two men played dominoes. At regular intervals Babs's raucous laugh would fill the saloon and the Captain's eyes would flicker in the direction of the bar again.

"Are you ready for another pint?" asked Sixpence when he'd won five easy games in a row and both their glasses were drained.

The Captain nodded.

"I'll order them on my way to the cloakroom," said Sixpence, standing.

The pub was fairly busy now, but he managed to attract Babs's attention and signal for another two pints as he passed the counter.

Babs poured the beer quickly, and, to the Captain's horror, began making her way to his table.

"There you go, Captain," she said.

"Thank you, Barbara," he managed.

She leaned down low in front of him to plonk the glasses on the table. He tried very hard not to look at the secret flesh she was revealing, but failed. Her perfume reached his nostrils and he almost stopped breathing.

"Well, Captain," she said, looking straight into his face, close enough for him to feel her hot breath, "you just let me know if you need anything else."

The Captain was lost.

8

"Are you quite sure you don't want to go to the pub, sir?" asked Sixpence.

It was extremely rare for the Captain and Sixpence to miss their evening walk to the pub, but the Captain was adamant; he didn't want to go.

As Sixpence cleared away the dinner plates and tidied the kitchen, he tried to figure out the cause of the Captain's refusal.

If I didn't know better, he thought to himself, *I reckon it's got somethin' to do with that new barmaid, Babs.*

He shook his head, concerned.

Meanwhile, the Captain sat in the drawing room, replaying the events of last evening over and over again.

Barbara.

First that wink.

What did it mean? Why had she singled him out and winked at him in such a familiar way?

And then, *you just let me know if you need anything else. What did she mean by that?* He remembered her hot breath on his face and felt his palms sweating.

"I'll find us somethin' nice to watch on the TV," said Sixpence, fiddling with the dials. "Won't do us any harm to miss a night at the pub."

The Captain watched the flickering screen but absorbed nothing.

When he retired to bed he struggled to sleep for a second night. Owls hooted in Sixpenny Woods and the moon travelled slowly across the sky. The Captain tossed and turned, but every time he closed his eyes, Barbara's painted face floated in front of him.

You just let me know if you need anything else, the vision whispered, and in slow motion, one eyelid lowered in a suggestive wink.

The next day saw a clear sky and the air felt warmer than it had for months. The hedgerows were alive with songbirds, and the ducks on the village green were building nests.

After breakfast, Sixpence visited his rose garden. He smiled at the neat rows of rose bushes before examining the new buds for any sign of insect or fungus attack. The bushes, severely pruned for the winter but now bursting with vigorous growth, looked the picture of health.

"Well," said Sixpence, "with a bit of luck, they'll win me some more First Place rosettes at the fête in June."

The Captain, too, was feeling more positive with the new day. He had come to a decision. He would brood no more about the barmaid. He would accompany Sixpence to the pub that evening, just as they always did, and he would ignore her. He must have imagined her interest in him. Why would a woman like that take a special interest in him?

Of course, if she made another move, then he would reconsider.

When Yewbridge Town Council handed over the flat to its latest tenants, the walls had been painted a fresh magnolia. Now the walls were nicotine-stained and the rooms stank of stale cigarettes and smoke. Hardly surprising, as the occupants were rarely without a cigarette between their fingers and the windows were seldom opened.

Husband and wife sat side by side on a sofa covered with a grubby blanket, their feet up on a shared vinyl pouffe. The man was leafing through *The Sun* newspaper, staring awhile at the topless pin-up girl on page three.

"Don't know why you're gawking at her, Rick," exclaimed the woman, "she must be half your age."

She went back to examining her own face in a hand-held mirror.

"Well, I can look, can't I?" he replied, before glancing at the news stories. "Still can't believe we have a woman for prime minister," he growled. "Gawd, that Maggie Thatcher should never be allowed to run the country."

His wife didn't reply, she'd heard it many times before.

"Would you look at this! A blooming Egyptian has bought Harrods! *Mohammed Al Fayed buys Harrods*. Whatever next! Probably sell Buckingham Palace to the Americans next."

"Why should you care?" asked the woman. "You've never been into Harrods once in your life."

"It's the principle of the thing," he said, stubbing out his cigarette in the overflowing ashtray between them.

"Hey, who knows," said Babs. "Maybe we'll be able to afford to shop in Harrods too, some day, what with my new job going so well. Which reminds me, my roots need seeing to. Gotta look my best now that I'm working."

The woman who sat on the sofa beside her husband in that dingy Yewbridge flat bore no resemblance to the Dew Drop's new barmaid. Gone were the stockings and high heels. Instead, Babs's thick white legs were bare and pushed into grimy slippers that may have been pink once. The short skirt and plunging blouse that had so caught the Captain's eye hung from a coat-hanger hooked onto the picture rail that ran around the room. Now Babs wore a faded, floral, quilted dressing-gown that gaped between the button holes, revealing patches of dimpled grey flesh. Her face, devoid of make-up, was blotched and her eyes were small and unremarkable.

She drew out a pack of cigarettes from her dressing-gown pocket, selected one and put it between her lips before lighting it and inhaling deeply. She belched comfortably.

"Let's have a few beers tonight, Rick," she suggested, "and then get ourselves a takeaway pizza. Might as well enjoy my night off."

"Can I pour anybody another coffee?" asked Sara Ridsdale, the vicar's wife, looking round the table.

Everybody politely refused.

The organisers of the annual Sixpenny Cross fête were attending a meeting in the vicarage. The vicar, Thomas Ridsdale, was checking his notes.

"Well, I think we have everything covered. The marquees have been booked. Jayne, you'll get the flyers printed?"

Jayne Fairweather nodded. "I'll keep a stack in the Post Office to give out, and I'll make sure they're pasted on lamp posts and different spots closer to the time. I'll also get the certificates printed for the home produce competitions and the flower arrangements. I'll organise the entries, too, if you like."

"Jayne, you're a marvel," smiled the vicar. "Daisy, are you happy to run the cake stall again?"

"No problem, vicar, I'll get some volunteers to bake for it, too. And I'm sure Abigail Martin will help out on the day."

"I'll bake some cakes," said Emily Draper, the farmer's wife.

"And Simon, you and Archie did a wonderful job last year, sorting the trestle tables and the stalls on the day. Are you happy to do that again?"

Simon Grainger and Archie Draper both nodded.

"Stan, raffle?"

The policeman nodded.

And so the meeting progressed as it had done every year for generations.

"Well, I think we have all the basics covered," said the vicar, closing his notebook. "We have more than two months to prepare, lots of time, hopefully, although we always seem to be in a panic at the end. Put your thinking caps on for next week's meeting, and we'll make a list of stalls and who to ask to run them."

He stood and the meeting broke up amidst a buzz of chatter. Some headed home, others for a quick drink at the Dew Drop.

At the same time, the Captain and Sixpence were also preparing to visit the pub.

9

The Dew Drop Inn was often busy on a Sunday evening, and tonight it was busier than usual. When the Captain and Sixpence arrived, the bar was crowded with people.

"Evening, Captain, evening, Sixpence," called Angus McDonald. "Sit yourselves down and I'll be right over."

"Good evening, Captain, hello, Sixpence, were your ears burning?" asked Jayne Fairweather, smiling, as the two men passed her on their way to the inglenook seats.

"Hello, Jayne, ears burnin'? No, why?" answered Sixpence.

The Captain said nothing. His eyes and ears were searching and listening for any sight or sound of Babs's presence in the pub. His hands were shaking.

"Well, we were just wondering how your roses are coming along this year and whether you were going to walk away with all the first prizes at the fête again. We had a fête meeting at the vicarage this evening."

"Ah! That explains why the pub's so busy tonight," said Sixpence, grinning. "I have to say, I'm pretty pleased with my rose bushes so far, thank you for askin', but it's early days. A lot can go wrong in two months. Next year I'm going to have a go at chrysanthemums, too, so look out!"

"I'll never enter my roses in the village fête, but I wish they grew better than they do. Have you any tips for me?"

"Bananas," said Sixpence, lowering his tone. "Chop up banana skins and spread them round the base. Roses love the potassium, you see. We always save our banana skins for the roses. Isn't that right, Captain?"

But the Captain had already taken his seat in the inglenook.

"I can see you're rushed off your feet," said Sixpence, catching sight of Angus bringing their beers. "I'll take those off your hands."

"Thanks, mate. It's Babs's night off, and I'm a bit pushed."

Sixpence joined his companion in the inglenook and set down their drinks.

"Poor old Angus has his work cut out tonight," he remarked. "It's the new barmaid's night off."

He saw the Captain's shoulders tense, then relax.

I was right, thought Sixpence. *He's got that wretched woman on the brain.*

Unfortunately, Sixpence's suspicions were correct. The Captain's simple nature had a tendency to obsess, much like a child's. The barmaid occupied his mind entirely, leaving little space for anything else.

The next night, when they arrived at the pub, the Captain managed to greet Babs civilly and he tried hard not to watch her as she worked. Although determined to ignore her, his intentions were thrown to the wind by a tiny incident that anyone else might have brushed aside as meaningless.

Early in the evening, while they were engrossed in a game of dominoes, Babs approached unnoticed from behind.

"Well, gentlemen," she said, standing between them and laying a hand on each of their shoulders, one broad, one bony.

The Captain nearly jumped out of his skin, and the hand on his shoulder felt as hot as a cattle brand.

"Who's going to buy me a drink, then?" she wheedled. "It's gone quiet, and I'm spitting feathers."

"Please pour yourself anything you like, Barbara," he said, "and put it on my bill."

"Thank you kindly, Captain," she replied, laughing loudly and leaving her hand on his shoulder for just a little too long. "I'll do that and come right back and enjoy it with you. I'm due a break."

"Well, actually, we're just..." said Sixpence.

"You are very welcome, my dear," cut in the Captain, giving Sixpence an icy look.

True to her word, Babs returned and sat with the two men. She hung on every word the Captain uttered and her raucous laugh rang round the pub.

When they walked home that night, the Captain's heart was beating faster.

He *wasn't* mistaken.

Barbara *had* taken a shine to him.

Beside him, Sixpence said nothing, but he was worried.

That evening set the pattern for future weeks. Every day, the Captain would occupy himself with writing letters, paying bills, or walking round the grounds, but he was whiling away the hours until he could return to the pub and see Babs. Sixpence cooked and carried out his duties as usual, but as he tended his roses in the walled garden, he worried.

Every evening, the Captain and Sixpence would take their seats in the pub and begin to play dominoes. Then the Captain would buy Babs a drink, often more. She'd pour herself a generous gin and tonic then join the two men in the inglenook. Dominoes forgotten, the Captain beamed and went pink whenever she laid her hand on his arm to emphasise a point.

Gradually, Sixpence detached himself. He'd make excuses and linger at the bar, chatting with other customers, and when the two men walked home, it was often in silence.

"I tell you," said Babs to her husband, "I reckon I've got the Captain eating out of my hand. The old goat's got the hots for me!"

They both laughed uproariously.

"Well," said Rick, "you ought to put it to some use. We've got bills to pay, you know."

"Yes, I think it's about time. What do you suggest?"

Rick was quiet for a moment, then an idea struck him.

"Let's test it. Why don't you say it's your birthday? Let's see if he gives you a nice present..."

"Perfect!" crowed Babs.

To Sixpence's consternation, the Captain's obsession with Babs didn't diminish. On the contrary, Sixpence thought it was intensifying. He watched his companion become almost hypnotised by the barmaid, and he shook his head.

"Well, Captain, you'll never guess what day it is next Wednesday," said Babs, tilting her head at him coyly and treating him to a wink.

"No, I'm sorry, Barbara, I have no idea," said the Captain.

"It's my birthday!"

"Is it? I'd like to get you a gift, what would you like?"

"Oh no, I'm not that kind of girl!" squealed Babs, and her laughter rang out.

Sixpence rolled his eyes, but neither the Captain or barmaid noticed.

"You don't have to buy little *me* a present!" she said, leaning into him and patting his knee.

The Captain's face flushed red at her touch.

"But I'd like to!"

"Well, Captain, if you must..."

That night, the Captain and Sixpence walked home in silence. The Captain, deep in thought, cleared his throat.

"Sixpence, you remember those ornaments you packed away years ago?"

"Yes, sir, I do."

"Do you remember where you stored them?"

"Of course. I wrapped them in newspaper and packed them into tea chests. They're in the cellar."

"Right! Good, good."

He said no more, but he didn't need to. The Captain was entirely devoid of any guile, and Sixpence could read him like an open book.

"Is there something you were looking for in particular?" Sixpence asked.

"Er, not exactly. I just wondered if some of that cut glass, or crystal stuff was to hand…"

"I expect I could find it without too much trouble, sir."

"Well, if you could, old man. Actually, I was thinking of that blue crystal peacock, do you remember it?"

"I do, sir. You told me it was one of your mother's favourites. Very valuable, I seem to remember."

"Ah, yes. That's the one. Could you locate it for me, please?"

"Of course, sir. May I ask what you were planning to do with it?"

The Captain's face darkened, taking on an expression that Sixpence had never seen before.

"If you *must* know, I'm planning to give it to Barbara on her birthday," he snapped.

Sixpence's jaw dropped in astonishment. Not because the Captain had admitted his plans for the crystal peacock.

No, Sixpence had already guessed that.

It was the Captain's tone of voice that astonished him. In all the years they'd been together, the Captain had never spoken to him like that.

10

"What is it?"

"Hang on! Give us a chance. Let me get it out of my bag. It's worth waiting for, honestly."

"It's all wrapped up in newspaper."

"I know, he apologised, but he said he didn't have any proper wrapping paper handy."

She peeled away the old newspaper.

"Look at this!" said Rick, holding up a scrap. "It's dated 1969 and the headline is about the Kray twins being found guilty of murder."

"1969? Well, the present he gave me is much older than that. He said it belonged to his mother."

Babs pulled away the last piece of newspaper and the crystal peacock was revealed. Rick gasped and took it from her, turning it over in his hands.

"Wow, that's an antique. It'll be worth a pretty penny."

"I know! When he gave it to me, I says to him, I says, 'Ooooh, Captain, that's so beeeutiful!' And he says, 'Oh, I'm very pleased you like it, dear lady.' So then I gave him a big kiss on the cheek, and the poor feller nearly fainted." Babs roared with laughter at the memory.

"So what did you say next?"

"So I says, 'Ooooh, Captain, how did you know I collect these?' And he says, 'Do you? Then I'll bring you some more.' Honestly, Rick, as long as that sidekick of his, Sixpence, doesn't stick his oar in, I think we've found ourselves a golden goose!"

Easter had long passed, and clumps of faded daffodils swayed on the village green. April showers had made the grass lush and vibrant.

The cricket season had started, and weekends saw villagers dressed in white, playing the ancient game on the green. The sound of willow hitting leather, and cries of "Howzat!" followed by spontaneous little bursts of applause rang round the village.

The date of the village fête was approaching, and the committee was finalising arrangements for the weekend in June when the fête would take place on the village green.

Babs had become accepted at the pub, and Angus was delighted that his takings were on the rise. It seemed that the clientele of the Dew Drop Inn liked the brashness of the woman and enjoyed seeing her behind the bar.

However, one man eyed the barmaid suspiciously. Sixpence had watched the collection of crystal ornaments stored in the cellar diminish, one by one. Each time Babs had unwrapped another, she squealed with delight, rewarding her admirer with a kiss on the cheek, rendering him pink with pleasure.

When the crystal had gone, the Captain presented her with other ornaments: buddhas, carved animals, ornate boxes and trinkets, all precious items that his grandfather had brought back from India.

Sixpence's heart sank lower daily. His employer was no judge of character and Sixpence was quite convinced that no happiness would result from this dalliance. Babs was a coquette, but a clever one. Sixpence had witnessed her winking at other customers and flirting outrageously but only when she was sure that the Captain couldn't see her.

Something, too, had shifted in his own relationship with the

Captain. No longer were they so easy in each other's company, and something unspoken lurked between them.

I've got to try and stop this, make him see sense before he gets in too deep, he thought to himself as he tended his roses. *Who is Babs Mason anyway? Where does she come from, and what is her history?*

The more he thought about it, the more he was resolved to carry out some detective work and prove that she was not a woman to be trusted.

And there were only two people who could answer his questions.

Her employer, Angus McDonald.

And Babs Mason herself.

Sixpence leaned on the bar next to Stan Cooper. He had left the Captain and Babs to their own devices in the inglenook. He stole a guilty look over his shoulder to ensure that neither was watching him. To the contrary, the pair were absorbed in each other. Babs was throwing back her head and laughing, while the Captain patted her hand fondly.

"Ah, Sixpence, can I get you anything?" asked the landlord.

"Thank you, Angus, but I don't need a drink. I did wonder whether you could help me with a rather, um, delicate matter."

"Shall I leave?" asked Stan, stepping back. He apologised profusely as his steel-capped size ten boots crushed another customer's toe. Stan's keen detective mind hadn't cured his clumsiness.

"No, no, Stan. Please stay. It isn't a criminal matter, exactly, but I wouldn't mind your opinion."

"Fire away, old man," said Angus. "We'll do our best to help."

Angus, Stan and Sixpence put their heads together, and Sixpence took a deep breath. He shuffled from one foot to the other.

"It's like this," Sixpence began in a low voice, then plunged on. "I'm worried about the Captain."

"Why?" asked Angus.

"The Captain hasn't had much experience with women," said

Sixpence carefully, "and I'm really worried that he's been taken for a ride."

Stan said nothing, but he was listening intently. Another peal of Babs's laughter rang out behind them.

"You mean his friendship with Babs?" asked Angus.

"Yes, I'm afraid so. He's absolutely smitten by her."

"Well, there's no law against that," said Stan, smiling.

"I know!" said Sixpence hurriedly. "It's just that he's givin' her a stream of presents. Valuable antiques from the manor. Stuff that's been packed away for decades."

"No law against that, either," said Stan, but he was no longer smiling.

"It's just, I wondered whether either of you knew anything about her or her past," finished Sixpence. "I mean, you read in the papers about these professional fraudsters... Perhaps I'm completely wrong, but it just doesn't feel right. Do you know what I mean?"

Angus and Stan nodded.

"Well," said Angus quietly. "She said she's a single woman. She came with two glowing references from other pubs. Somerset area, I think. To be honest, I didn't check them out at the time, I was so busy, but I could look them up in the Yellow Pages and give them a ring. Nobody needs serving at the moment, I'll pop out the back and do it right now. I hope you're wrong about this, because she's a good barmaid!"

"I'd be really grateful," said Sixpence.

Stan said nothing, but he was deep in thought. If he turned sideways, he could see Babs quite clearly in the inglenook. Her left hand rested on the Captain's knee. He focused on the third finger. No wedding ring, but her finger was indented, the way a woman's finger becomes when she's worn a ring for years.

Was Sixpence right?

Was Babs Mason hiding some secrets?

"Hello, am I through to the White Hart?"

"Yes, you are, how can I help you?"

"I'm sorry to disturb you, but I was wondering if you could help me. My name's Angus McDonald and I'm the landlord of the Dew Drop in Sixpenny Cross, Dorset. Who am I speaking with, please?"

"My name's Sarah, I'm the landlady here. How can I help you, Mr McDonald?"

"I've recently hired a new barmaid, Babs Mason. She worked for you, and she gave me a reference signed by the landlord, David Leech."

The line went silent for several seconds. Then Sarah spoke again.

"I'm sorry, but are you sure you have the right pub? There's no David Leech here. My husband is the landlord, and his name is Daniel Falconbridge. We've had the White Hart for twelve years and I'm quite sure we've never had a barmaid here called Babs Mason."

11

*A*ngus McDonald put the telephone down, perplexed.

Good gracious!

He ran his fingers through his hair.

Was Sixpence right? If Babs was lying about her past job at the White Hart, what else was she hiding?

Sixpence had returned to the inglenook, and Babs was back behind the bar.

"Ah, there you are, Boss," she cried, "I thought you'd been whisked away by aliens!" And she threw her head back, laughing.

Stan Cooper watched her with interest, then turned to Angus, raising his eyebrows in question.

Angus leaned in to him and whispered, "The pub in Somerset."

"Yes?"

"They've never heard of her."

Stan's brow furrowed but he wasn't very surprised.

"Don't tell her what you know yet," he instructed. "When you get the chance, phone the other pub, check out their reference too. That'll give me time to make a few enquiries of my own."

"Do you need some more time to think about it?" asked the salesman.

"No, I don't think so, do you?" Babs turned to check with her husband.

"If you can knock a bit more off the price, we'll take it," said Rick. "We'll pay cash, of course."

"Wise decision," said the salesman. "You can't go wrong with these Ford Escorts. Very reliable cars. This one may be secondhand, but it'll go on for ever."

They agreed on a price and Rick pulled out a wad of banknotes from his pocket. He counted them out on the desk, licking his finger occasionally and placing the notes in neat one-hundred piles. Then he passed them over to the salesman to count. Satisfied, the man unlocked a drawer and put the money away before handing Rick the car's keys and logbook.

"A pleasure doing business with you," said Rick, as they left.

"Oooh, Rick! It's so nice to have a car of our own again, isn't it? I'll be able to drive myself to work now instead of taking the bus," cooed Babs as they drove away. "And I saw you watching where he keeps the money! You're not thinking of turning the place over, are you?"

Rick laughed, and patted her knee.

"Once a con, always a con," he chuckled. "I learned in prison it's always a good idea to use your eyes. You never know when you might need to know where people stash their cash."

"Thanks to the Captain, I think we have happy days ahead," laughed Babs. "It's my night off, let's raise a glass or two to our golden goose tonight, thank him for our new car."

"Good idea. And it's time we started to think about how to get you inside that manor house of his. I reckon it's packed with valuables, and I bet he wouldn't even notice if some went missing."

"I don't think he would either," agreed Babs, smiling at the thought, then sobering. "I think his companion, Sixpence, is a lot more switched on, though. We can't rush into anything."

"Hmm," said Rick thoughtfully, "it would be even better if we could get rid of our friend Sixpence altogether."

"Yes, that's right, Sixpenny Cross, near Yewbridge. Am I speaking with the landlord of the King's Arms?"

"Indeed you are, how can I help?"

"Just a quick staff question, if you don't mind. Did you have a Babs Mason working for you at any time? Maybe she called herself Barbara?"

"Barbara? No, definitely not. My ex-wife's called Barbara, and I'd remember *that* name, no question. We've never had a Barbara, or Babs, working here."

Time marched on, and May saw the first swallows arriving from Africa. A cuckoo called from Sixpenny Woods. Angus no longer lit the fire in the Dew Drop, but the Captain and Sixpence still sat in their customary seats in the inglenook, often joined by Babs.

The month of June brought out all the wildflowers in the surrounding meadows. Garden beds burst with blooms all the colours of the rainbow.

The Captain gazed out of the drawing room window onto the wide lawns edged with herbaceous borders. In his mind's eye he saw Sixpence's father using twine and stakes to tie up and support the tall lupins, foxgloves and gladioli, preventing them from falling over in strong winds.

So many years ago!

Now a professional landscaping company tended the grounds. Except, of course, for the roses and kitchen garden which were Sixpence's pride and joy.

The place needs a woman, thought the Captain. *It's too late to fill the house with children, but at least I can keep my promise and bring home a wife.*

Yes, it was time to take action.

Meanwhile, outside, Sixpence gazed at his roses. There were several buds that he had his eye on, lavishing them with time and attention. Any of these might be the blooms he would choose on the morning of the village fête, to enter in the Best Roses competition. He smiled, confident that he'd win another red rosette. His roses never failed to lift his sagging spirits. This business between Babs and the Captain was driving him to distraction lately.

Should I talk to the Captain about my suspicions? he mused. *No. Not yet.*

Stan Cooper had asked him and Angus to maintain silence for the moment while he investigated further.

"After all," Stan had said, when Angus had reported back about the second pub Babs had allegedly worked in, "she lied, but she hasn't actually broken the law. And she has no criminal record that I can find. But mark my words, people like her may be very clever, but they always make a mistake. For the moment, we just watch and wait."

Angus was only happy to agree. Babs was an excellent barmaid and attracting an ever increasing clientele. The pub was thriving and, despite her lies, he was reluctant to fire her.

But it was hard for Sixpence to see the Captain fall ever more deeply under Babs's spell. The man was mesmerised by her, oblivious to her lack of breeding and her brassiness. The thought that the Captain might be considering making the wretched woman the lady of the manor made him shudder.

"Sixpence, is that you?" called the Captain from the drawing room, when Sixpence entered the kitchen through the back door.

"Yes, sir."

"Can I have a quick word?"

"Of course, sir."

Sixpence entered the drawing room and waited.

"Ah, there you are, old man. I've been thinking I'd like to hold a dinner party some time, would you have any objection?"

The Captain's tone was light but Sixpence was astute enough to detect a hint of uncertainty in his employer's voice, as though he was nervous of Sixpence's reaction.

"No, of course not, sir. How many guests?"

"Oh, just one, I think."

Sixpence's heart sank. He didn't need a planetary-sized brain to guess the identity of the proposed guest.

"May I ask who?"

"Of course, I was thinking of asking Barbara from the pub. She said to me only the other day that she'd love to see Sixpenny Manor and that she really enjoys looking at antique furniture."

I bet she does, thought Sixpence, but managed to keep his features impassive.

"Nothing too fancy," continued the Captain. "Just a nice homemade soup perhaps, and maybe roast chicken to follow. She's a simple creature."

Simple? That woman is more cunning than a starving fox.

"Perhaps, if you wouldn't mind, you could unpack a couple of the silver candlesticks, and cut a few roses for the vases?"

"Very good, sir. When were you thinking of holding this little, um, soirée?"

"I thought Thursday next week. That's Barbara's next evening off. Would that suit?"

"Indeed, sir."

"Sixpence, perhaps I shouldn't ask, but I get the impression that you don't like Barbara very much. Am I right?"

12

Sixpence opened his mouth. Here was his opportunity. The Captain had asked him a direct question. He could answer with the truth.

That woman is a lying fraud. In my opinion, she's after your money.

That was what he wanted to say, but he held his tongue.

"Sixpence?"

"It's not for me to say, sir."

"Very well. If you have any reservations, I'm sure you'll let me know in your own good time."

"Yes, sir."

"He's invited me to dinner at the manor house next Thursday," crowed Babs.

"Oh, lah-de-dah!"

"Yeah, I'll have to get myself a little black dress!"

"Never mind that, you just make sure you take a good look round. Case the joint, memorise the layout. See which rooms have good stuff in them."

"I will, don't worry. Have I ever let you down?"

"Nope, we're a great team. I just wish we could get rid of the golden goose's mate, he's the only fly in the ointment."

"You'll think of something, Rick, you always do."

***

It was five o'clock when the telephone on the counter rang. Stan reached for the receiver but his elbow caught his mug of tea, sending it spinning before it smashed in two on the floor. Tea splattered over the counter, threatening a pile of paperwork, and a growing, brown puddle collected at his feet.

He rolled his eyes in annoyance but grabbed the receiver just before the telephone stopped ringing.

"Sixpenny Cross Police Station, PC Cooper speaking."

"Ah Stan, thought I'd missed you. It's PC Holman here at Yewbridge cop shop. Thought I'd give you a quick bell."

"How are you?" asked Stan, watching with dismay as his papers began to soak up the spilled tea.

"Fine, thank you. You wanted us to check out a Barbara Mason, I think, a few weeks ago?"

Stan forgot about the tea.

"Yes, that's right. You couldn't find anything on her. She had no rap sheet."

"That's true, but we've just come across something else. I thought it might be worth telling you."

Stan waited, unaware he was now standing in a pool of tea.

"Barbara Mason kept her maiden name, but she's actually married to Richard Kane. And he's got a rap sheet as long as your arm."

"Really? What for?"

"Just about everything. He's a nasty piece of work. Burglary, car theft, fraud, grievous bodily harm, you name it. He's had a few stretches inside. He was also the main suspect for a homicide back in the seventies, but the case was dropped through lack of evidence. It was a bungled burglary. The homeowner surprised the burglars so they clobbered him over the head with a crowbar. He died of a heart attack."

"And Babs Mason is married to this thug?"

"Yup, looks like it. They live together in a council flat in Yewbridge."

"Well, thank you. You've been most helpful."

Stan stood still for several minutes, deep in thought. It was time to have a word with the Captain. Better still, he'd first have a chat with Sixpence and together they'd work out the best way to break the unwelcome news to the Captain.

Yes, he decided. *I'll catch Sixpence at the pub tonight and bend his ear.*

Decision made, he locked up and went home, unaware of the great, wet footprints he left criss-crossing the floor.

———

But PC Stan Cooper didn't see Sixpence that evening. It was Thursday and neither the Captain nor Sixpence were at the pub. They were entertaining Babs at the manor house.

The Captain had taken extra care with his appearance. His sparse hair was slicked down with water, and his fingernails were spotless. He wore a crisp white shirt and cravat, feeling they were in keeping with the occasion.

What exactly was the occasion? he asked himself.

He had no precise answer to this question but planned to see how the evening went. For some reason he felt that something huge was about to happen.

Sixpence, in spite of his misgivings, had worked hard. He had uncovered the dining room table and chairs and polished the wood until it gleamed. White candles flickered in silver candlesticks, and he'd arranged some of his roses in vases. The table was set perfectly and the silverware sparkled.

"You'll dine with us, of course, old man?" the Captain had asked, but Sixpence had politely refused.

"No, sir, I'll leave you two in peace. It'll leave me free to serve, too."

The truth was, he didn't think he could stomach watching Babs fawn all over the Captain. He didn't want to listen to her peals of fake laughter while the Captain gazed at her as though she was Miss World 1985.

Babs had swept up the gravel drive in her new Ford Escort, and the Captain had welcomed her. She was wearing a tight black dress that hugged her ample curves. A necklace drew the eye to her décolletage, and her scarlet lips pouted. She tilted her head, allowing him to kiss her cheek, and he walked her through to the drawing room.

"Can I get you a drink, Barbara?" he asked. "Perhaps a sherry?"

"Oooh! Perhaps a sweet sherry, thank you! Just a little one, mind, don't want you getting me tipsy!"

A peal of empty laughter rang out, and, in the kitchen, Sixpence grimaced and rolled his eyes.

The Captain stuck his head round the kitchen door.

"Sixpence, I'm just going to show Barbara round the house, we shouldn't be long."

"Very good, sir, I'll have the first course waiting for you when you get back."

As he stirred the homemade vegetable soup, he could hear her laughter reverberating from different parts of the house. Many of the rooms were closed, but she seemed to want to see them all.

When the pair had returned and seated themselves at the dining room table, Sixpence served the soup, ensuring each bowl had a sprig of watercress garnish and a final dash of cream.

"Thank you, Sixpence, that looks very good," said the Captain.

"Look what the Captain just gave me," said Babs, showing Sixpence the exquisitely carved ivory elephant that usually sat on the hall table next to the telephone.

Sixpence said nothing.

"My grandfather brought that back from India a hundred years ago. It has a raised trunk which is supposed to be lucky," said the Captain. "It was much prized by my mother. She always said that if it stood facing the front door, it would protect all who live here. I'm glad you like it."

"I'll put it here, out of your way," said Sixpence, moving it to the sideboard before returning to the kitchen.

When they had finished, Sixpence cleared away the empty soup plates.

"Excellent soup," said the Captain. "It's a pity you can't enter it in the fête this weekend, I'm sure it would win a prize."

"Thank you, sir," said Sixpence and brought in the next course.

The fragrant roast chicken steamed as he served it. He was lifting off the lids to the fresh vegetables when the telephone rang.

"Who can that be? You get it, Sixpence," said the Captain, "we can manage."

Sixpence hurried to the telephone in the hall, trying to ignore Babs's voice behind him.

"Let me serve you, Captain. You just tell me when to stop…" and her laughter rang out.

The hall table looked strange and empty without the ivory elephant.

"Sixpenny Manor," he said into the telephone receiver. "Who's calling?"

"Sixpence, is that you?"

13

"Sixpence speakin', who am I talkin' with?"

"Sixpence, it's me," said the voice, "Stan Cooper. Can you talk or might you be overheard?"

"It's not a good time," Sixpence said quietly.

"Right, answer yes or no. I'm guessing the Captain and Babs Mason are within earshot?"

"Yes."

"Listen carefully. I found out something rather disturbing today. I was going to tell you at the pub but Angus just told me that you and the Captain were holding a dinner party for Babs tonight. It's just possible that you and the Captain may be in some danger. Babs Mason is married to a villain."

Sixpence gasped and found himself glancing over his shoulder.

"She's married to an old con with a record as long as your arm. He's a thief, but that's not all, he's violent. I'm guessing that he's sent her to case the manor. Has she walked round the house?"

"Yes."

"As I thought."

"What shall I do?" whispered Sixpence.

"Nothing. Don't do anything yet, leave it with me. I don't think you have anything to fear from her, it's what her husband is planning that worries me. Make sure you lock all your doors and windows tonight, and stay on the alert."

When Sixpence replaced the receiver, his hand was shaking.

I knew it! he whispered to himself. *I just knew it!*

He stood for a moment, digesting this latest news, then entered the dining room.

"Ah, there you are, old man," said the Captain. "Who was it? Anything important?"

Always the gentleman, the Captain had been doing his best to be as pleasant as possible, aware that Babs and Sixpence were wary of each other.

"No, no. Just my old mother calling from Worthing. I'll phone her back another time for a proper chat. How's the roast chicken?"

"Delicious, old boy! You surpassed yourself. Barbara is really enjoying it, too. Aren't you, my dear?"

Babs nodded as she chewed.

"I'm a good cook, too, Captain. You'll have to let *me* cook for you one day," she said, her mouth still full.

"Nothing would give me more pleasure, my dear," said the Captain gazing at her fondly, and his tone spoke volumes.

Sixpence retreated to the kitchen as fast as etiquette would allow.

The evening dragged on.

Sixpence served the dessert, followed by coffee and liqueurs in the drawing room. Then he tidied the kitchen, waiting impatiently for the evening to end.

At last he heard the Captain call.

"Sixpence, Barbara is leaving. She'd like to thank you."

"I bet," he growled, but joined them on the gravel driveway.

Although it was after ten o'clock, it was still quite light, as is the norm during British summers. Babs was already sitting in her car with the window wound down and the engine running.

"Thank you for the meal, Sixpence," she called.

"Don't mention it."

The Captain patted her hand which was resting on the steering wheel, then leaned down through the window to peck her on the cheek.

Suddenly, her hand flew to her mouth in alarm.

"My elephant! I forgot my elephant!"

"Don't you worry, my dear," said the Captain, swinging round. "I'll get it for you in a trice. I know exactly where it is."

He hurried past Sixpence and into the house, intent on his act of chivalry.

Babs looked up at Sixpence and her eyes widened a little.

"Who are you staring at?" she asked.

The rage that Sixpence had been trying so hard to keep in check was threatening to bubble over.

"You, actually."

He stepped forward then leaned down into the car, bringing his face close to hers.

"What … what do you …?" she stammered.

"I know who you are, Barbara Mason, and I know what you're tryin' to do. If you, or that villain you're married to, harm a hair on the Captain's head, I swear, I'll…"

But he never finished his sentence.

Babs's foot stamped on the accelerator pedal and the car shot away, showering him with gravel and leaving gouges in the driveway.

Sixpence turned to see the Captain standing on the doorstep, white-faced, frozen in astonishment, the elephant still clutched in his hand. He ran over to his employer and, taking him by the arm, guided him back into the house.

"What happened?" asked the Captain. "Why didn't she wait for me?"

"Captain, I think we need to talk…"

"Wait! It was something you said, wasn't it? You chased her off!"

"No! Sir, that woman isn't right for you. Please listen, I'll explain!"

"That woman? Did you just call Barbara *that woman?*" The Captain held onto the mantlepiece for support. His complexion had turned from white to red.

"Sir, I…"

"I was planning to ask *that woman* to marry me," spat the Captain. "I think you guessed that and you're jealous, aren't you? You don't want her to join us here, do you? I don't know what you said to her, but I can tell you this, Peter Anderson, my debt to you ends now."

Sixpence gaped, but the Captain hadn't finished. His eyes narrowed to slits as he hissed his next words.

"You may have saved my life back in London all those years ago, but I've repaid you. Remember, I pulled you out of the gutter. I employed you. I gave you a roof over your head. I shared my home with you. Now I intend to ask *that woman* to be my wife."

"Captain!"

"But you can't let that happen, can you?"

"No! Captain! Babs isn't who you think she is! I beg you, please listen…"

"You ungrateful, scheming wretch! I will *not* listen to you," he said through clenched teeth, his lips bloodless with fury.

He slammed the elephant down on the mantlepiece and folded his arms.

"Listen to me carefully, Peter Anderson, I intend to give Barbara this elephant tomorrow, and I'm planning to ask for her hand in marriage."

"I'm sorry, Captain," said Sixpence gently, "but I don't think that's possible."

He hoped that his tone might calm the Captain, make him listen to reason and return him to his senses. Unfortunately, it had the opposite effect.

"Do you intend to stop me?" asked the Captain, barely able to contain his rage.

"Not me, Captain, but the law. I believe that Babs is already married."

"Now you've gone too far. I think it's better if you go. I want you to leave Sixpenny Manor," he said, his eyes glittering. "Pack your things and go. I never want to lay eyes on you again."

"You must listen to me, Captain! Babs Mason cannot be trusted! She's playin' you for a fool…"

"Get out!" the Captain shouted. "Get out!"

"Captain…"

But the Captain was bereft of all reason.

"Get out!" he screamed.

14

*I*t was Friday evening and the Dew Drop Inn was buzzing.

"On your own tonight?" asked Angus when the Captain entered the pub. "No Sixpence?"

"No," said the Captain shortly, then took a breath. "Sixpence has left Sixpenny Cross."

"Oh, really? Problems with his mother in Worthing?"

The Captain didn't reply. His eyes were downcast and his face was expressionless.

Jayne Fairweather had overheard the exchange.

"Captain," she said, "the entries are closed now for the produce and flower competitions for the fête on Sunday. Did I hear you say Sixpence has gone away?"

"Yes, that's right."

"That's good news!" chipped in Archie Draper, always the comedian. "Now my Emily has a chance of winning this year's rose competition."

Everybody laughed, except Babs, who stood behind the bar, listening and watching intently. Without looking up, the Captain made his way to the inglenook and sat down. Only then did he raise his head to search for Babs. His eyes lit up when he spotted her behind the bar. Babs treated him to a wink and a little wave of her hand. The Captain blushed.

PC Stan Cooper stood in the shadows, watching. He saw Babs pull back the handle of the pump, allowing beer to rush into the pint glass she held.

"Mind your backs," she called, pushing through the crowd to reach the Captain.

"There you go, Captain. How are you today?"

"I brought you your elephant," he said awkwardly, relishing her nearness as she leaned down to place the pint in front of him.

"Oh, you darling man!" she said, putting her hand on his arm and enjoying seeing him blush. "You shouldn't have!"

The Captain put the elephant down and reached for her hand.

"Barbara, I'm so sorry about last night. I don't know what Sixpence said to you, but he had no right, no right at all."

"Well, I don't think he's ever liked me…"

"I told him that I didn't intend to give you up."

"Oh!"

"He's gone now, and won't trouble you again. And I hope you will continue to spend time with me."

"Of course I will, silly, it'll be my pleasure."

The Captain beamed, then looked more serious. "Barbara, I need to talk to you about … about matters close to my heart…"

"Babs! Customers!" called Angus, and Babs turned away.

"We'll talk later," she said, with a wink. "Don't want to lose my job!"

"If you'll be mine, my dear, you'll never need to work again," he said under his breath, as Babs walked away.

The bar was particularly busy that evening, as the fête committee had just had their final meeting.

"Weather forecast looks okay for the weekend," commented Daisy Grainger, "thank goodness."

"We've been lucky most years," said Jayne Fairweather. "The marquee company will be here tomorrow to put the marquee up, and, fingers crossed, I think everything is pretty much in place."

"Yes, I'll get the tractor out and give the green a final mow in the morning before they come," said Archie. "The vicar has done a good job of pulling it all together, as usual. Barring an act of God, it should all be smooth sailing on Sunday. But then we *do* have the vicar on our side," he added, and everybody laughed.

Talk of past fêtes, interspersed with cries of, "Who's for another drink?" filled the pub, and Babs was spared only a few minutes to chat with her admirer. Realising he was unlikely to enjoy much private time with her that evening, the Captain left early.

"I'll see you tomorrow," said Babs, and squeezed his hand.

"Yes, yes! Good night, my dear. I shall look forward to it."

Stan Cooper remained in the shadows, one hand in his pocket, fiddling with the books of raffle tickets that Jayne had handed him earlier. He waited for a lull, then approached the bar.

"Excuse me, Babs," he said lightly. "Totally out of interest, you know. I wondered if you knew where Sixpence had gone."

Babs jumped, reddening.

"How should I know?"

"Weren't you having dinner at Sixpenny Manor last night?"

"Yes, but…"

"Well, did Sixpence say anything about leaving the village?"

"Not to me, he didn't."

"So you don't know where he went?"

"No, why should I? But he did get a phone call from his old mother in Worthing though."

"Did he, indeed. Thank you for that information."

Babs backed away, but Stan beckoned her forward again.

"Just one more thing," he said quietly. "Not many people know who you really are, Babs. But I do. And now that Sixpence has gone, the whole village will be looking out for the Captain. He's very well liked here."

Babs's eyes widened.

"Oh, and Babs, give my regards to Rick."

Jayne Fairweather eyed the skies on Saturday morning as she opened the post office and general store. All clear, she decided, and therefore a good day to prepare for the village fête the next day. Archie Draper waved as he rumbled his tractor onto the green, the attachment he towed already scything through the lush summer grass. Jayne sniffed. She loved the smell of newly mown grass.

A steady stream of customers kept her busy that morning, but she noted the arrival of a truck with *Marilla's Marquees* emblazoned on the side. The village always used the same company. Six men jumped out and, after consulting a map, identified where the marquee should be set up on the far side of the green.

When Jayne next looked, she saw the men marking out the site, driving pegs into the ground. Even at this distance, the rhythmic hammering filled the air.

Suddenly, a man shouted. The banging stopped and, to her amazement, the men flung down their tools and ran as though chased by bulls. The first two burst through the shop doorway.

"Quick, phone the police! We've come across an unexploded bomb!"

Jayne didn't need telling twice and grabbed the telephone.

"Stan? Jayne here. I'm with the marquee people. They've found an unexploded bomb on the green."

Following a short conversation, Jayne put down the receiver and looked up. The men had crowded into the shop, waiting for her to speak.

"PC Cooper is alerting the bomb disposal unit now," she said. He's on his way but he's asked if we can make sure nobody goes near the area. Unfortunately this isn't the first time unexploded shells have been found around here."

The men nodded and went outside. They stood in a huddle for a moment then fanned out, keeping a healthy distance from where they had been working.

Jayne snatched up the receiver again and dialled the rectory's number.

"Vicar? Jayne here. We've got a bit of a crisis. The marquee men found an unexploded bomb on the village green."

"Good heavens! Has Stan been told?"

"Yes, he's informed the bomb disposal squad. Everything is under control. But the big problem is, I doubt we'll be able to use the green for the fête!"

"Oh my goodness. You're right, by the time they diffuse the bomb there'll be no time to put the marquee up."

"And the bomb people will want to scour the whole green in case there are more."

"Yes, yes," the vicar thought for a moment. "Well, we can't move it here, the rectory gardens are just too small. There's only one other place really."

"Sixpenny Manor?"

"Exactly."

"Do you think the Captain will agree?"

"I think so. I'll reassure him, tell him that nobody will disturb him or invade his privacy. We only need the gardens and I'll promise him that the committee will make sure everything is as we found it when we leave."

Saturday had been a rough day for the Captain. The visit from the vicar had turned his world upside down. As if he didn't have enough on his mind, with Babs and Sixpence, now he was being asked to allow the general public into the grounds of the manor house.

"We'll put *No Entry* signs up," the vicar had said. "The public will only be allowed on the lawn, not the walled garden, and definitely not in the house. Just keep all the doors locked, Captain, and nobody will bother you."

The Captain knew that his parents would have agreed immediately, as would Sixpence, had he been there, so he reluctantly relented. A simple man, he found it difficult to cope with any changes to his routine, Lately, there had been just too many.

From the drawing room window he saw the marquee go up. Then Archie Draper arrived on his tractor, pulling a trailer heaped with trestle tables and chairs. Simon Grainger helped him unload and the pair carried the tables into the marquee to set up. In and out, in and out, like bees in a hive.

It was enough to make a man dizzy.

Members of the committee kept arriving all afternoon, bringing items like blackboards and stacks of white tablecloths.

But the Captain's mind was only partially diverted. Most of his thoughts were centred on one person: his passion, his hope for the future.

Barbara.

The pub will be busy again tonight, he mused, *and I doubt I'll be able to get Barbara on her own. I'll just pop in for a quick pint. But when the fête is over, then I'll ask her if she'll be mine. Nothing will stand in my way.*

The thought made him tremble almost uncontrollably but also warmed him from the top of his head to the tips of his toes.

15

At the pub that night, conversation centred around the discovery of the unexploded shell. Dorset had been a major target during the second world war and, years later, the discovery of unexploded bombs was a common occurrence.

The bomb disposal unit arrived from nearby Bovington. They removed the bomb and then conducted a thorough search of the village green. All the cottages skirting the village green, including the pub and post office, were evacuated. Many hours later, the area was declared safe and everyone was allowed back.

When the Captain entered the pub, a cheer went up.

"Pour that man a drink!" shouted Archie Draper. "If it wasn't for him, the fête wouldn't be going ahead tomorrow."

Hands clapped the Captain's back.

"No, no," he protested, awkward as always, "it's nothing."

The Captain was too socially inept to interact easily with the villagers, even though he had known most of them all his life. The attention was too much for him, and he soon left, having only enjoyed the briefest of glimpses of his love behind the bar.

Never mind, he told himself, *I must be patient. Soon Barbara and I will be together for ever.*

Early the next morning, the stall-holders began to arrive, and the Captain observed the activity from the drawing room window. True to his word, the vicar arrived and hung *No Entry*, and *Private* notices on all the manor house doors, and on the gate into the walled garden.

On the outer lawns, a coconut shy was erected, as well as a skittle alley and a hoopla stall. Cloths were flung over tables, and posters and placards fixed up proclaiming "Guess the weight of the cake" and "How many sweets in the jar?" A tombola appeared, and also a 'Test your strength' machine.

A long, thick rope was laid on the ground in readiness for the tug-of-war, and vans began to arrive that would serve burgers, popcorn and candyfloss. An inflatable bouncy castle began to pulse and raise itself from the ground as air was pumped into it.

Unseen, the Captain watched it all.

Blast it, Sixpence! he couldn't help thinking. *You would have enjoyed all this!*

But then he remembered Barbara, and the way her soft hand felt in his.

Villagers began arriving carrying cake tins, jam and pickle jars, vegetables, fruit, flowers and all manner of produce. They disappeared into the marquee to set up their entries on the tables, ready for judging.

Somebody else would win the *Best Rose* competition this year, while Sixpence's prize roses would be left to wilt and rot unseen within the walled garden.

Suddenly, the Captain felt an overwhelming urge to see his lady love.

He looked at his watch. It was one o'clock and the pub would remain open until two. Plenty of time. He could walk down to the Dew Drop and order himself a Ploughman's Lunch from the menu. A good slice of thick, crusty bread with cheese and pickle and a salad garnish would make a nice change for lunch. And he could feast his eyes on Barbara, even if she was busy.

He couldn't remember the last time he had visited the Dew Drop at lunchtime. The thought of surprising Barbara put a little spring in his step and his heart raced faster as he locked the house and headed towards the pub.

He didn't hear the telephone in the hall ringing.

PC Stan Cooper was uneasy. The Captain wasn't answering his telephone.

"He's probably in the grounds, watching the preparations for the fête," his wife, Sally, said. "I wouldn't worry."

"Yes, I'm sure that's what it is. I'm going to walk over there soon anyway, those raffle tickets won't sell themselves."

He and Sally had been discussing the Captain's obvious passion for Babs. Both had agreed that, although the Dew Drop's barmaid hadn't broken any laws, it was probably wise to tell the Captain what they had discovered about her.

"It's for his own protection," said Sally.

"I don't think he'll take it very well," said Stan, shaking his head. "He's not really a man of the world."

"I think you *have* to warn him," said Sally. "Imagine if the manor house was broken into, or worse, and you'd known about her and her husband all the time. You'd never forgive yourself!"

"No, you're right. I must have a chat with him, man to man, and sooner rather than later."

Outside the Dew Drop Inn, wide red parasols advertising beers shaded wooden tables. People were seated enjoying cold drinks and pub snacks.

Even before the Captain entered the pub, he heard laughter ringing out through the door that had been flung open to let in the summer breezes. He smiled, recognising her voice mingling with others.

Always the life and soul of the party, he thought fondly. *So unlike me! Whatever does she see in me?*

He stepped into the pub and stood still, scanning the interior, his eyes adjusting to the dark, eager to see her. The hilarity he had heard emanated from one particular table.

And Babs was at the centre of it.

Three men sat round the table, drinking and laughing. A fourth man had Babs perched on his knee, her back to the Captain. The man's arm encircled her waist.

The Captain froze.

"Go on," the man begged, "one more kiss and I'll buy you another drink."

"Just one, then," Babs exclaimed and landed a long kiss on the man's waiting lips. "There you go!" she shrieked, and threw back her head, filling the pub with peals of laughter.

The men were all cheering and raising their glasses, but the Captain had seen enough. He turned and blundered out of the pub, past the outside tables, in the direction of the manor house.

Images flashed through his head, so vivid that they almost blinded him, making him stumble as he headed home.

Barbara.

Barbara flirting with men.

Barbara kissing another man.

Margaret.

Margaret in Kensington Gardens.

Margaret telling him she had met somebody else.

His dying father.

His promise to his father.

And finally, Sixpence.

16

Blind to everybody and everything, the Captain staggered home and pushed the key into the lock. He turned it and entered the coolness, shutting out the sounds of the fête. Leaning his back against the door, he felt more protected from the outside world, but waves of nausea swept over him and he found breathing difficult.

Gathering his strength, he lurched to the kitchen, drew the bolt and opened the door to the walled garden.

The fête was in full swing. Madonna's latest song, *Crazy for You,* blared from a loudspeaker. Children screamed as they bounced on the inflatable castle, and adults called each other.

"Hold tight!" yelled parents to their youngsters as they trotted past on Shetland pony rides.

"Sorry, missed! Have another go," urged stall holders when punters lost their money attempting to hook ducks or throw hoops over targets.

But the Captain heard nothing.

He stumbled past the neat rows of vegetables that Sixpence had grown from seed. Lettuce, spinach and clambering broad beans, all ready for picking. As he passed the herb bed, one shoe brushed the pungent mint plants, but he smelled nothing.

A spade leaned against the wall, soil still clinging to it.

Panting, he finally reached his destination.

The rose garden.

On an ordinary day, the Captain would have enjoyed and admired the blooms. Perfect buds, poised, and others already open, showing the sun their velvet petals and exquisite colours.

The Captain stepped off the path and into the bushes, paying no heed to the cruel thorns that scratched his skin.

He stood, tears coursing down his cheeks, aware of a growing pressure and tightening of his chest.

"Sixpence!" he mouthed. "What have I done?"

Stan Cooper had already completed one circuit of the fête, selling raffle tickets. Having forgotten to bring a box, he stored the bought tickets in his upturned police helmet, much to everybody's amusement. It was a good plan, except that sometimes the breeze sent the tickets hurtling across the grass.

"I'm going to try and have a word with the Captain," he told his wife, handing her the helmet and unsold books of raffle tickets. "I shouldn't be long."

"Good luck," said Sally, "and see if you can borrow a box or something. We can't be chasing raffle tickets across the lawn all afternoon."

"Ah, a box! I'll use that as my excuse."

Aware that the Captain was unlikely to answer a knock on the front door, Stan headed for the gate to the walled garden. He ignored the large *Private, No Entry* sign and tried the handle. It was unlocked. He quietly let himself in and walked up the path to the kitchen door. Despite it being slightly ajar, he rapped it lightly with his knuckles.

No answer.

He stuck his head round the door and glanced into the empty kitchen.

"Captain? Are you there?"

No reply.

"Captain? PC Stan Cooper here. Sorry to bother you, but I wondered if you had a box or something I could borrow."

Nothing.

"For the raffle tickets…"

He listened carefully, but nothing stirred in the house. Stan pushed the door open and entered, all his senses alert.

"Captain?"

He checked the dining room, but that was empty, too.

"Captain, are you there?" he called as he entered the drawing room.

The heavy velvet curtains were drawn, shutting out the sunlight and deadening the sounds of the fête. It took a moment for his eyes to adjust to the darkness.

Stan's finger flicked the light switch, flooding the room with artificial light.

"Ah, there you are, Captain," he said, seeing the figure in the armchair. "Sorry to disturb you, but I was…"

He never finished the sentence.

Neither did the Captain answer.

The Captain's eyes were wide open, staring ahead at a spot above the mantlepiece. His hands, already cold, were clenched in his lap.

The Captain was dead.

The ambulance had to come from Yewbridge, so Stan had plenty of time to look around while he waited for it to arrive. He was sure the Captain had died of natural causes, but he knew better than to tamper with anything. His keen eyes and sharp detective brain missed nothing.

Without touching them, he examined the Captain's clenched fists. His eyes scanned the room, absorbing every detail. He walked back out into the walled garden and prowled around. Before long, he believed he knew exactly what had happened, and was filled with sorrow.

The ambulance swept up the gravel drive, and the attendants ran up the steps.

"There's no hurry," said Stan. "I'm afraid he's already passed away."

They checked for a pulse, but there was no sign of life.

"Looks like he's had a heart attack," commented one of the attendants, "but the doctors at the hospital will confirm that."

Stan nodded.

The blue flashing light and siren had attracted the attention of the crowds at the fête, and news of the Captain's death spread like wildfire. As the body was carried down the steps on a gurney, the onlookers fell silent.

"I saw the Captain go into the Dew Drop Inn at lunchtime," somebody said in a low voice.

Stan heard the comment, and felt he probably now held the last jagged piece of the jigsaw puzzle.

When the ambulance pulled away, and the crowds had dispersed, Stan entered the house again and, with a heavy heart, contacted Yewbridge police station.

"Hello, PC Stan Cooper of Sixpenny Cross here. I wish to report a murder."

17

Angus McDonald, Stan Cooper and his wife, Sally, sat around the kitchen table at the police house.

"What I'm telling you now must go no further," said Stan. "It'll all come out in the open soon enough, but I thought you'd probably need to know, Angus, as you've been in on it from the beginning."

"Of course, but I don't understand anything," said Angus, bewildered. "You say there's been a murder, but I thought the Captain died of a heart attack?"

"Yes, that's right."

"The Captain wasn't murdered, was he?"

"No."

"Then who was?"

"I'm coming to that."

"I take it my barmaid has something to do with all this, am I right?"

"Yes. I don't believe it would have happened if it hadn't been for Babs and her villainous husband. But no, I don't think they murdered anybody."

Sally frowned but said nothing, knowing that her husband would explain all in good time.

Stan took a gulp of tea from his mug.

"Sixpence told me long ago about the Captain's promise to his dying father to bring back a wife to Sixpenny Manor. But we all know that the Captain had no idea about women."

"Or anything really," remarked Sally.

"He was like putty in Babs's hands," agreed Angus. "I never liked her, but she's a jolly good barmaid."

"Exactly. The Captain fell for her, hook, line and sinker. As you know, Sixpence was very protective of the Captain. He'd saved the Captain's life once before, long ago, and I think Sixpence felt kind of responsible for him ever since."

"They were genuinely fond of each other," said Sally. "And we all know the Captain was not exactly worldly wise."

"I think the murder occurred last Thursday, the night of the dinner party," said Stan. "I phoned Sixpence that night because I had just found out about Babs and her husband's background. I was worried that they might target the manor house, and that Babs was casing the joint. I told him not to tell the Captain yet, but I think he did. And it was too much for the Captain, which is why I think the Captain killed Sixpence."

"What?"

"The Captain killed Sixpence?"

"Yes, I believe he couldn't accept that Babs wasn't genuine. Maybe Sixpence even told him he suspected Babs was already married. The idea drove him completely insane."

"So Sixpence never went away? Have you found Sixpence's body?"

"No. But I'm pretty sure I know where it is. And I know how he was killed."

"Where?"

"How?"

"Let me explain. During the time before the ambulance arrived, I had a chance to have a good look around, and I found several things that told the story."

"Like what?"

"I looked round the walls, and there were lots of slightly darker squares and rectangles where pictures used to hang long ago. The wallpaper had faded less behind the pictures. But in one place, right above the mantlepiece, there was another, similar, much darker mark on the wall, as if something used to hang there, but had recently been removed."

"A picture?"

"No, a curved shape. I think an Indian scimitar used to hang there. A souvenir brought back by the Captain's grandfather."

Sally and Angus stared at Stan, who continued.

"In death, the Captain's eyes were open, staring at that point on the wall."

Both listeners gasped.

"I looked at the carpet. It's one of those brown, ornate Persian affairs, and there was a big stain on it. I took my handkerchief out of my pocket, moistened it with water, and rubbed at a corner of the stain. I'm positive it's blood."

Stan drew out a white handkerchief and showed them.

"It does look like blood," agreed Sally.

"Also, his hands were clenched tightly in his lap. I could see he was holding something and at first I thought it was scraps of white paper. But it wasn't."

"What was it?" breathed Sally.

"Rose petals. White rose petals. It was almost as if he was trying to confess, trying to tell us something. His expression in death showed such pain and sorrow..."

Stan stopped. The memory was a sad one. Then he took a deep breath and continued.

"The rose petals led me outside, and I found an area in the walled garden, next to Sixpenny's rose bushes. It had been cleared and well dug over recently."

"Didn't Sixpence say he was planning to cultivate chrysanthemums? Perhaps that's the spot he had chosen?"

"Yes, I think that's it. But I think that's where they will find poor Sixpence's body, and the scimitar, probably. I think the Captain killed Sixpence in a moment of blind rage, then carried him to the walled garden and buried him. It's very sad. I believe he caught sight of Babs flirting in the pub at lunchtime, and he realised he'd made a terrible mistake."

"He realised that Sixpence was telling the truth?"

"Exactly. And the shock of his dreadful mistake, and grief for Sixpence, brought on a massive heart attack."

Of course, when the police investigated, little one, they found everything just as Stan said they would. Poor Sixpence's body was buried in the patch where he had planned to grow prize chrysanthemums. With him was the Indian scimitar that killed him.

Stan Cooper had a fine policeman's mind, no question about that.

People still talk in whispers about the village fête of 1985. First it was almost cancelled because of the unexploded shell, then two bodies were found at the manor. As you can imagine, Sixpenny Cross made national news that month.

Babs and her husband, Richard Kane, left Yewbridge. Some say they went up north but nobody missed them, except perhaps Angus who had to advertise for a new barmaid. As Stan always said, the couple hadn't committed murder or broken any law. Even so, everyone felt that the whole sorry affair was Babs's fault. It was her greed that made her act the way she did, and caused the Captain to become unhinged.

Angus McDonald put the box of dominoes away in a dark cupboard. He always told my friend Jayne that he couldn't bear to see anybody else play with them.

Lots of people still believe that Sixpenny Manor is haunted by the ghosts of the Captain and Sixpence. I don't know about that, little one, but I do know that nothing ever grows in that spot where Sixpence was once buried, except roses. No vegetables, no chrysanthemums, no weeds, nothing.

Only roses would grow, and the white ones grew best of all.

At first, no living relatives could be found to inherit Sixpenny Manor, but the Captain's lawyers eventually managed to track down a distant cousin.

Next time I watch over you, little one, I'm going to tell you the story of young Dexter. What a remarkable tale that is! It's remarkable because Dexter surprised everyone, including himself.

Yes, D is for Dexter, but that story is for another day.

SIXPENCE'S CREAMY
SUMMER VEGETABLE SOUP

"*E*xcellent soup," said the Captain. "It's a pity you can't enter it in the fete this weekend, I'm sure it would win a prize."

INGREDIENTS

- 1 cup sweetcorn kernels
- 1 cup green beans, sliced
- 1 cup peas
- 1 cup chopped carrot
- 4 cups vegetable stock or broth
- 2 medium potatoes, cubed

- 3 stalks celery, chopped
- 1 large onion, chopped
- 4 tbs butter
- 1 tbs garlic powder
- 1 tbs basil
- 1 tbs oregano
- 3 tbs lemon juice
- Cream, sour cream or Greek style yogurt for serving
- Parsley or watercress for garnish

METHOD

Melt the butter in a large pot over medium-high heat.
Sauté the onion and celery for 2 minutes.
Add spices.
Continue cooking, stirring frequently for a further 2 minutes.
Add the stock and remaining vegetables.
Bring to the boil.
Reduce heat to medium-low. Cover and simmer 30 minutes, or until the carrots, potato and celery are cooked.
Sieve or blend the soup until it has reached your desired consistency.
Return the soup to the stock pot. Mix well and reheat if necessary.
Stir in the lemon juice.
Serve with a dollop of cream, sour cream or natural Greek yogurt on top.
Garnish with parsley or a sprig of watercress.

PREVIEW OF CHICKENS, MULES AND TWO OLD FOOLS

BY VICTORIA TWEAD

If you enjoyed the Sixpenny Cross series, please join Victoria and Joe in the bestselling, awardwinning Old Fools series. The series starter is *Chickens, Mules and Two Old Fools*.

PREVIEW

1

THE FIVE YEAR PLAN

"Hello?"

"This is Kurt."

"Oh! Hello, Kurt. How are you?"

"I am vell. The papers you vill sign now. I haf made an appointment vith the Notary for you May 23rd, 12 o'clock."

"Right, I'll check the flights and…" but he had already hung up.

Kurt, our German estate agent, was the type of person one obeyed without question. So, on May 23rd, we found ourselves back in Spain, seated round a huge polished table in the Notary's office. Beside us sat our bank manager holding a briefcase stuffed with bank notes.

Nine months earlier, we had never met Kurt. Nine months earlier, Joe and I lived in an ordinary house, in an ordinary Sussex town. Nine months earlier we had ordinary jobs and expected an ordinary future.

Then, one dismal Sunday, I decided to change all that.

"...heavy showers are expected to last through the Bank Holiday weekend and into next week. Temperatures are struggling to reach 14 degrees..."

August, and the weather-girl was wearing a coat, sheltering under an umbrella. June had been wet, July wetter. I sighed, stabbing the 'off' button on the remote control before she could depress me further. Agh! Typical British weather.

My depression changed to frustration. The private thoughts that had been tormenting me so long returned. Why should we put up with it? Why not move? Why not live in my beloved Spain where the sun always shines?

I walked to the window. Raindrops like slug trails trickled down the windowpane. Steely clouds hung low, heavy with more rain, smothering the town. Sodden litter sat drowning in the gutter.

"Joe?" He was dozing, stretched out on the sofa, mouth slightly open. "Joe, I want to talk to you about something."

Poor Joe, my long-suffering husband. His gangly frame was sprawled out, newspaper slipping from his fingers. He was utterly relaxed, blissfully unaware that our lives were about to change course.

How different he looked in scruffy jeans compared with his usual crisp uniform. But to me, whatever he wore, he was always the same, an officer and a gentleman. Nearing retirement from the Forces, I knew he was looking forward to a tension-free future, but the television weather-girl had galvanised me into action. The metaphorical bee in my bonnet would not be stilled. It buzzed and grew until it became a hornet demanding attention.

"Huh? What's the matter?" His words were blurred with sleep, his eyes still closed. Rain beat a tattoo on the window pane.

"Joe? Are you listening?"

"Uhuh…"

"When you retire, I want us to sell up and buy a house in Spain." Deep breath.

There. The bomb was dropped. I had finally admitted my longing. I wanted to abandon England with its ceaseless rain. I wanted to move permanently to Spain.

Sleep forgotten, Joe pulled himself upright, confusion in his blue eyes as he tried to read my expression.

"Vicky, what did you say just then?" he asked, squinting at me.

"I want to go and live in Spain."

"You can't be serious."

"Yes, I am."

Of course it wasn't just the rain. I had plenty of reasons, some vague, some more solid.

I presented my pitch carefully. Our children, adults now, were scattered round the world; Scotland, Australia and London. No grandchildren yet on the horizon and Joe only had a year before he retired. Then we would be free as birds to nest where we pleased.

And the cost of living in Spain would be so much lower. Council tax a fraction of what we usually paid, cheaper food, cheaper houses… The list went on.

Joe listened closely and I watched his reactions. Usually, *he* is the impetuous one, not me. But I was well aware that his retirement fantasy was being threatened. His dream of lounging all day in his dressing-gown, writing his book and diverting himself with the odd mathematical problem was being exploded.

"Hang on, Vicky, I thought we had it all planned? I thought you would do a few days of supply teaching if you wanted, while I start writing my book." Joe absentmindedly scratched his nether regions. For once I ignored his infuriating habit; I was in full flow.

"But imagine writing in Spain! Imagine sitting outside in the shade of a grapevine and writing your masterpiece."

Outside, windscreen wipers slapped as cars swept past, tyres sending up plumes of filthy water. Joe glanced out of the window at the driving rain and I sensed I had scored an important point.

"Why don't you write one of your famous lists?" he suggested, only half joking.

I am well known for my lists and records. Inheriting the record-keeping gene from my father, I can't help myself. I make a note of the weather every day, the temperature, the first snowdrop, the day the ants fly, the exchange rate of the euro, everything. I make shopping lists, separate ones for each shop. I make To Do lists and 'Joe, will you please' lists. I make packing lists before holidays. I even make lists of lists. My nickname at work was Schindler.

So I set to work and composed what I considered to be a killer pitch:

- Sunny weather
- Cheap houses
- Live in the country
- Miniscule council tax
- Friendly people
- Less crime
- No heating bills
- Cheap petrol
- Wonderful Spanish food
- Cheap wine and beer
- Could get satellite TV so you won't miss English football
- Much more laid-back life style
- Could afford house big enough for family and visitors to stay
- No TV licence
- Only short flight to UK
- Might live longer because Mediterranean diet is healthiest in the world

When I ran dry, I handed the list to Joe. He glanced at it and snorted.

"I'm going to make a coffee," he said, but he took my list with him. He was in the kitchen a long time.

When he came out, I looked up at him expectantly. He ignored me, snatched a pen and scribbled on the bottom of the list. Satisfied, he threw it on the table and left the room. I grabbed it and read his additions. He'd pressed so hard with the pen that he'd nearly gone through the paper.

Joe had written:

- CAN'T SPEAK SPANISH!
- TOO MANY FLIES!
- *MOVING HOUSE IS THE PITS!*

For weeks we debated, bouncing arguments for and against like a game of ping pong. Even when we weren't discussing it, the subject hung in the air between us, almost tangible. Then one day, (was it a coincidence that it was raining yet again?) Joe surprised me.

"Vicky, why don't you book us a holiday over Christmas, and we could just take a look."

The hug I gave him nearly crushed his ribs.

"Hang on!" he said, detaching himself and holding me at arm's length. "What I'm trying to say is, well, I'm willing to compromise."

"What do you mean, 'compromise'?"

"How about if we look on it as a five year plan? We don't sell this house, just rent it out. Okay, we could move to Spain, but not necessarily for ever. At the end of five years, we can make up our minds whether to come back to England or stay out there. I'm happy to try it for five years. What do you think?"

I turned it over in my mind. Move to Spain, but look on it as a sort of project? Actually, it seemed rather a good idea. In fact, a perfect compromise.

Joe was watching me. "Well? Agreed?"

"Agreed..." It was a victory of sorts. A Five Year Plan. Yes, I saw the sense in that. Anything could happen in five years.

"Well, go on, then. Book a holiday over Christmas and we'll take it from there."

So I logged onto the Internet and booked a two week holiday in Almería.

Why Almería? Well, we already knew the area quite well as this would be our fourth visit. And I considered this part of Andalucía to be perfect. Only two and a half hours flight from London, guaranteed sunshine, friendly people and jaw-dropping views. It ticked all my boxes. Joe agreed cautiously that the area could be ideal.

So the destination was decided, but what type of home in Spain would we want? Our budget was reduced because we weren't going to sell our English house. We'd have to find something cheap.

On previous visits, I'd hated all the houses we'd noticed in the resorts. Mass produced boxes on legoland estates, each identical, each characterless and overlooking the next. No, I knew what I really wanted: a house we could do up, with views and space, preferably in an unspoiled Spanish village.

Unlike Joe, I've always been obsessed with houses. I was the driving force and it was the hard climb up the English property ladder that allowed us even to contemplate moving abroad. In the past few years, we had bought a derelict house, improved and sold it, making a good profit. So we bought another and repeated the process. It was gruelling work. We both had other careers, but it was well worth the effort. Now we could afford to rent out our home in England and still buy a modest house in Spain.

"If we do decide to move out there," said Joe, "and we buy an old place to do up, it's not going to be like doing up houses in England. Everything's going to be different there."

How right he was.

Like a child, I yearned for that Christmas to come. I couldn't wait to set foot on Spanish soil again. We arrived, and although Christmas lights decorated the airport, it was warm enough to remove our jackets. Before long, we had found our hotel and settled in.

The next morning, we hired a little car. Joe, having finally accepted the inevitable, was happy to drive into the mountains in search of The House. We had two weeks to find it.

Yet again the mountains seduced us. The endless blue sky where birds of prey wheeled lazily. The neat orchards splashed with bright oranges and lemons. The secret, sleepy villages nestled into valleys. Even the roads, narrow, treacherous and winding, couldn't break the spell that Andalucía cast over us.

Daily, we drove through whitewashed villages where little old ladies dressed in black stopped sweeping their doorsteps to watch us pass. We waved at farmers working in their fields, the dry dust swirling in irritated clouds from their labours. We paused to allow goat-herds to pass with their flocks, the lead goat's bell clanging bossily as the herd followed, snatching mouthfuls of vegetation on the run.

Although we hadn't yet found The House, we were positive we'd found the area we wanted to live in.

One day we drove into a village that clung to the steep mountainside by its fingernails. We entered a bar that was buzzing with activity. It was busy and the air heavy with smoke. The white-aproned bartender looked us up and down and jerked his head in greeting. No smile, just a nod.

Joe found a rocky wooden table by the window with panoramic views and we settled ourselves, soaking in the atmosphere. Four old men played cards at the next table. A heated debate was taking place between another group. I caught the words 'Barcelona' and 'Real Madrid'. Most of the bar's customers were male.

Grumpy, the bartender, wiped his hands on his apron and approached our table, flicking off imaginary crumbs from the surface with the back of his hand. He had a splendid moustache which concealed any expression he may have had, and made communication difficult.

"Could we see the menu, please?" asked Joe in his best phrase book Spanish.

Grumpy shook his head and snorted. It seemed there was no menu.

"No importa," said Joe. "It doesn't matter."

Using a combination of sign language and impatient grunts, Grumpy took our order but our meal was destined to be a surprise. A basket of bread was slammed onto the table, followed by two plates of food. Garlic mushrooms - delicious. We cleaned our plates and leaned back, digesting our food and the surroundings. In typical Spanish fashion, the drinkers at the bar bellowed at each other as though every individual had profound hearing problems.

"We're running out of time," said Joe. "We can carry on gallivanting around the countryside, but we aren't going to find anything. I very much doubt we'll find a house this holiday."

Suddenly, clear as cut crystal, the English words, "Oh, bugger! Where are my keys?" floated above the Spanish hubbub.

THE OLD FOOLS SERIES

Book #1

Chickens, Mules and Two Old Fools

If Joe and Vicky had known what relocating to a tiny mountain village in Andalucía would REALLY be like, they might have hesitated...

Book #2

Two Old Fools - Olé!

Vicky and Joe have finished fixing up their house and look forward to peaceful days enjoying their retirement. Then the fish van arrives, and instead of delivering fresh fish, disgorges the Ufarte family.

Book #3

Two Old Fools on a Camel

Reluctantly, Vicky and Joe leave Spain to work for a year in the Middle East. Incredibly, the Arab revolution erupted, throwing them into violent events that made world headlines.

New York Times bestseller three times

Book #4

Two Old Fools in Spain Again

Life refuses to stand still in tiny El Hoyo. Lola Ufarte's behaviour surprises nobody, but when a millionaire becomes a neighbour, the village turns into a battleground.

Book #5

Two Old Fools in Turmoil

When dark, sinister clouds loom, Victoria and Joe find themselves facing life-changing decisions. Happily, silver linings also abound. A fresh new face joins the cast of well-known characters but the return of a bad penny may be more than some can handle.

Book #6

Two Old Fools Down Under

When Vicky and Joe wave goodbye to their beloved Spanish village, they face their future in Australia with some trepidation. Now they must build a new life amongst strangers, snakes and spiders the size of saucers. Accompanied by their enthusiastic new puppy, Lola, adventures abound, both heartwarming and terrifying.

Book #7

Two Old Fools Fair Dinkum

Wall Street Journal Top 10 and New York Times bestselling author "If you enjoyed The Durrells and James Herriott, you'll love the Old Fools series." Life is good. The grandchildren are thriving despite swallowing magnets and sticking crayons up their noses. Joe and Vicky plan a road trip with their dog, Lola. However, after disturbing dingoes, entering zombie zones and breaking the law, they learn life on the road is rarely relaxing. Even worse, after a terrible drought, bushfire season arrives early, and flames rage across the land. Will love and laughter be enough to keep the Two Old Fools and their family safe from harm?

One Young Fool in Dorset (PREQUEL)

This light and charming story is the delightful prequel to Victoria Twead's Old Fools series. Her childhood memories are vividly portrayed, leaving the reader chuckling and enjoying a warm sense of comfortable nostalgia.

One Young Fool in South Africa (PREQUEL)

Who is Joe Twead? What happened before Joe met Victoria and they moved to a crazy Spanish mountain village? Joe vividly paints his childhood memories despite constant heckling from Victoria at his elbow.

Two Old Fools in the Kitchen, Part 1 (COOKBOOK)

The *Old Fools' Kitchen* cookbooks were created in response to frequent requests from readers of the *Old Fools series* asking to see all the recipes collected together in one place.

NEW! THE STILLWATER MURDERS BY VICTORIA TWEAD

DEAD OF NIGHT SERIES BOOK 1

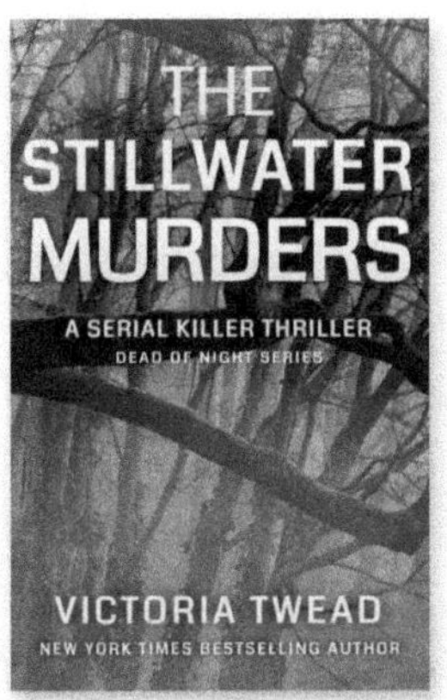

THE STILLWATER MURDERS

Stillwater Cove is a town built on quiet.

When a string of unexplained deaths shatters the calm of Stillwater Cove, detective Lara Lennox is sent from Sydney to investigate. Each victim is found carefully posed, a small paper star left behind.

The Stillwater Murders (Chapter 1)

This is my time.

I am calm, but ready, prepared.

The dead of night, when the world exhales and falls utterly still. When darkness gathers like a velvet tide, drawn quietly over the earth. The sky becomes an ink-deep ocean without horizon or seam. A place where the stars seem to hesitate before shining. Even the gulls tuck their heads beneath their wings and stay quiet, surrendering to the dark.

There is a moment just before dawn, when the world forgets to breathe. The sea holds still. The reeds stop whispering.

I wait for that moment.

It is the best time a person can cross from this life to the next without struggle. Without fear. Without the burden of the weight of the world pressing in behind their ribs.

The old woman couldn't sleep. She sits on her veranda swing, wrapped in a faded, knitted shawl.

Her eyes are closed, her hair silvered by the moon.

I've been watching her. She didn't see me. I heard her trying to hum a tune she no longer remembered.

Her voice trembled.

Her hands trembled.

Her soul trembled.

But not now.

Now she is still. Perfectly still. Her heart no longer beats.

Now she is beautiful in her quietness.

I kneel beside her, careful not to disturb the blanket tucked around her knees. A faint night breeze lifts a strand of hair from her cheek, and I smooth it gently back into place.

Warm. Soft.

She earned this.

She carried her burden for so long that the weight bent her shoulders. No one noticed how tired she had become.

But I noticed. I always notice.

There is no fear in her face. Only the softness and peace that comes when the world finally releases you, lets you go.

I take the small, red paper star from my pocket.

It is imperfect. Torn by my fingers. A little crooked at the edges. The first star I ever made was for her, the woman who taught me how to say goodbye.

I place it gently under the old woman's hand, letting it rest on the shawl.

I breathe in.

A new beginning always starts with a quiet ending.

I stay with her until the light begins to rise behind the drowned forest.

Until the world remembers to breathe again.

Then I stand.

Gently close her eyes.

And leave her to her peace.

No one should die alone.

Amazon Link: https://bit.ly/Stillwater-Murders

REVIEWS

“I’m going: ‘Nooooo! Don't go out, lock your door, don't let anyone in!’ If this was TV I would be shouting at the screen.”

“Totally wowed with it!”

“A brilliant edge-of-your-seat read.”

“Totally and utterly gripping. I got nothing done while reading this.”

NEW! THE BONE GARDEN
BY VICTORIA TWEAD

DEAD OF NIGHT SERIES BOOK 2

THE BONE GARDEN

Some patterns should never be completed.

Bodies are turning up, posed with impossible care, surrounded by spirals built from bleached bones.

Detective Senior Constable Lara Lennox expects a straightforward hunt. Instead, she finds a killer who seems to know her team's next move before they do.

The Bone Garden (Chapter 1)

The bucket of bones stood waiting. He inhaled, controlling his excitement. Allowed his hand to dip in. Eager, trembling fingers gripped the first bone. He drew it out.

Not too long, not too short. Good. Almost silky to the touch.

He fumbled and it slipped from his fingers and disappeared into the dark soil.

He hissed with annoyance, crouching to find it again by touch, feeling for its smooth curve. The lantern at his feet threw a shallow circle of light, not quite reaching the treeline. Beyond that, the night pressed in: a black wall of trunks and wet leaves and insect sound.

"Focus," he murmured.

His breath ghosted white in the cool air. He found the bone at last, pinched it between thumb and forefinger, and set it in place.

Now he worked steadily, almost oblivious to the night sounds and the woman's motionless body.

The last bone completed the curve of the spiral, almost perfect now. He studied it critically, head tilted, then nudged one of the vertebrae a fraction to the left.

Much better.

The line flowed again.

The woman in the centre of the pattern didn't move. She would never move again. Never breathe, blink, smile or speak.

He kept an eye on her anyway. The lantern's light softened the harshness of her features, turned them almost peaceful. Straw-coloured hair spilled across the flattened grass like fluid, poured. One of her hands lay palm-up beside her head, dead fingers curled. He tried to uncurl them, arrange them more neatly.

He stepped back, heels sinking slightly into the mulch. His boots made no sound. The small clearing was quiet now.

"This one is important," he told the corpse on the ground. "The first impression matters. You understand."

She did not answer, of course. They never did, not at this stage. That was all right. He wasn't really speaking to her anyway.

He moved around the spiral, placing the last few bones from the bucket. They were small ones, birdlike, scavenged months ago and saved for this. He had cleaned them himself, boiled and bleached and dried, his kitchen thick with the smell for days.

The last bone fell into place with a tiny, satisfying click against its neighbours. The spiral was complete. A pale, graceful swirl encircling the woman's body, curling inward as if to claim her.

He stepped back until his shoulder brushed the rough bark of a tree. From this distance, the whole design came together. The body was the centre point, the axis. The spiral drew the eye straight to her pale, dead face.

He felt a thrill rise, sharp as cold water. It was so… Right.

Better than the practice layouts in his cottage, better than the chalk mock-ups on the concrete floor. Better than the rehearsals in dense bushland where human feet rarely trod.

Those had been exercises.

This was the *real thing.*

ABOUT THE AUTHOR

Victoria Twead is the New York Times bestselling author of *Chickens, Mules and Two Old Fools* and the subsequent books in the Old Fools series. She is also the founder of Ant Press and the popular Facebook group, We Love Memoirs.

After living in a remote mountain village in Spain for eleven years, and owning probably the most dangerous cockerel in Europe, Victoria and Joe retired to Australia to watch their new grandchildren thrive amongst kangaroos and koalas.

More joyous life-chapters are unwinding.

For photographs and additional unpublished material to
accompany this book, download the
Free Photo Book
from
www.victoriatwead.com/free-stuff

CONTACTS AND LINKS
CONNECT WITH VICTORIA

Email: TopHen@VictoriaTwead.com (emails welcome)
Website: www.VictoriaTwead.com
Old Fools' Updates Signup: www.VictoriaTwead.com
This includes the latest Old Fools' news, free books, book recommendations, and recipe. Guaranteed spam-free and sent out every few months.
Free Stuff: http://www.victoriatwead.com/Free-Stuff/
Facebook: https://www.facebook.com/VictoriaTwead (friend requests welcome)
Instagram: @victoria.twead
Victoria's Cut-Price Paperback Bookstore: Books.by/Victoria-Twead

We Love Memoirs
Join me and other memoir authors and readers in the We Love Memoirs Facebook group, the friendliest group on Facebook.
www.facebook.com/groups/welovememoirs/

VICTORIA'S BOOKSTORE

If you prefer to read paperbacks, and would like to pay lower prices by buying direct, do visit Victoria's own cut-price bookstore. Shipping anywhere in the world is a flat fee of $5.

Bookstore Link: Books.by/Victoria-Twead

Scan me

MORE ANT PRESS MEMOIRS
AWESOME AUTHORS ~ AWESOME BOOKS

If you enjoyed this book, you may also enjoy these other Ant Press memoir authors. All titles are available in ebook, paperback, hardback and large print editions from **Amazon**.

These two booksellers offer FREE delivery worldwide.
Blackwells.co.uk and Wordery.com
More Stores
Waterstones (Europe delivery), Booktopia (Australia), Barnes &
Noble (USA), and all good bookstores.

VICTORIA TWEAD
New York Times bestselling author
The Old Fools series

1.Chickens, Mules and Two Old Fools
2.Two Old Fools ~ Olé!
3.Two Old Fools on a Camel
4.Two Old Fools in Spain Again
5.Two Old Fools in Turmoil
6.Two Old Fools Down Under
7.Two Old Fools Fair Dinkum
8.Two Old Fools Find their Tribe
8.One Young Fool in Dorset (Prequel)
9.One Young Fool in South Africa (Prequel)

Dear Fran, Love Dulcie: Life and Death in the Hills and Hollows of Bygone Australia

BETH HASLAM
The Fat Dogs series

Fat Dogs and French Estates ~ Part I
Fat Dogs and French Estates ~ Part II
Fat Dogs and French Estates ~ Part III
Fat Dogs and French Estates ~ Part IV
Fat Dogs and French Estates ~ Part V
Fat Dogs and French Estates ~ Part VI
Fat Dogs and Welsh Estates ~ The Prequel

DIANE ELLIOTT
Lady Goatherder series

Butting Heads in Spain: Lady Goatherder 1
El Maestro: Lady Goatherder 2

EJ BAUER
The Someday Travels series

1.From Moulin Rouge to Gaudi's City
2.From Gaudi's City to Granada's Red Palace
3.From an Umbrian Farmhouse to Como's Quiet Shores

For more information about stockists, Ant Press titles or how to publish with Ant Press, please visit our website or contact us by email.

WEBSITE: www.antpress.org

EMAIL: admin@antpress.org

FACEBOOK: https://www.facebook.com/AntPress/